FICTION
Denni
Denning, Susan

Far Away Home

D1295792

FAR AWAY HOME

FAR AWAY HOME

by

Susan Denning

No Limit Press

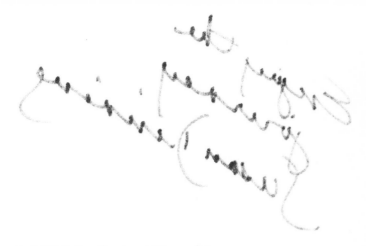

No Limit Press
PO Box 284
Mendham, NJ 07945
Email address: farawayhomenlp@gmail.com
Website: www.nolimitpress.com

ISBN 978-0-692-00039-7
Library of Congress control number 2008911151
Printed in the USA

This book is for TD and Timmy,
for all you are and all you have given me.

FAR AWAY HOME

Chapter 1

September, 1867
New York City

"You don't belong here, Aislynn Denehy," Jimmy Tully shouted. " 'Tis a man's meeting."

While the huddle of men surrounding him voiced their agreement, Aislynn pointed to the announcement tacked to the church door. She addressed them collectively, "The sign says everyone is welcomed in the West."

"Everyone who's not a woman," Jimmy joshed.

Aislynn knew each man and through all her sixteen years, made it a habit to dismiss their good-natured taunts. Yet as she approached the Parish Hall, she saw they were correct; the entryway was clogged with men. Spying a woodpile, she dragged a log to the door and stood

1

it on its end. Holding the doorframe, she hoisted herself up and surveyed the sea of masculinity. The bare-beamed room seethed with the unemployed and the adventurous. Some greeted each other, shaking hands and slapping backs, while others elbowed and nudged their way through conversations punctuated by outbursts of laughter and amiable insults. The smell of sweat and ale drifted toward her on a thin cloud of cigar smoke. Aislynn's eyes searched the throng.

On the stage, a dark haired man stepped up to the podium and cleared his throat. "May I have your attention?"

The sound of the speaker's voice quieted the crowd.

"Gentlemen, my name is Liam Moran, and I am so glad to see you all here tonight. My colleagues and I have come to offer you the opportunity of a lifetime, the chance to go west. The chance to be a part of a new world, a new way of life, the chance to fulfill your dreams."

Moran exhorted the gathering like a preacher. "You," his arms stretched out as he roared, "all you Irish, you've dug the canals for a pauper's wage. You've built this city and gained little more than your broken backs."

With narrowed eyes and a sneer across his lips, he jabbed his cigar at the audience, "You fought the great Civil War. You freed the slaves. Now they've come north and taken your jobs. I've been around. I've seen the signs, 'No Irish need apply.'" Moran leaned on the podium and scanned the assemblage, "The War's been over for two years. What did you get for all your efforts? You earn three hundred dollars a year, a mere pittance! Is that why you and your fathers came to these shores?"

He straightened and paused until the murmuring died down. "You see these men?" His hands swept toward the speakers seated at the long table behind him. "They're rich, wealthy. Do you know how they got rich? They went west, to the great American West. They cashed in on the abundance of natural resources just waiting for a man

2

with a dream. Why, the forests are so thick the trees are falling down by themselves. The ground is so fertile you just have to scatter seeds and watch them grow. There's grass everywhere just waiting for cattle to graze."

A buzz of excitement rose from the audience. Moran motioned the crowd closer as his voice became softer, "And, of course, there are precious minerals just floating in the streams, hinting at the lodes below the surface, waiting to be struck."

After a pause to catch his breath, Moran continued in a solemn tone. "This nation is ready to explode again. Not into war this time. No, it's going to explode with expansion. That expansion is going to move on a bed of rails that's fixing to run clear across this continent. When it does, that ribbon of rails is going to tie our ranching, logging, mining, and farming to all the big markets. You," he called, waving his cigar, "you can be a part of it. Now, my associates will step up and tell you about the opportunities they have to offer. They'll pay your fare, give you a decent wage, and all you have to do in return is give them a year of solid work."

As soon as the last speaker completed his sales pitch, a mass of men pressed toward the stage to volunteer. One burly young man with broad shoulders bulging under his worn shirt approached Aislynn. Hands on hips and a hint of sarcasm in his voice, he demanded, "What brings you here?"

"I brought myself, Johnny Maher," she replied, as he eyed her. Aislynn liked Johnny and his constant pursuit flattered her. She found him agreeable and good-humored. Although his round face always brightened for Aislynn, his looks did not appeal to her. Fair and freckled, he was too big and bulky for Aislynn's taste.

"This is no place for a girl."

Aislynn sighed with frustration. "The sign says everyone is welcomed in the West. Didn't the speakers say it's the land of equal opportunity?"

"I guess any place asking for Irish would take women, too."

Aislynn had to smile knowing the stigma they all bore. Regardless of their looks, intelligence or talents, they felt the sting of discrimination. It was one of the things binding them together and driving them west.

Johnny continued, "But I didn't hear them offerin' any women's work."

"I'll just have to find work on my own."

"I suspect you just want to follow Tim Nolan wherever he goes."

"Is he here?" Aislynn tried to sound calm.

"Seems everyone's here."

"Did you see Tim?" Aislynn asked pointedly.

Johnny looked over the crowd, "No, but I'm sure he's here; he's unemployed like the rest." Returning his gaze to Aislynn, he stated, "If you're goin' west, you'd be better off travelin' with a man like me. I might not have the mind of Tim Nolan, but I've a sturdy back and strong hands and from what I hear, they're far more valuable in the West."

"I don't believe Mr. Moran or any of those men up there got rich with their big fists, Johnny Maher!"

"Aye, so it's money you're wantin'?" He leaned closer, "Let's combine our talents. We could go far."

Blushing, Aislynn replied, "I am not interested in going where you want to go."

Johnny guffawed. "We'll see Aislynn Denehy. When Tim marries Emma Greene, you'll come lookin' for me," Johnny stated. "Bein' the fool I am, I'll be waitin'. If I'm dismissed, your Royal Highness, I'll take my leave." Johnny lifted her hand to his lips saying, " 'Til we meet again, your Majesty."

Snapping her fingers from his grip, she suppressed a smile and ordered, "Oh, just go."

As Johnny departed, Aislynn glanced toward the action on the stage and saw Moran eyeing her. When he rose to the podium, Aislynn noticed he was attractive, for an older man, tall, well-built, with hair as black as hers combed back from his face, which was decorated with an equally dark mustache and closely-trimmed beard. The darkness of his hair set off his light blue eyes giving him an almost sinister look. He seemed a man who could make a pact with the devil confident he could retract his pledge when it suited him. Aislynn thought it unseemly for a man twice her age to look at a girl of sixteen in this way. She turned her gaze away from him, but movement in his direction brought Aislynn's eyes back. She saw Tim approach Moran.

"No!" she screamed. Her tiny voice could not penetrate the din. She jumped down and tried to push her way through the tangle of men who smelled of hard work and limited means. They were packed tightly up against the stage. She attempted to squeeze through small gaps between elbows and legs, pleading, "Pardon me. Excuse me. I have to get through, please." The hoop in her skirt slowed her progress. It needed space and the men were reluctant to yield any. When some men stepped aside, it would snag on the others who were pressing to get ahead.

She slowly advanced through the mass of men, reaching the stage as Tim was shaking hands with Moran. "Tim!" she called.

Tim's head jerked in the direction of her voice. "Aislynn?" A puzzled look crossed his face, but it quickly changed to a smile. He extended his hand to her, "Come meet my new employer."

Chapter 2

Aislynn hurried out of the Parish Hall with tears brimming in her eyes. Scurrying down the sidewalk, her pace slowed when she reached the front of the church. From behind, she heard Tim calling her name, "Aislynn, stop! Aislynn!" She recognized his tone, and it indicated she should obey.

Aislynn turned and cried, "You're going?"

Tim grabbed her arm and led the reluctant Aislynn to the church stairs. "Sit," he commanded. It was darker and cooler in the stone portico. The steps felt damp. The church doors were sealed, and the smell of the old wood and moist stone filled the entryway. Seated, she turned and glared into his bright blue eyes.

"We were supposed to go together and now you're going by yourself."

Tim wiped the tears from her cheeks and said,

"Aislynn, I have to find work."

"You said we'd make our fortune together."

"Things change."

"You let them change."

"Aislynn, I didn't cause the war or the lack of jobs. I feel like I just returned from the war; do you think I want to go away again?"

"You made a promise."

Tim searched her eyes, "Surely I've kept my promise. We were children then and you needed me. Now, I'm grown and you're," he hesitated, "you're almost grown." Aislynn straightened, trying to look taller than her five feet. He continued, "Let's not fight, Aislynn. I have to go. I have no future here."

Tears rose in Aislynn's eyes. "What about me and my future?"

"You'll be fine. You have your father, my father and all my brothers to take care of you."

"In truth, I take care of them and you."

"You're right. I'll suffer your absence more than you'll suffer mine." Tim stood and pulled Aislynn to her feet. "Now, stop this crying. Run on and get dinner." Tim planted a quick kiss on her head and turned her in the direction of home. "I've got to tell Emma."

Aislynn's sadness switched to anger. *Emma, what does he see in such a frail bird of a girl?* Hearing a commotion coming from the street behind her, Aislynn made an about-face. Three exquisite carriages, with groomed horses clopping their hooves and jangling their ornate harnesses, pulled up to the curb. The speakers clambered in. As the carriages jerked forward, wheels grinding on the cobbles, Aislynn's eyes caught Moran's. His glance slowly swept down her body and up again. She felt her face redden. Reflexive modesty caused her arms to cross over her breasts. Giving him her back, she walked toward Worth Street.

Aislynn found her father seated at the kitchen table,

reading the newspaper and waiting to be fed. The tiny, yellow kitchen, so bright in the daylight, was dim and shadowy under the glow of a single oil lamp suspended from the ceiling. The fire in the stove had faded. Although the wood was stacked within easy reach, neither her father nor any of the Nolan men would deign to feed the flames. "'Tis woman's work," they would declare, and for the past eight years, Aislynn, the only female between the two families, was responsible for all chores falling into that category: washing, ironing, mending, marketing, cooking and anything else they deemed fit only for a woman. Aislynn stirred the stew and let the sweet, sour scent of bacon with red cabbage, onions, apples and potatoes fill the air.

Her father sat up and filled his lungs with the aroma. "You're a wizard, you are, my sweet daughter. Are we ready to eat?"

"In a few minutes." While Aislynn had his attention, she planned to use it. Seating herself at the wooden table, she asked, "Da, do you remember how we used to talk about going west, getting a ranch so you could breed horses?"

"Aye, the dreams of my youth."

"You're still young, Da."

"Not so young as all that. I know I talked, but that's all it was."

"Couldn't we think about going west again?"

"Aislynn, you can't just start walkin' toward the settin' sun, you know. You'd have to cross the Hudson River, and you can't swim," he joked.

"Da, I'm serious."

"Are you, then? Well, give some serious thought to the cost of such an adventure. You'd have to buy a wagon and some horses and provisions. Why, you'd need hundreds of dollars just to leave New York. And how would we buy land and horses once we got to wherever we're goin'?"

"Money, everything comes down to money. I hate it."

9

"You'd not hate it if you had it." He patted her hand.

"And how will we ever get it?"

"Are we doin' so poorly, daughter? I've steady work and you've a roof and food."

"I'm not complaining, Da. I just wish for more, like our own house, and I'd work for it."

"Ha, there's no work for men and even less for women. That's why Tim's gone to the meetin'." A look of recognition spread over Brendan's face. "I know what you're about. You want to follow Tim."

"We always planned to go west." Aislynn fought her tears. "Now, he's going alone."

Aislynn leaned on the table and cradled her chin in her hands. "We were supposed to be partners for life."

"Oh girl, Tim's been a fine friend since the day you were born, but it's time he went his way and you went yours."

"And what's my way? I've planned my whole life around Tim."

Scowling, Brendan warned, "You can't live your life for someone else. You have to follow your own road, hard as that may be, and it can be hard. I know that. But here, in this country, you have a chance."

Aislynn could hear the anger in his voice. When Brendan thought of his homeland, it raised the dark specters of troubling times. "Why in Ireland, we starved; we had nothing. Couldn't dig a hole for shelter or eat dirt 'cause the English claimed all the land."

His eyes narrowed and she could feel his entire body grow taut. "We had no rights. They made the rules and enforced them as they would. Here, there's a place for us. All those people who call us names won't be sayin' such things forever. In this country, we make strides with every generation. You're a part of that. You're born here. You and your children will have American stories, and they'll be better than any sorrowful Irish tales. At the end, you will be strong and independent, and no one will hold you down or deny you freedom."

Aislynn leaned across the table and challenged him. "And how much freedom extends to a woman?"

Brendan thought for a moment, "That's why you need a man, a man who'll respect you and give you what you need."

"I can get what I need myself."

"Ha, a woman needs a man, love. You know what they say, 'A woman without a man, ain't a woman.' "

"And do I get to decide which man?"

"Of course you do," Brendan paused, "as long as I agree."

"Da, you talk of independence and freedom, and then, you don't give them to me."

" 'Tisn't me Aislynn, 'tis a man's world. You know that. You can't make your way in it alone."

"Well, if I have to have a man, I want Tim. I'll find some work, and we'll get money and a home."

"Now daughter, at sixteen, you think marriage is all love and romance but at twenty-six, when you've babes to feed, you'll not want a man who reads and talks about ideas like Tim; you'll want a man who can provide for you."

The words "babes to feed" made Aislynn a bit queasy. She had minimal knowledge about reproduction. At the Church of the Transfiguration School, she learned the three "Rs" and how to speak and behave like a proper American, but there were many unasked and consequently, unanswered questions. With no woman to query, Aislynn remained ignorant and preferred not to think about that part of marriage.

"Now, take Johnny Maher," Brendan offered. "Hasn't he been askin' after you?"

Aislynn lowered her hands and sent a sour expression his way.

Brendan persisted, "He's a good man. Didn't waste his time in the war gettin' shot at. Oh no, he learned a

11

trade and a good trade smithin' is."

"He lied to enlist; he was too young to fight."

"There's no shame in that. He wanted to serve his country. It wasn't his fault they found out and pushed him to the back of the lines with the farriers. It was his good fortune. Shows he's lucky." Brendan winked, "A lucky Irishman, imagine that."

"Da," Aislynn tried to object.

"He's makin' good money and supportin' his dear, widowed mother and that deaf sister of his."

"How is it you know so much about Johnny Maher?"

"He's been courtin' me for months. Been buyin' me draughts every night."

"Then you marry him."

"Don't you be fresh with your Da. Goodness, when these boys know how saucy you are, I may never get you married!"

"Fine. I'll make my own way in life."

The scent of the boiling stew reached the Nolans in their apartment across the hall. It signaled dinnertime. Their arrival and their greetings brought her conversation with her father to a close. Each man took a seat around the table, and Aislynn served them as custom dictated, her father first, then Papa Nolan. With young Frank married and living apart from the family, twenty-eight- year-old Sean was next in seniority, then Michael, followed by Brian. The men wiped their plates with the buttermilk biscuits Aislynn had baked as Tim arrived. Just seeing his sweet face and golden hair made Aislynn smile. She watched him take his place at the table and rushed to prepare his plate.

"Well, how did it go at the hall?" Papa Nolan asked.

"I had great success. The man I approached has a vast ranch in Utah." The men nodded their approval as Tim talked on. "He has interests in timber and the railroads, the Central Pacific to be exact."

"Sounds wealthy," Brendan interjected.

"Very. He was looking for ranch hands." This caused laughter from Tim's audience. Although Tim was built tall and strong, everyone in the room knew he was more cerebral than physical. "I know, I'll never be a bronco buster but I mentioned I hoped to earn enough money to attend college. He asked about my skills with figures. I told him I have a talent for mathematics. He said he needed someone to check his accounts and be his paymaster. I said, 'I'm your man. I'm good with sums and I'm honest. Ask any man here and he'd vouch for my integrity.' So I'm off to Utah."

Sean interrupted, "Utah, you say? Do you know you can have as many wives as you want in Utah? You could have a dozen wives."

"Oh, no, Sean," Tim replied derisively, "I don't think the law applies to us."

Sean challenged him, "And why not?"

"First off, we're Catholic, in case you've forgotten. It's a Mormon rule. And secondly, I can't afford one wife," holding up his index finger, "what would I do with a dozen?"

Michael, the contrary middle brother, replied, "I could think of a dozen things you could do with a dozen wives, but not all at the same time."

A palpable silence followed Michael's remark. His brothers' eyes darted from their father's to Aislynn's Da. Michael, unlike his four tall, fair brothers, was short, dark, and disagreeable. Papa Nolan upbraided Michael for being crude in front of Aislynn.

Undaunted, Sean continued, "I still think it would be wonderful. Imagine having twelve women to wait on you all the time."

Brian added, "Sean, you can't get one woman to marry you. How would you get a dozen?"

As the group laughed at Sean, Tim rose from the table and brought his empty mug to Aislynn quietly standing at the stove, listening to the banter. With one hand on her shoulder, he said, "Sean, you're imagining all the women in Utah have the green eyes and pretty, little face of our Aislynn; when in truth, I hear most of them closely resemble Michael." He ruffled Michael's brown hair to everyone's amusement but Michael's.

"And it would be my luck to get twelve of them."

Aislynn knew what lay beneath the joking. Humor masked their pain and their losses. When things like long, possibly interminable separations were too difficult to discuss, the subject would be relegated to jokes. The Nolan men and Aislynn's Da did not cry. Laughter substituted for tears.

"So when do you go, son?" Brendan asked.

"Tomorrow, I take the night train out of Hoboken."

"Tomorrow?" Aislynn could not contain her disappointment. The men could see her tears rising. Brendan stood and announced he had to meet a friend at the pub. Papa Nolan concurred. Sean, Michael and Brian headed for the door, as well. Tim returned to his chair and told Aislynn to take a seat.

"Mr. Moran said tomorrow. I have to leave before winter sets in and the way is impassable."

"But it's so soon."

"I know Aislynn, but this is a wonderful opportunity, and I have to take it."

Tears slipped down her face. "So I'm left here. What am I to do?"

"You write to me regularly, long detailed letters so I don't feel so far away from all I love."

Aislynn sensed his sadness. She suddenly realized he was not simply leaving her. It was like the war all over again. He was the one going far from home, alone, in harm's way. Aislynn felt ashamed of her selfishness. "How can I help?"

"You can help me pack my meager belongings. But, right now, you might cut my hair. I don't know when I'll have the chance again."

14

With the barbering finished, Aislynn sat at the table across from him holding a snip of his hair. She opened her locket and extracted her mother's black ringlet. Under his despondent gaze, she twined them together and said, "Our bond is tighter than blood; we are bound by the history of the life we've shared."

Her words brought tears to his eyes. She snapped the locket closed and rushed to hold his head against her heart.

"No matter where we are, or what happens, we'll always be a part of each other," Tim said.

Chapter 3

Five-year-old Tim Nolan sat on the floor outside his apartment waiting for his four older brothers to return from school. He watched while a beautiful, young lady ascended the stairs in the stream of sunshine that radiated through the building's skylight. She glowed, luminescent in the shaft of heavenly rays. Tim thought she was an angel or a fairy princess.

"Hello," her voice sang to him.

Enchanted, he could not speak.

"I'm your new neighbor, Katherine Denehy," she said. "I hope we'll be friends." Her green eyes smiled as she extended her hand to him. It was soft and cloud-white with perfectly buffed nails. This was no mortal woman. Women washed laundry, scrubbed floors and had hands that showed their labor. He held her fingers in his and bowed, like the knights in his books.

Recovering his voice, he whispered, "Tim Nolan, ma'am, at your service."

The small, dark-haired woman seemed to float into the flat across the hall from his and disappeared behind the door. He stared after her in reverential silence. A few seconds later, a man bounded up the stairs.

"Hey, boy!" the man greeted him loudly. Tim thought the man was the cocky sort, too pleased with himself. The man entered Katherine's apartment. Tim immediately became concerned about the man's intentions and formed an instant dislike. He jumped to his feet. Thinking she might need protection from this intruder, Tim ran for his wooden sword. He knew how to kill dragons and demons and wanted to be prepared to sacrifice himself for this lady fair.

It took no time for Tim to become Katherine's constant companion. Five boys and the weight of many chores did not allow Mary Nolan to give her last child the attention he craved. Tenderhearted Mrs. Denehy recognized the five-year-old's needs and quickly adopted him into her life. She was the perfect antidote for an ignored child. Tim fell in love with the woman who always referred to him as "my love."

In January, Katherine's husband Brendan was called to Florida. Training for the horseracing season had begun in the South, and Brendan, a jockey, had to return to his profession. They decided the pregnant Katherine should stay home. The prospect of having Katherine to himself thrilled Tim.

After Brendan's departure, diarrhea, a deadly urban illness, struck Katherine. She suffered wrenching pain and dehydration, losing the baby and nearly her life. Mrs. Nolan and Tim cared for her, and she slowly recuperated.

Spring showed one bright day in early March. Warmth replaced the damp, chill air of February, and the promise of new life pushed through the ground in the privy-yard. The sound of children playing rose up to

Katherine's kitchen window where she and her habitual companion sat at the kitchen table planning their day. It was still too cold to open the windows and let in fresh air, so they decided to make gingerbread and fill the apartment with its sweet, spicy smell.

After a trip to the egg man and the flour seller, Tim and Katherine returned home, arms laden with everything they needed for baking. Entering the apartment, they found Brendan emerging from the bedroom. He was in his undershirt, with his suspenders hanging from the waist of his pants. He wordlessly took the bundles from her and placed them on a parlor table. Taking her in his arms, he said, "I can't live without you."

Katherine pulled away and turned to Tim. She bent down and sweetly asked, "My love, would you leave Brendan and me alone for a short while? We have something to discuss. I will come for you as soon as we are finished."

"What about the gingerbread?" he protested, scowling at Brendan.

"We'll bake later. I promise."

Katherine walked Tim to the door while he shot suspicious sideways glances at the interloper. He went home pouting and angry.

Tim found his mother doing the wash. She had a bar of brown soap in one hand and his father's pants in the other. A pile of his family's laundry, stacked at her feet, declared that she would not have time for gingerbread. The disappointed boy reluctantly sauntered into the parlor that served as a bedroom for all five boys and took out his notepad and a pencil to start a list.

The list enumerated all the reasons he believed Katherine loved him more than Brendan. First he wrote, "loves me," because she always called Tim "my love," and she referred to Brendan by his name.

Second on the list was "time." He reasoned she spent far more time with him than with Brendan. He went away and stayed away for weeks. When he was home, he left in the morning and did not return until Tim's bedtime. All the intervening hours, Katherine spent with Tim.

At number three, he wrote "speshal," because Katherine gave him little presents and did many special things just for him. She taught him to read and write. She bought him candy. She would sit beside him and put her arm around his shoulders and read to him, sometimes on her big bed. Tim knew that the big bed was a grownup place. He deduced that for Katherine to let him sit on the bed with her meant he was just as close to her as Brendan.

Finally, he never saw Katherine approach Brendan and give him a kiss or a hug. He reveled in the thought that she repeatedly bent over, opened her arms to him and asked him for a kiss. Tim loved to kiss Katherine. She smelled like lavender. Her hair was always soft and shiny. Her fingers were cool and her arms warm. When her lips touched his cheek, it was like a blessing from God. With "kiss and hug" at number four, he was absolutely sure she loved him more than she loved Brendan.

The belief that his place in Katherine's heart was far more secure than her husband's allowed the child to endure Brendan's persistent presence. It scared Tim that Brendan had returned with the intention of staying. Tim feared his time with Katherine would be limited, but Brendan quickly found work at the stable of the New York City Police Brigade. Much to Tim's approval, the job kept Brendan busy and out of the apartment for long hours every day.

By August, Katherine was pregnant. When she announced her condition to young Tim, she explained that "we" were having a baby. In Tim's immature and uneducated mind, he assumed the "we" referred to him and Katherine. Tim did not know how this miracle had occurred, but as a Catholic, he believed that miracles were a part of life. That a miracle had happened to him was no surprise. Katherine always referred to the child she was carrying as "our" baby. Tim was very pleased and proud. Whenever he spoke about "our" baby, no one understood his meaning; therefore, no one corrected his misunderstanding.

The baby arrived in February of 1851. The Nolans were all bewitched by the introduction of a girl into their lives. Mrs. Nolan welcomed a girl after being blessed with five boys. The Nolan boys were also intrigued by the baby's presence. They were old enough to appreciate other people in their world. Frank Junior was nearly fourteen-years-old, Sean was a curious twelve, Michael, the resentful middle child, was eleven and Brian, an active eight. They all found the baby a fascinating, albeit alien, life form.

Tim saw the child as a responsibility. He believed the baby was his and he had an obligation to take an active role in nurturing her. Katherine, in her sensitive style, never made him feel subordinate to the baby. She considered his feelings and included him whenever possible in every aspect of her care. Katherine wanted Tim to love the baby and be her guardian, and she told him so.

They named the baby Aislynn, after an ancient Celtic Goddess. She was round and pink with a tiny bow mouth. Her eyes were deep green and her hair was black. Aislynn grew slowly but matured quickly. At eleven months, she could climb out of the little basket bed, which sat on the floor, and crawl across the hall to find her friends. Words came by fourteen months. Her male admirers found everything she uttered amusing. Their vocal responses encouraged the young child to perform. Aislynn was center stage in a small, two-apartment theater. She grew confident, assertive and indulged. Only Katherine and Tim set limits on her.

*　　*　　*

The summer of 1854 hung on hot and humid. All day, in the brutal sun, the tenements inhaled heat. When darkness fell, the pent up energy of the day could barely be exhaled through small windows and few doors. On Worth Street, Katherine Denehy was confined to bed. Swollen from pregnancy, she was having difficulty breathing. She tried to lie still keeping the pressure of the baby off her chest. This pregnancy seemed to be taking over her whole body. Unlike Aislynn, who was eager to escape confinement and pushed down on her pelvis, this baby continually pushed up on her lungs. The repeated pressure made it difficult to breathe.

Katherine had curtailed all of her activities, spending most of her days in bed. Mrs. Nolan did her shopping, cooking and washing. Brendan helped with the cleaning. Tim began to assume complete responsibility for Aislynn: feeding, dressing and supervising her.

Almost ten-years-old, Tim was able to assist Katherine, too. The serious child sat with Katherine, quietly conversing or reading to her during Aislynn's naptimes. He lovingly applied cool, wet towels to her forehead and fanned her, shooing flies and the insistent heat away while showing his enormous affection for her in every attentive act.

On the morning of September 1st, Aislynn sat up on her cot and discovered her sleeping mother. With great self-satisfaction, she relieved herself and pulled on a dress. She toddled across the hall to find Tim. Mrs. Nolan and Tim were the only ones in their stuffy flat. The older boys and Papa Nolan had gone off to work and the younger two were swimming in the East River, trying to keep cool. After a light breakfast, the three crossed the hall.

Upon arrival, they found Katherine awake and in pain. She lay on the bed, clothed in a thin nightdress. Even in her distress, she looked like an angel to Tim. Her bright green eyes were large and glassy. Her hair, a riot of

22

dark curls, draped over the stark white pillow. The thin film of perspiration covering her body made her shine in the morning light like a heavenly body.

Mrs. Nolan asked Tim to take Aislynn to the stables and inform Brendan about the impending birth. Tim felt his stomach flip. He believed that having one baby was entirely sufficient. With school starting soon and his chores, he worried about the burden of a second child.

The two children started off in the sweltering heat toward the East River. Their route brought them into the dismal, deteriorating Five Points section of the city. Tim looked up at the foreboding buildings, the huge warehouses that stored humans too poor to afford adequate housing. He wondered why the city's fathers allowed such conditions. Landlords packed ten to a dozen people into one flat. Privies lined the basements and backyards, standing right next to the common wells that served as the only source of drinking water for the hundreds who inhabited each building. Garbage covered the streets. Rats ran through the narrow, eight-foot passageways that separated the buildings. At this time of the morning, not even the sun could slide through the tight alleys. To Tim, it was a dark, sinister looking forest of tall, dingy buildings. In Aislynn's mind, it was a mysterious, threatening fortress that could hold a princess or a little girl prisoner forever.

She followed Tim hesitantly into the dreariness. The stench of human and animal excretions blended with the smell of the rotting, fly-covered garbage strewn in the street and on the sidewalks. Aislynn balked at the filth and the horrid smells, refusing to go any farther. Tim halted for an instant, but he knew he had to obey his mother. He also knew that Katherine was suffering and depending on him to bring Brendan to her side. Patiently, he explained to Aislynn they were on an important mission. Aislynn was accustomed to getting her own way and would not budge. Tim pulled Aislynn's arm until she cried out in protest.

"Won't go! Smelly and dark!"

"I know it's scary, but I am with you. Remember Aislynn, no matter where we are or what is happening, if we're together, we can survive anything."

Aislynn considered her idol's reasoning. Although she wanted to believe she would be safe with Tim, her strong, practical side made her cautious about testing her theory. She chewed her lower lip and gazed around her. Her love and trust won out. She lifted her tiny hand and placed it in his. They trudged off into the unknown.

The walk was long for short legs. Aislynn struggled to keep pace with Tim. She repeatedly cried for him to slow down but Tim, carrying his own trepidation, tramped onward. He walked quickly and avoided eye contact with the people they passed. However, his eyes were busy; they searched in every direction for danger. He peered sideways into doors and alleys watching for vagrants who could hurt them. Looking upward, he checked for garbage dropping from windows. The sidewalk, cluttered with debris, also had to be examined. They were on an obstacle course he was determined they would maneuver without calamity.

Arriving at the stable, they found the doors were stretched open. Brendan was standing in the center of the huge, vaulted, brick building. The sun streamed down through a skylight, surrounding him in a square of gold. He was reaching up, brushing a horse's mane. To Aislynn, he looked like a knight in his castle, grooming his trusted steed. She released Tim's hand and ran to her father with her short arms spread wide, calling "Da!"

Tim joined her as Brendan bent to lift the child up over his head. Before Brendan could pose the question, Tim released his message in one long breath. "Katherine's havin' the baby. Mama sent us for you."

Brendan placed Aislynn on her feet. He said, "I'll be back."

Brendan disappeared for a few moments leaving the

children to admire the stables. The inside of this barn was a striking contrast to the streets of Five Points. The barn smelled of fresh hay and oats, lineament and soap. The vastness and the majesty of the structure fascinated Aislynn. She twirled, arms extended, trying to grab hold of all there was to see. Stalls of shiny reddish-brown mahogany lined the walls. Each cubicle was trimmed with polished brass fixtures. Bricks stretched across the entire floor. All of the horses were strong, straight, and neatly filed in their own spaces. It seemed like a palace for horses. Aislynn was so proud that it was her father's.

"We can leave." Brendan announced when he returned. He perched Aislynn on his shoulders and waved for Tim to follow. They made their way quickly back to Worth Street. Brendan flew into the bedroom leaving Aislynn and Tim standing in the parlor. Momentarily dejected, Tim felt forgotten. Suddenly, Tim heard Katherine's sweet, strained voice call him. His heart soared knowing that even with Brendan present, Katherine remembered him. He pushed past Brendan to be by her side.

Katherine reached out her cool fingered hand to Tim, and he grasped it in both of his. She smiled up at him and said, "Thank you, my love." Tim was rapt by the near-whisper and leaned close to her beautiful face. "Tim, will you take care of our girl? Read to her. Keep her safe. I just can't."

Without any hesitation, Tim agreed.

"You are a love. I knew I could depend on you." She brought his hands to her lips and softly kissed each one. Tim left the flat wearing Katherine's scent.

The day dragged on in the unrelenting heat. Tim tried to amuse Aislynn with his few toys, but his mind was in the Denehy apartment. He could hear periodic groans followed by soft voices and silence. Bringing Aislynn into the hallway, they sat on the floor pretending with her dolls. Mr. Rattawitz descended from the third floor, complained about the heat and inquired why they were not outside.

25

Tim explained that the baby was on its way and they wanted to be home for the birth.

"Mazel Tov!" Rattawitz exclaimed and went on his slow way out of the building. Tim listened as the old man padded down the ten front steps, his ears straining for sounds.

The hallway's varnished floor was tacky from the un-ending humidity and their sweaty bodies seemed to stick to it. Despite the opened doors, no air was moving. From their outpost, Tim watched the dust lazily floating up the stairway toward the skylight. *Somewhere at the end of that shaft of light is God.* Imagining a direct line of communi-cation, Tim prayed, "Please watch over Katherine."

Declaring her hunger, Aislynn whined for her lunch. Tim was grateful for her timing. He wanted to know what was occurring in Katherine's bedroom. Aislynn's hunger gave him an opportunity to enter the Denehy apartment and assess the situation.

Tim brought Aislynn into her kitchen and made her some bread and jam. He sat her at the table, and they qui-etly ate together. The meal fortified and emboldened Tim. He approached his mother for some news. Seeing his con-cern, she explained that it was normal for such things to take a long time.

At his mother's suggestion, Tim took Aislynn to their apartment. He stripped off her sweat-soaked dress, stood her in the laundry sink and rinsed her off. Aislynn liked the water and stood splashing until they were both cool.

He lifted the small girl into his arms and playfully dropped her on his parents' big bed. She jumped up and started to bounce until Tim stopped her, "Don't make a mess. We'll both get hanged." He pulled her damp dress over her head. "Sit and don't get heated again. I'm going to read to you."

Propped on his parents' pillows, Tim opened a book and began reading to her. Aislynn leaned her moist, baby-scented body against his chest. After several stories, she fell asleep. Though he wanted to get up and investigate the happenings across the hall, he did not want to wake her. He looked down at the soft lines of her small, round face. She was breathing through her tiny mouth that hung slightly open. Her wet hair was stuck to her cheeks.

Gazing at Aislynn, he remembered his promise to Katherine. For the first time, the thought that Katherine could die struck him. *She has to live. She can't leave me with this girl.* Fear swelled in his chest. Tim wrapped his arms around the sleeping child. Holding her made him feel stronger. He rested his head on the pillow and started to recite the prayers he had learned in school. The monotony of the recitation, the heat and the exhaustion from worry overcame him, and he slipped into a troubled sleep.

Tim woke to find Aislynn with one arm and one leg flung across his body. He carefully slid out from under her and emerged drowsy and disoriented to find his brothers in the kitchen, scouring for food. Remembering Katherine and her baby, Tim stumbled out into the hall and crossed into the Denehy flat. Standing in the doorway, Tim could see his mother's dark, sweaty back; her hair was tentatively pulled into a loose bun with wet locks randomly hanging down. He heard his mother encouraging Katherine and knew the trial continued.

Tim sat on the floor and waited. In his flat, he could hear Aislynn awake and playing with his brothers, oblivious of the struggle. Darkness began spreading its ominous wings and descending on the dying day. The constant worry and fear added to the wretched heat made time drag as though it towed a heavy weight. Still, he waited.

A high-pitched scream cut the thick air. He listened breathlessly as frantic words were exchanged inside the Denehy bedroom. With Katherine's scream, Tim felt a river of perspiration flow down his back. He was burning hot and shivering cold. The boys volleyed into the hall and stood wide-eyed and silent. Sean held Aislynn's face against his chest as the child, sensing disaster, whimpered. Mrs. Nolan appeared looking frantic. Her eyes caught Frank Junior's, and he jumped to attention.

"Go get the doctor quickly!" she commanded like a general in the pitch of a battle. Frank Junior responded to the order like a well-trained soldier. He flew down the front stairs, his footsteps quickly drowning in the din of the street as he ran to complete his directive.

Mrs. Nolan turned to reenter the Denehy apartment when she suddenly stopped. The boys could see from the tilt of her head and her arms suspended in midair, that she was contemplating additional action. She turned back to the boys and took a deep ragged breath, "Michael, go get the priest."

Getting the priest meant someone was dying. Tim closed his eyes and prayed through his tears. He knew it was wrong, but every part of him cried out to strike a bargain with God. "Please, take that baby. We don't need another baby. The priest can come, baptize that brat and I swear to You, I will never do anything bad in my whole life. Just please, please don't let Katherine die," he supplicated.

The screaming grew louder. He could hear his mother saying words like breech, cord, and something else about suffocating. Tim wanted to cry, but he could barely breathe for fear he might miss some vital information.

As Katherine's screaming stopped, Brendan began to wail. The sound cut through Tim like a saber. It struck deep at a place in his heart he had never felt before. A weeping man was not a part of Tim's world; men did not cry. With that thought, Brendan's sobbing was muffled.

Frank Junior returned with the doctor. He entered the bedroom, and an "Oh, dear!" burst into the hall. Frantic movement commenced within the room. Katherine screamed. They heard the doctor yelling at Katherine as though she were deaf. "Stay with me, Mrs. Denehy. The child is dead. I'm going to break the skull. I'm going to use

28

this instrument, just stay with me now. Relax your muscles. Keep her awake there, man."

The boys were strewn around the hallway in various levels of distress. Frank Junior took charge and lifted Aislynn from Sean's arms. "Come on, Lovey. You come with me. You boys come home, too."

Tim watched his brothers disappear into the Nolan parlor. The door slowly swung closed with a soft snap. Numbness set in as Tim listened to the stunning sounds and inhaled the nauseating smells emerging from the flat. Tim felt weak and feared he would vomit.

Bustling up the stairs and fumbling with his bag, the priest entered the dim hall with Michael close at his heels. He rushed into the flat and cried, "Blessed Jesus."

Tim needed to see what was happening. He quietly crept into the Denehy flat and hid under their kitchen table, watching the legs of the people who remained in the bedroom. From his post, Tim could hear the conversation clearly. Katherine was hemorrhaging. There was some movement on the part of the doctor. "I could give her some morphia and ease her pain, and then she can slip away in her sleep."

"She'll not slip away!" Brendan cried. "Katherine, please stay with me." Brendan sat on the bed, amid the mess of birth and death. He put his arms around Katherine, "Stop bleedin'. Please stop bleedin'. Take me strength. I give you every drop. Please take it, me love, take all of it."

An airy whisper floated from Katherine's lips, "I'm so tired, Brendan."

"I know love, rest. I'm right here. Just don't give up. Stay with me, Katherine. Stay with me." His pleading drove Mrs. Nolan from the room. She stumbled, tearblind, into the parlor. Tim could hear the doctor close his bag and saw him leave the bedroom. He heard his mother thank the doctor as he fled the scene. His mother fell to her knees on the parlor rug and doubled over in tears and prayer.

Tim heard Katherine speak again. "I'll always be with you," was followed by hollow, breathless silence. He craned his neck trying to get closer to the bedroom without being discovered, straining to see.

Katherine's breathing was ragged. Between painful gasps, she said, "If you need me, just close your eyes. I'll be right here with you."

Tim heard Katherine struggling for air. He saw the bed shaking and heard Brendan's frantic voice, "Let me hold you, me love. I'll hold you and everything will be fine. You're not goin' anywhere...stayin' with me."

No sound came from Katherine or Brendan, but the priest began to mumble last rights. The dark angel had descended and it was not leaving alone. Mary Nolan wearily rose from the floor and, on leaden legs, returned to the bedroom. She bent over Katherine's body and felt her neck for its life-affirming throb. Touching the pulseless girl sent Mary into a wail that made Tim snap his head up, cracking it on the table. His entire body was perspiring. It seemed his grief leaked from all his pores, flowing down his back and his forehead, dripping down his face. His head fell into his hands, and he cried.

Looking up, Tim could barely recognize anything in the dark flat. Night had fallen hard and moonless. A single candle burned in the bedroom. His eyes searched the void. Trapped in his hiding place, he needed a chance, just a moment to see Katherine.

Neglected and lonely for her mother, Aislynn boldly strode into the Denehy flat and pushed her way into the bedroom. She hastily climbed onto the bed and demanded a hug from her mother. She lifted her mother's arms, which lay lifelessly over Brendan's shoulders, attempting to wiggle under them. When no response came, she started to pitifully plead for a hug. "Mama, I need hug, Mama please." Not meeting any success, she tried to move the arm her father had wrapped around Katherine. "Da help me. I need hug. Mama, please." In frustration and anger, Aislynn began pulling at Brendan's hair to lift his head. The priest and Mrs. Nolan stood in shocked silence, yet neither one moved.

Tim heard the commotion and realized that he had not kept his pledge to Katherine. The very day she charged him with the responsibility of Aislynn, he had failed to fulfill his promise. Guilt moved him.

Unfolding, Tim emerged from under the kitchen table. He straightened, steeled himself and entered the bedroom. The scene nearly overcame him. Katherine lay amid the blood and filth. Her body was twisted in the stained sheets. Her legs and feet, which he had never seen bared before, were partially revealed. Ashen, stonelike, her head rested on the soiled, damp pillow. Katherine's tangled hair reached across her expressionless face. Aislynn was straddling her mother and leaning over her father begging for attention. Swallowing hard, Tim took two sharp breaths. With his eyes riveted on the girl, he said, "Aislynn, let's kiss your mother good night and I will give you all the hugs you need." He closed his eyes and brushed his lips across Katherine's gaping mouth. He could feel his heart collapsing, as his throat made odd choking sounds, and he struggled for breath. While rising from his kiss, Tim caught Brendan's disoriented gaze. Putting aside the jealousy he had held toward the man, the boy paused near Brendan's face. With as much empathy and compassion his young heart could muster, he whispered, "It's time to let her go."

Aislynn, watching Tim, responded to his command and to his emotion. She kissed her mother's cheek and with bewildered sympathy, reached her chubby arms up to embrace Tim. He lifted the child off her mother. With her legs wrapped around his waist, he held her against his chest. He knew her hug was the only thing that was keeping him from coming apart and scattering like fallen leaves around the room. She was keeping him whole. Yet, he believed that everything in her narrow life rested on him. He had to do the right thing.

While the family attended the funeral, Tim stayed home with Aislynn. For two days, Tim had been in mourning; however, no one seemed to notice. Everyone was concerned about Brendan and Aislynn; no one understood his pain. His parents expected him to help prepare for the funeral and care for Aislynn. Katherine would not have forgotten his needs. He felt disconsolate without her. A piece of himself was missing. He had heard that when people lost a limb, an arm or a leg, they continued to feel its presence. He felt this way about Katherine. He knew she was gone, but he believed she was still there, somewhere. Tim put Aislynn into his parents' big bed for a nap and went across the hall to find Katherine.

In the Denehy apartment, he found Katherine's belongings. Her rocker rested in the parlor next to the window. He sat in her chair and rocked for a minute, stroking the chair's arm. The sun blazed and at this time of the year, it streamed into the flat. *Katherine loved the sun.* He rose and wandered into the bedroom.

Tim looked at the bed. The soiled linens had been burned in the stove. All evidence of the tragedy had been removed and a void remained.

Approaching the dresser at the foot of the bed, Tim gently caressed the lace covering the top. His fingers ran around the mirror's frame and came to rest at the daguerreotype Katherine had placed there. Tim lifted the wedding portrait and squinted at Katherine's tiny, faded face. The blurred photo did not relieve any of his longing.

Tim boldly lay upon the bed and looked out the window to the sky. He closed his eyes. He could see her, but he could not feel her. Stretching his arms, he ran his hands over the covers. He thought about her last touch, her cool fingers and her soft lips. Tim felt a need for her run the full length of his body. He needed more; he wanted something to hold.

He sat up in frustration. At the end of the bed, the dresser called to him. Crawling across the covers, he reached the foot of the bed. He swung his legs down and sat on the edge. Tim opened the top drawer. Brendan's belongings filled the space. Tim slammed it shut and pulled on the lower knobs. Looking into the gaping drawer, Tim could not have experienced greater awe if he had discovered a religious relic. Linens, laces, silks and cottons in the form of underdrawers, camisoles, negligees, stockings, and handkerchiefs lay folded. He had uncovered a treasure of feminine unmentionables. Completely forgetting he believed Katherine to be watching, his young male curiosity took over. Tim's hands reached for the shiny silk. The entire piece quivered at his slight touch. He snatched his hand back. When he fully reassured himself that it was lifeless and not bewitched in any way, he lifted the camisole up to view it in its entirety. He was excited by the softness in his hands. He leaned back and draped it over his face. Katherine's scent clung to the garment, and it sent a thrill through his short body.

Tim quickly realized that prying into Katherine's private cache of clothes was disrespectful, as were the feelings he was having for her. He folded the silk and returned it to its place. Still tempted by the array of intimates, he cautiously ran his hand under the lace negligee and quickly discerned that one could have seen Katherine's breasts through something that sheer. Feeling strangely aroused, he tried to suppress the crude vision. Shame and tiny traces of guilt fell like snow in his consciousness. The recollection of Katherine watching from heaven made his cheeks burn with embarrassment. As he made excuses to himself, he was comforted by the thought that Katherine would understand. Katherine knew he loved her, and she knew he had not meant to be indecent.

Looking over the contents in the drawer, Tim wondered what Brendan would do with Katherine's belongings. He reasoned that they should be saved; every last piece should be preserved, as in a museum, in tribute to Katherine. Someday, he imagined, they could be presented to Aislynn with great pageantry to mark her transformation into a woman like Katherine. Tim picked up a delicate handkerchief. The silk shimmered. It was the color of peach ice cream and just as cool and smooth. A small "K," embroidered in deep green thread, shone from one corner. He drew his finger over the letter, knowing that Katherine had pushed every millimeter of thread through the silk and pulled it out again to form her initial. Glancing about, like the thief that he was, he folded the hankie and placed it into the pocket over his heart, all the while telling himself that Brendan had so many of Katherine's things, he would never miss this one small item.

With his eyes closed, Tim fell back on the bed, his hands crossed over his heart. His tears rolled down the side of his face, past his ears and dropped on the bed where they were instantly absorbed by the coverlet. He lay alone in the apartment, alone on the bed; yet, he finally felt her presence. He could feel her in the room, her aura settling around him. He heard her soft, tiny voice calling his name. He turned his head expecting to see a glowing, diaphanous apparition floating gracefully before him. Instead, Tim found a little girl, with black curls and big, green eyes. For a moment, disappointment surged through him. Tears of anger brimmed in his eyes. Aislynn tilted her head and looked at him. She smiled a familiar smile and brushed his face with her cool, little fingers, saying, "My love." A gentle acceptance rose from Tim's heart and he reached out his arms.

Chapter 4

With Tim in Utah, Aislynn waited for the mail to arrive every day hoping for a letter. The Christmas Eve delivery left her disappointed and late for the communal dinner at the Parish Hall. When she opened the door of the hall's kitchen, she stepped into the smell of stew and a wall of heat that made the windows sweat.

The kitchen had only one occupant. Mrs. Tully stood at one of the four large stoves. Her body, heavy and wide from bearing seven children, heaved when she saw Aislynn. "I have been waitin' on you, Miss. Your men are starvin' out there. Everyone else is bein' served."

"I'm sorry. I've just been so busy," Aislynn replied. To expedite her reunion with Tim, Aislynn decided she had to earn money to either help him return or pay for her passage to Utah. She took the only job she could find, as a companion to elderly Mrs. Pearson. She diligently saved her one dollar a week.

Mrs. Tully said, "I'm sure you have, love and t'will be a busier year. I do wish you every happiness."

The comment flew past Aislynn's ears and she gave a standard reply. "Happy Christmas to you, too."

Aislynn lifted the tray holding bowls and a tureen of stew. With her foot, she opened the door to the hall and searched the room for her family's table. Ropes of pine boughs and strips of white paper draped the bare wooden rafters. Candles sitting on beds of evergreens perched on every sill, threw halos of light on the watery windows. A small tree stood proudly in the corner of the hall, dotted with candles and red bows. For a moment, the excited air in the room cheered Aislynn, and she forgot how much she missed Tim. He had been gone nearly three months, and thoughts of him ceaselessly crowded her mind.

When she located her men, she noticed the Mahers were seated with them. At first, Aislynn thought it was nice that the Mahers were joining their group, but her thoughts shifted to suspicions. *Da invited them. He's pushing Johnny on me again.* A dread rose and her body started to tingle with tension. *Dear God! He couldn't have made any promises, not without asking me.* She tried to calm herself. *No, not even my Da, inconsiderate and immature as he is, would make promises and neglect to consult me.*

Convinced she was right, Aislynn exhaled with relief and approached the empty seat next to Johnny. She greeted her family with a "Happy Christmas" as she settled the tray at her place. With a quick curtsey in Mrs. Maher's direction, she said, "It's so nice you could join us."

Mrs. Maher leaned her broad frame toward Aislynn. Her wide, freckled face smiled, "Aislynn, we're so thrilled to be here, sharin' Christmas with our new family."

Aislynn's eyes flew open. A great gasp escaped her lips. She wheeled around and glared at her father. On the rim of rage, her hands gripped the edge of the table; her locked arms were the only things keeping her upright.

The eyes of everyone at the table began darting, looking for an explanation. Sean stood. All attention veered toward his movement. He picked up the empty pitcher of ale and said, "Aislynn, take Brendan into the kitchen and fill this. Brendan, go!"

Brendan rose, and propelled by Sean's shove, he stumbled toward the kitchen. Aislynn followed. She was numb and could barely feel her feet pad across the trail to the door.

Without thinking, Aislynn directed Brendan out of the kitchen, onto the snowy stairs and closed the heavy door behind them. Grabbing the frosty railing for strength, she leaned into her father's face. "What have you done?" she cried.

"I consented to the boy payin' court to you," Brendan replied with his nose in the air.

"You know I don't want Johnny."

"I'll not have you moonin' over a man who don't want you. He's not comin' home and if he does, it won't be to you," he insisted.

"But I love Tim."

"I know you think that. But you'll grow to love Johnny. You know in Ireland many families make these arrangements and the couples end up lovin' each other."

"This is America and I'm an American. You can't make arrangements. Besides, you married for love; I should be able to do the same."

Brendan's face grew red. He set his feet on the slippery snow, his hands on his hips and announced, "Our parents weren't here. We had to make our own decisions. But I am here and I'm your Da. I can do what I think best, and this is best. Aislynn, I'm gettin' old. I don't have much to leave you. Let me go to my grave knowin' you'll be taken care of."

"You're not going anywhere."

"When I do, I want you well married, and he's the best I can do!"

Aislynn felt weak as a new fear swept over her, "Da, did you promise I'd actually marry him?"

"No, but if you want to humiliate me before the whole parish, you'll refuse the choice your ol' Da has made for you. 'Tis up to you. Now I'm cold and I'm goin' to eat me dinner." He brushed past her and disappeared into the kitchen.

Aislynn stood on the landing shivering and biting her lip. She fought tears while she tried to think of an acceptable way to disengage herself without insulting the Mahers or humiliating her father. Although her father's heart was in the right place, she just wished he would let her make her own decisions. In Aislynn's mind, if she wanted to hold on to the hope of Tim, why should anyone interfere with her choice?

Melting snow was seeping through her thin shoes. Her cold feet reminded her she must move them in one direction or another. She composed herself with the thought that given time, she could find a way to get what she wanted.

As Aislynn entered the hall, old Mr. Malloy was squeaking his fiddle into tune. Sean's eyes caught hers and she saw him report her return to the table's occupants. The conversation stopped and Aislynn was greeted by silent expectation. She threw her shoulders back and stood at her place, feeling the anxiety radiating from Johnny's body and hearing his short breaths. With her eyes focused on the stew, she ladled a bowl for her Da and shoved it at him; only its thickness kept it from sloshing over into his face. Following custom, she filled the next bowl for Papa Nolan, her second father. Everyone waited to see whom she would serve next. As a guest, Mrs. Maher was in line but as her intended, Johnny took precedence over his mother and the other men. She could feel their anticipation and knew what they wanted, but Aislynn believed she should make her own choices. Aislynn looked up at Sean; his eyes pleaded with her as they shot toward Johnny. Grimacing, she closed her eyes and handed the stew to Johnny.

Johnny took the bowl in both of his hands and turned his face up to Aislynn's. "Thank you," he said, sending her a grateful grin.

Aislynn could feel her heart softening, her anger draining into pity. With a long, calming breath, she gave him a sympathetic smile and said, "Happy Christmas."

The Mahers joined the Denehys at midnight mass. Kneeling between her father and Johnny, Aislynn felt trapped. On one side, she could feel her father's critical gaze. On the other, she could feel Johnny's discomfort in the taut muscles of his arm and his thigh as they pressed against her in the crowded church. If she looked out of the corner of her eye, she could see the muscles in his jaw were tight. She leaned back against the pew, and with her head bent, feigning prayer, she studied him from under her lashes. He was just a hair taller than Tim, but everything about Johnny was big: his legs, arms, back, shoulders and head. He had a round face and when he smiled, a chipped tooth, broken in a fight, was revealed. His grey eyes, sandy hair and pink-toned skin were not features Aislynn found attractive.

Disinterested in Johnny, Aislynn's attention shifted. She watched the smoke from the candles and incense rise to the ceiling. Among the beams, Aislynn imagined thousands of prayers still swirled, waiting to be answered. Sometimes she feared if she took too large a breath, she might inhale someone else's wishes, requested long ago but still held captive under the thick slate roof with no escape. Aislynn added her own request, asking God to let her join Tim or let him come home.

Her eyes wandered and found other distractions to engage her imagination. Two rows ahead, the Tullys sat with their array of children and grandchildren. *That's what I want. I want a real family with children, and I want it with Tim. We could work together and buy land, have our own home.* Her eyes fell on the O'Mallys. Mrs. O'Mally had her head down and a veil draped over her face. Aislynn wondered what was hidden beneath. She knew in her world, marriage reigned supreme, regardless of the conditions. Women stayed in marriages through drunkenness, violence, and neglect. They stayed, bound by canon and civil law, and to maintain social standing. Women without men were pitied. It seemed better to be in a bad marriage than in no marriage. *My marriage will be wonderful; if it's with Tim.*

Aislynn folded her hands and placed them on the pew in front of her. Johnny's hands rested next to hers and she studied them. His thick fingers were entwined. Black, ash-filled lines ran chaotically through his skin, abruptly halting at the places where smooth scars had been burned into his flesh. His thumbs stood sentinel, guarding his palms that were thick with calluses, the natural armor against the tools of his trade. Aislynn gazed at the soot embedded around his thumbnails, shaped in the form of little ebony smiles. *As big as they are, they seem to be kind, gentle hands.*

Christmas morning mass was a repeat of midnight mass. The Mahers joined the Denehys and the Nolans at church, and they all proceeded to Worth Street for Christmas dinner. Aislynn had decorated the shelves and sills of both apartments with holly and pine. She hung two evergreen boughs tied with red ribbon on the doors of both apartments. Presents trimmed with ribbons were stacked in the Nolan's parlor. The Nolan's kitchen table had been moved into the Denehy parlor, which would allow everyone to eat in the same flat.

Once home, Aislynn retreated to the kitchen. Since Tim's departure, Aislynn found diversion in cooking. She planned a meal starting with beet soup, called borscht, one of the many recipes she copied over the years from old Mr. Rattawitz. After the soup, she presented a roasted goose dripping fat over its potato stuffing to her appreciative diners. Applesauce, green peas and cranberry preserves were served with the goose. For days prior to this main event, Aislynn had baked whiskey cake, fruitcake and apple pies.

After the meal, everyone squeezed into the Nolan parlor to open gifts. Frank Junior and his wife, Patsy, brought their young son, who delighted the group by wrapping himself in discarded ribbons and twirling among the presents. When all the packages were opened, Brendan announced that Johnny had a gift for Aislynn. Johnny, standing outside the circle, shot a surprised look at Brendan and shook his head. Patsy squealed, "Let's see! Let's see!"

Johnny's pale skin went red and looking across the room, he searched Aislynn's face. Her eyes were wide, her mouth taut. They looked at each other as though they had been caught committing a terrible crime. Aislynn heard Patsy coaxing Johnny and silently wished the woman would be struck dumb.

Brendan said, "Come on, Son. It's fine." He directed Johnny toward Aislynn with his arms raised high like Moses parting the sea. Scowling at Brendan, Johnny turned back to Aislynn, who gave him a weak smile. Onlookers murmured encouragement. With a sigh, Johnny took the seat next to Aislynn. Looking over the crowd, Johnny pulled a small box from his shirt pocket and passed it into her waiting palm.

Aislynn said, "Thank you." She rested the present in her lap and covered it with her hands.

"Open it!" Patsy cried.

Please God, just render her unconscious for a few minutes.

Aislynn bit her lip and looked up at Johnny for some direction. Johnny shrugged.

She untied the bow and removed the top. Peering inside, she saw a small, gold Claddagh ring in the shape of a heart wearing a crown. Embedded in the crown was a small diamond chip. Aislynn gasped loudly as her mouth dropped open and her hand flew to her breast. "Oh, Johnny, this is far too dear."

Johnny grinned and whispered, "I wanted you to have it."

Aislynn chewed her lip, biting her way through three phases of emotion: guilt, remorse and fear. The ring and its meaning terrified her.

Patsy rushed forward and grabbed the box, "Oh, my heavens, look at it. It has a real diamond, not that I would know what a real diamond looked like because I don't have one," she glowered at Frank Junior, "but I'm sure it's real."

Patsy pushed the box at Johnny and commanded, "Put it on her."

"She can wear it when she's ready." Johnny mumbled in Aislynn's direction handing her the gift.

"Kiss him, Aislynn! You have to give him a kiss!"

Aislynn's wide eyes strafed the room. "God," she prayed silently, "strike her down or I will."

She heard Johnny say, "We'll do our kissin' in private, Patsy."

She accepted the reprieve gratefully. She knew it was not a full pardon and she would have to talk her way out of this ever-escalating mess.

Johnny slapped his hands on his thighs and stood over Aislynn. "I think I'd like to get some fresh air."

Aislynn slipped the ring in her apron pocket and rose. Looking up at Johnny, she said, "I have to start cleaning up," and began walking toward her apartment.

"He wants you to go with him, you ninny." Patsy informed Aislynn.

"I have the whole kitchen a mess," she explained.

"Don't worry, love," Mrs. Maher interjected, "we women will clean up the dishes. You worked so hard preparin' such a lovely meal. 'Tis the least we can do. You two run along."

Aislynn's legs were like lead. Johnny took her hand and they descended the steps to the sidewalk. She wordlessly followed his quick pace through the quiet street as their shoes squeaked on the fresh snow. Aislynn did not know where they were going, but she knew they were going together.

They arrived at the church. The thick, wooden doors were unlocked. Johnny pulled one door open. With his free hand on Aislynn's back, he guided her inside. The church was dark and deserted. Candles had been extinguished and the sunlight was dying with the day. He took her arm and walked her down the main aisle. They automatically genuflected in front of the altar and took seats in the first pew.

Johnny settled back on the bench, crossed his arms and stretched his legs. "Your father didn't tell you," he began in an offhanded way.

Aislynn balanced on the edge of her seat, facing him with her hands folded in her lap. She shook her head. Without time to prepare her defense, Aislynn's mind was grasping for valid, compassionate justifications to explain why their union could never happen.

"You've known for a very long time I was goin' to ask."

She nodded. Impelled to get the truth out, she blurted, "You know how I feel about Tim."

"Aislynn," he smiled, "you have plenty of room in your heart for both of us."

"You don't understand; I really love him."

"I do understand. It's expected and I'm not askin' you to stop lovin' him."

Aislynn stared at him for a moment sure he had no comprehension of her true feelings. She decided to take a different approach, "We can't get married now; we're too young."

"I agree. We have to wait for at least a year, maybe

more. I found some property I think would be good for a smithy. It's uptown but the price is too high. If I can get the owner to come down, I'll buy it. Even then, it will be a while before I can build much more than the shop. I was thinkin' of puttin' two rooms on the back for us to use just 'til we can afford a house."

Aislynn brightened when she heard the word "house." She wanted a home. However, with or without a house, she did not want to marry Johnny and she did not feel he understood. Before she could respond, he said, "Let's just wait and see what happens."

She nodded, believing the longer they waited the more time she would have to find a way to convince Johnny and her father this was not a good match.

Johnny rose and pulled her to her feet. "Let's say a prayer before we leave."

He knelt at the altar. Aislynn sank to her knees next to him. She looked up and saw the last light of day floating through the stained glass window depicting the Holy Family. The Blessed Virgin, glowing in the pale light, was smiling at her infant son while her adoring husband gazed down on them. *How serene and secure she appears. She had no idea what heartbreak awaited her.* Praying the Virgin and her Son would watch over her family and keep everyone safe and healthy, the Mahers included, she made a particular plea to God to keep Tim warm through the notoriously cold Utah winter.

When she crossed herself, Johnny asked, "Where's the ring?"

"In my apron."

"Let me have it."

Aislynn was reluctant to return such a precious gift but she dug in her pocket and extracted the ring. Johnny took her right hand in his and placed the ring on her finger with the heart pointing away from her heart, symbolizing the ring was given in friendship. He said, "When you're ready, you can turn it around." With the heart pointing toward hers, the ring would signify engagement. She was sure he expected her to move it to her left hand on their wedding day.

Aislynn accepted his gesture and thought, for now, she could live with the arrangement. He stood and helped her up from the kneeler. Johnny lifted her hands and released them around his neck. Quickly, he reached around her back and pulled her close. "Have you ever been kissed?" he grinned.

"Of course not," she whispered. "Who would kiss me with you threatening any boy who ever spoke to me?"

"Ah," Johnny smiled, "my plan worked."

Aislynn twisted her mouth and stuck her nose in the air.

"Well, I'm goin' to kiss you."

Aislynn thought kissing Johnny might be exciting and educational. When she saw Tim again, she thought it would be advantageous to know how to kiss. Aislynn puckered her lips tightly as Johnny's came down on hers.

He pulled back and shook his head.

"What's wrong?" she asked.

"That wasn't very good."

Furious, her hands slipped to his shoulders and she tried to push him away. Johnny tightened his grip, as she demanded, "What did you expect? Unlike you, I haven't been practicing all over the neighborhood with the likes of Patty Downs and Linda Gallagher."

Johnny laughed, "Aislynn, a man needs some experience and someday you'll be grateful I've had it."

"As though I'm interested in anything you'll ever know." She pushed him again.

"Just relax your mouth; don't try so hard." Acquiescing, she allowed Johnny to kiss her.

"That was much better, but you'll need to practice," he coaxed. Johnny's hand slipped into her hair as his lips moved slowly over hers. His other hand pressed on her back until her breasts were crushed against his chest. In her heavy coat, Aislynn began to feel warm and uncomfortable. When he lifted his mouth, she squirmed in his arms saying, "That's enough."

"I've got at least a million more."

Aislynn's curiosity was roused. She lowered her eyes and tilting her head to one side peered at him. "Save them," she suggested in a voice that carried an invitation.

It soon became Johnny's habit to keep company with Aislynn each evening after her family finished eating dinner and went on their way to Quigley's Pub. While Aislynn washed dishes, ironed, mended, sewed or knitted, they talked or Johnny read aloud. On rare evenings when her chores were done, they would play checkers or card games. Aislynn found him amusing and could admit to being fond of him. Despite these feelings, Tim occupied a deeper place in her heart and her imagination. Through time and distance, she could attribute all the bright, good things he was and deny the negative. When she looked at Johnny, real and flawed, he fell short of her romantic desire.

The winter of 1867-68 was an unusually harsh one. It brought heavy snow and low temperatures. For Aislynn, the sun emerged and the world warmed on February 20th. Tim sent a telegram for her birthday. It was short, but one paid by the word. "Happy Birthday. Miss you."

Aislynn read much more into the four words. The telegram told her he loved her and could not live without her. It said he would return to New York or she could join him. She would see him again and when she did, everything between them would be the way she fantasized it to be. It gave her hope and her love thrived on hope. She carried the missive in her apron pocket all day and checked it periodically to confirm his affection. At night, it was kissed and gently placed under her pillow. There was no more important piece of paper in her world.

A few warm days brought a brief thaw in March. The damp smells of spring rose in the air. The streets became a slushy mess, with puddles hiding ice. On the night of March 2nd, the men returned from work to a kitchen redolent with the scent of bread pudding. Although Brendan was absent, Aislynn fed the men their meals. They boisterously argued the impeachment of President Johnson throughout the main course.

As Aislynn served the bubbling dessert, the door opened and Johnny stood solemn faced, twisting his hat in his hands. Aislynn was surprised to see him so early but she casually asked him to sit and share their pudding. Johnny's eyes narrowed and raced across the cheerful group. His gaze held a question as it locked on Aislynn. She crossed the room and extended her hands, pulling him toward the table. Suspecting Johnny held a secret, she teased, "What is it?"

Johnny's face fell, his mouth moved wordlessly.

Chapter 5

Brendan had died instantly. While grooming a horse, he slipped on an invisible sheet of ice. Brendan's excited flailing spooked the mare. She reared and caught him in the chest, crushing his ribs into his heart and his lungs.

Aislynn passed through the wake and the funeral with complete equanimity. She repeatedly admonished Sean, Papa Nolan and Johnny for all their fussing about her. Knowing the Police Brigade made the funeral arrangements, she busied herself cooking in anticipation of her father's mourners. Aislynn cooked for two days. When the crowd departed, she cleaned. She stood un-supported at the burial, holding her head high. Although she acknowledged being an orphan, Aislynn knew she was resourceful and capable and assured those concerned she could carry on without her father.

After the funeral, she strove to get her life back in

order. She sent the Nolans to work with their supper pails filled and promised a fine dinner upon their return. When they were far down the street, Aislynn returned to her room, lay on her bed and cried herself blind.

A knock on the door brought her into control. She wiped her eyes and hurried to the door. She opened it on a police officer dressed in his blue uniform, buttons shining in the sun from the skylight. Assuming he came to express his condolences, Aislynn felt honored by the man's personal visit. He spoke formally, "Miss Denehy?"

"Yes," Aislynn answered, "Won't you come in?"

"No, ma'am. I'm just here to deliver this. It's from Sergeant James." He handed her an envelope.

Aislynn thanked the officer and watched him leave, listening to his quick, sharp steps as they struck the stairs. Closing the door, Aislynn sat in her mother's rocker in the parlor and opened the letter. Sergeant James had been a friend to her father. Knowing the police took up collections when one of their members died, she expected the envelope to contain money.

Aislynn pulled out a bill for the funeral amounting to the sum of sixty-four dollars. She blinked and shook her head. *This must be a mistake.*

Pulling on her shawl, she dashed to the Commissioner's Office on Mulberry Street. A solid stone arch etched with the words "Police Brigade" formed a portico on the front of the granite building and shaded the entryway. It felt degrees colder as she mounted the steps and pushed open the thick wooden door. Inside, the vaulted stone ceiling amplified the sound. There were about a dozen people casually milling and talking, but it sounded like an unruly crowd.

Aislynn approached an officer seated alone at a desk and asked to see Sergeant James. Her anxiety waned as James appeared and extended his arms to embrace Aislynn. "May I please speak to you privately?" she inquired.

James led her to a seat in a quiet corner. Aislynn produced the bill and asked if there were some mistake. "Oh, no. The brigade made the arrangements, but they would never pay for the funeral; that is a privilege reserved for officers."

"But sixty-four dollars, where would I get that kind of money?"

"I wouldn't know, but if you'd like, I could take up a collection. We do that for the needy."

Aislynn had never considered herself among the ranks of the poor. With her seven years of Catholic education, few nice clothes and three-room flat, she considered herself above those wretched souls packed into slums. Feeling her status had devolved a notch, she felt the need to redeem her place. Straightening, she spoke in a cool, businesslike tone, "No thank you, sir." James bowed his head and apologized for his suggestion.

She threw her head back and held her chin up, "Officer James, I must also inquire about the annuity the Brigade extends to orphans."

"That, too, is only offered to officers' children, and they must be under the age of sixteen."

Aislynn met the news without reaction. The words sank in but she would not allow him to see her disappointment. "Thank you for your time, Sergeant. I appreciate you sharing this information." She rose gracefully and strode across the broad stones paving the floor with her head held high, balancing her station in life on the tip of her nose.

Panic rose from her belly, and she could feel it tingling in her limbs as she rushed through the slick streets to return home. She threw the door open and flew into her bedroom. Sitting on the edge of the bed, she faced the dresser she and her father had shared. Opening his top drawer, she started to fling its contents on the bed. Lying under the clothes, she found a tiny pistol. Examining it, she considered the reasons why Brendan might own a gun. *He must have acquired it while running from the law in Ireland.* It seemed useless to her. She placed it next to

51

a small pile of bullets and disregarded it. Slamming the drawer closed, she attacked the one below. Tucked on one side she discovered an envelope with her name on it. *Thank God, he has left me something.*

With a deep breath, she calmed herself and gently slipped her finger under the seal and broke it.

To My Dearest Daughter Aislynn,

If you're reading this I must be dead or close to it. Tim has consented to be your guardian; it seemed most fitting. I can trust him to always guide you to do what is right.

Your mother and I are sorry to have left you at such a young age but it was not in our power to stay. We will watch over you while you travel through your earthly life and we wait to see you again. Until that time, know you have all of our love and in some way, we are with you.

Your loving and devoted Father.

Aislynn gently ran her finger over the letter and folded it carefully. After a moment of thought, she slapped it on the dresser and looked up to heaven and shouted, "You gave me a guardian, did you? You should have given me money. Where is the money? How am I to live?"

Aislynn emptied the drawer and found some of Katherine's delicate clothing wrapped in tissue paper at the bottom. Her heart swelled when she remembered her parents' love. For a moment, she felt happy they were together. However, in seconds, she returned to her immediate concern. She began to quest the bedroom: dismantling the dresser, wiggling under the beds, shaking out boxes where she stored linens, and overturning the mattresses. Her search widened to the kitchen: rummaging through the cabinet, checking under the sink, and peeking behind the stove. In the parlor, she shook out every book, removed every cushion, and dug into her sewing box, yet nothing appeared.

Night had fallen when Sean and Papa Nolan walked into the Denehy parlor to find it ransacked. When Aislynn explained the circumstances surrounding the disruption, the men exchanged glances and agreed to help her pull up the rug and turn over the couch. Their efforts were no more fruitful than Aislynn's.

Aislynn allowed them to straighten the rooms as she went into the kitchen to start dinner. She worked silently, her mind spinning over her problems. She needed sixty-four dollars for the funeral debt, but she only had eighteen. Once she paid the bill, she had to make a living, but she did not know how. Tears spilled over as fast as she could brush them away with the back of her hand.

Brian and Michael returned home and they all sat down to a hasty meal of fried eggs and ham with apple fritters. While the men ate quietly, Aislynn moved food around her plate. Michael broke the silence, "Why don't you just marry Johnny?"

Sean's head jerked up, "She doesn't want to get married. She's only seventeen, for Christ sakes. And besides, when she does marry Johnny, who is goin' to take care of us?"

Aislynn shook her head and announced, "I have to get a job."

"You have a job," Sean said shortly, flashing an angry look at Aislynn, "You don't need another."

"One dollar a week won't pay for an apartment and food, not to mention shoes and clothes. And, good heavens, where am I to get sixty-four dollars?" She shook her head, "No, I've got to find work."

"I'm talkin' about your job here. We'll not have you goin' into some strange man's home and doin' for him." Sean nodded to his father.

Papa Nolan interjected, "Aislynn, your job is takin' care of us. You've been doin' the woman's work since my Mary,.. since you were a wee one. 'Tis time we started to pay you back. Now, you may not like the idea, but you must live with us. We can't go payin' for two apartments, you know. But, we can be comfortable together in one. And we will all give you fifty cents a month for your spendin' money. We could all skip a few pints," he glared at Michael who was leaning back in his chair and pouting, "and give you the money for all you do for us. Now that's the way I see it." He paused and looked around the table for nods of agreement. "What do you say?"

Aislynn looked down at the table biting her lip. Slowly, she rose and threw her arms around Papa Nolan, burying her face in his neck. She squeezed hard, trying to contain her tears. "Thank you," she whispered.

"You're our girl. You belong with us." Papa Nolan patted her on the back.

Aislynn went around the table and hugged each one of them. Michael burned red, Brian laughed timidly and Sean welcomed her with his arms wide. He pulled her down on his knee and asked, "Would you rather we all moved in here? This flat is sunny and the bedroom is already partitioned." Aislynn nodded and hugged him a second time.

At Sunday mass, Aislynn sat in the Nolan pew between Papa Nolan and Sean. When she and the Nolans emerged through the front entrance, Johnny, his mother and sister joined them on the front steps. Fellow parishioners approached Aislynn expressing their regrets and promising prayers for her and her father.

Upon their departure, she noticed the priest had waylaid Papa Nolan. They stood near the side of the church, away from the crowd, engaged in deep conversation. Sean put his hand on Aislynn's shoulder and said, "He'll meet us at home." Johnny took Aislynn's arm and the group walked toward Worth Street.

Dinner was nearly ready to be served when Papa Nolan returned. He fell into a kitchen chair, his head in his hands. The sight of him sitting in the chair elicited an automatic response in Aislynn and she poured him a draught. She sat across from him and asked, "Where have you been? I know I shouldn't be so nervous but I worry."

"I've been prayin'."

"Thank you, I'm sure Da hears you." Aislynn replied.

"I was prayin' for me and for you." His emphasis on the word "you" stayed suspended between them.

Aislynn could feel his body trembling against the table. She could see the sweat erupting through his forehead and upper lip. His eyes were focused on his worn hands. They had fallen on the table like a dead soldier's, on their backs with their palms up. He looked old and defeated. She surveyed him carefully as her stomach churned.

The boys had heard their father arrive and each one sauntered in from the parlor, expecting dinner would be served. Aislynn glanced up at them as they circled the table and took seats. Silence swelled in the room. "Why me?" she asked.

"The priest, he says you can't live with us. He says you're not family and t'would be too much of a..." he pursed his lips and looked away from her as he squeezed out the words, "a temptation for three single men."

Sean exploded, "The bastard! His mind's in the gutter!"

The elder Nolan's eyes burned into him. His words seethed through his lips, softly, as though he didn't want God to hear, "Sean, watch yourself. The man speaks for the Lord."

"He's a drunken ol' buggar!"

"Sean, stop," Aislynn cried. "Can't you see he's upset?" She grabbed Papa's hand.

"We'll talk to him," Brian offered.

Papa answered, "I just did. He says it's an improper, sinful arrangement. All of our souls would be in danger." He turned to Aislynn, his voice ragged, "You know dear, I love you like you were my own, but I do want to meet my Mary again."

"I know, Papa." She ran her fingers over the swollen blue veins on his hand. "I'll get a job, a "live-in" job. I'll find someplace to go."

"With strangers?" Sean turned to his father. "The priest wants us to send her to live with strange men. God knows what they'll do to a young Irish girl with no protection."

Papa Nolan's face contorted as he heard Sean's terrifying words. "What are we to do? Go against the priest, the voice of God?"

"Blast him! He doesn't live here. He doesn't know how things are!" Sean's arms gesturing wildly.

"Sean, we'll work it out. Maybe she can work for the nuns." Brian suggested.

Michael broke in, "And what are we to do? Who's goin' to cook and wash?"

"You selfish bastard," Sean shouted, "thinkin' about yourself when we're turnin' her out."

"It's your fault," Michael accused Sean, "If you didn't fawn over her so."

Sean's fist rose to the side of Michael's face. "What are you sayin'?"

Seated beside Sean, Aislynn grabbed his arm, "Stop it. Please. I'm not..." she choked on the word, "family. It's true."

Sean stood, dragging her with him. He shook her off his arm and took two strides toward the door. "I'll take care of the priest."

"Sean, no!" Her voice became shrill as she followed him to the door. "You'll disgrace us all."

"He'll not run our lives!" he declared as he moved down the hall.

Aislynn pivoted. "Brian, please?"

Brian pushed himself up from the table and ran after his brother.

Aislynn stood behind Papa Nolan. She rested her chin on his head and wrapped her arms around his neck, "Don't worry, Papa."

His head fell and his chin landed on her forearm. A tear splashed against her flesh. She rubbed her cheek on his thin hair and soothed, "I'll find a way to take care of myself."

Aislynn approached the first home on Madison Avenue displaying a sign advertising employment. She rang the front bell. The door opened to a world of dark wood lining the walls and twisting up a broad staircase. When she asked about the position, the maid said, "Go to the back," and slammed the door.

Aislynn trudged to the back door and the same maid opened it. She entered to a large green kitchen. A counter ran around the room under huge cabinets hanging high on the walls. Two Negro women chopping vegetables stopped their conversation and looked up at Aislynn. The older one asked Aislynn if she had ever worked in a kitchen before.

"I cook for my family."

"Dis here's different. You gots to know food. We gots some fine folks comin' here to eat and we gots to serve fine food. Now, you knowed what a consumay is?"

Aislynn shook her head.

"What 'bout galettes?"

Aislynn shook her head again.

"Ain't no sense sendin' you to the lady of da house. She ain't gonna take you."

Aislynn thanked the woman for her time and moved on. She thought she could find work as a governess but discovered a governess needed to know more than history, literature and mathematics. They were supposed to be masters of etiquette. Aislynn felt she had fine manners but several interviews revealed she lacked the knowledge wealthy young ladies required. She could not succeed as an upstairs maid because she did not know the difference between a sham and a pillowcase. A downstairs maid needed to be familiar with a wide array of glasses and various forms of silverware, information Aislynn lacked.

As Aislynn departed another disappointing interview, a small Negro woman pulled her aside and said, "Da lady cross da way loss a girl yesterday. She throwed her out for heavens only knows why. Run over and see if she take you on. Be jus' cleanin'.'"

Aislynn thanked the woman for her kindness and approached the house. The four-story limestone building had cast iron railings leading to the front door, but Aislynn scurried to the back. While she waited for someone to answer her knock, she straightened her hair and her coat. A man with an English accent led Aislynn through a long narrow kitchen to the back parlor and ordered her to sit.

A frail, long-faced woman entered the room. She wore a slim gray dress with a small train. Aislynn rose and gave the woman a quick curtsy. After the woman took her seat, Aislynn waited for instructions to sit. They did not come. Aislynn stood looking down at the woman, answering questions about where she lived, why she needed a job and references. References were a problem for Aislynn. She had a nice note penned by her companion, but Mrs. Pearson was without connections and unknown to Aislynn's prospective employers.

"Well, I am truly in need of cleaning help. We are entertaining this weekend and I must have this house immaculate. Now you understand it's six days a week, and you will have Sundays off. You will be given a bed in the attic with the other girls and two meals a day. There is no pilfering of food. I will pay you seven dollars a month and not a penny more."

Aislynn beamed. She folded her hands and brought them to her breast and thanked God and this mousy little woman. In four days, she had to leave her apartment and she had no rent money to extend her stay even one more week. This job was a blessing. She envisioned her parents watching over her as the parlor door opened and a portly, balding man entered the room.

"Herschel, I did not hear you come in. Welcome home, dear." The woman extended her hand to the man who brushed past Aislynn.

"How are you today, my pet?" the man asked with no

real interest.

"I am well." She smiled weakly at the man. "This," gesturing to Aislynn as though she were a piece of furniture, "is our new girl. She'll begin cleaning tomorrow. It's such a relief." The woman sounded as though a weight had been lifted from her.

Aislynn assumed Herschel was the woman's husband. He turned toward Aislynn and examined her from head to foot. His scrutiny made Aislynn feel uncomfortable. When his dark, fluid little eyes stopped at her breasts and her hips, she stepped back toward the door. Herschel looked down at the woman and in a syrupy voice said, "I'm sure she'll be a very interesting addition to our household."

He nodded at Aislynn as he left the room. Uneasy, Aislynn's eyes followed him out the door and she listened for his steps to die away. When she turned back to her employer, Aislynn discovered the woman standing directly in front of her. Aislynn heard the slap hit her cheek before she fully felt it.

"Get out, you slattern. Don't you dare come near this house again."

Aislynn reeled from the pain. In disbelief and fury she countered, "Are you insane?"

"Get out or I'll call the police!" the woman screeched.

Aislynn took her anger and her humiliation and left through the front door. The city was darkening. The buildings were shadowed and the fabulous homes with their unevenly lit windows seemed sinister and unbalanced. Soot and ash blackened the barrier of snow remaining on the curb. Puddles of filthy water stained the cobbles on the streets. As she walked alone, every sound made her start. She hurried home, fearing that in a few days she might be living on these streets.

While sitting in her mother's rocker, she looked out at the cold night listening to Papa Nolan snoring. He had decided she should not sleep in her apartment alone and had taken to spending the night in her father's bed. Soon, she had to leave the apartment and had nowhere to go but consoled herself with the thought that at least she would not have to listen to his snoring.

Aislynn looked around the room. Since the day her mother died, nothing had changed. Her father had not added one piece of furniture. Except for the addition of a small vase of paper flowers Aislynn received for her fine performance at school, she had not changed anything, either. It remained her mother's home. She pulled her shawl around her and wondered how her mother's arms must have felt when they hugged her. At times the Nolans and her father hugged her but she imagined a mother's touch would be different. She pulled her legs up into the chair and hugged herself as she rocked. *I've spent my life longing for my mother and now I'll spend the rest of my life missing them both.* She looked up toward heaven. *If you're watching, I could use some help.*

Aislynn's eyes searched the darkened room. Looking over its shadowed contents, she decided to sell the furniture and thought she could make enough to pay the funeral bill. *At least I'll be starting off without a debt. Now if I only had somewhere to go.* She rocked back against the wall and kept the chair suspended in the air. Closing her eyes, she imagined she was flying, flying to some place far away, some place she could have a home, a job. She lost her balance and the chair fell forward landing loudly on the wooden floor. Her eyes flew open with the jolt and she caught the glimmer of a solution sitting on the table in the corner of the room.

Chapter 6

As soon as the men left for work, Aislynn ran up the stairs to old Mr. Rattawitz's.

"I need some help. I have some things I want to sell." Aislynn needed a pawnbroker and after years of peddling on Orchard Street, she knew Louis Rattawitz could direct her to one she could trust.

"Vat are you selling?"

"I have silver, real sterling." He looked at her quizzically. "It's mine," she established. "Lady Falwell, my mother's employer, gave it to her. It's eight place settings of sterling and a genuine silver tea service, tray and all."

"So you vant to sell? But your mother?" he shook his head.

"They're the only things I own that are worth anything. I'm nearly destitute. I need money very badly."

"Your father, he loved you, but he vas not one to look

to tomorrow. It vas not his fault, some do, some don't."

"I know; he lived day by day. But now I have to live." She bit her lip and twisted her hands. "Help me?"

"Of course, but know you may never get these back."

Aislynn looked away from the old man and took a few deep breaths, calming her wavering resolve. "I know."

She wrapped the silver in soft towels. Together, they carried it to Orchard Street, a thoroughfare teeming with people, horses, pushcarts and noise. A hundred languages mingled into one loud roar. Strange, tantalizing smells floated in the air alongside wisps of grey smoke from stoves set up on steps and sidewalks for cooking and warmth. The atmosphere buoyed her spirits and made the impending separation more of a celebration.

They walked into a narrow, dark building displaying the sign "Freilischer's Pawn Shop." Bells rang as the door swung open. Behind the counter, a small, big-nosed man with graying hair peered over tiny glasses with his tiny eyes. He rose and extended his hand to Mr. Rattawitz.

"Louis, if these is your new vife, I drop dead right here."

"Al, if she vere my vife, I'd drop dead."

Mr. Rattawitz introduced Aislynn to the pawnbroker and explained her situation.

"Och! Such troubles for such a young girl." He examined the goods and declared, "I could not sell such things here. My customers don't buy silver, but I know another Jew, uptown, his name is Golden, vas Goldstein. I ask you, who is he trying to fool? In any case, silver is selling at a good rate. You leave it to me, I get you a good price."

"I'm sorry to rush you, Mr. Freilischer, but I have to be out of my apartment in three days."

"Lou, you vatch the store and I vill make the trip uptown today."

While Aislynn cleaned away the remnants of dinner

and Johnny sat reading at the kitchen table, a soft knock came to the door. Johnny volunteered to answer it, but she overrode his offer. Mr. Rattawitz stood in the hall clasping a wrinkled envelope. She stepped out and closed the door behind her with a snap.

"You're rich. Six hundred dollars rich."

Aislynn could not contain a squeal of delight. "Thank you, thank you, thank you. You are the best neighbor in the whole world. Please thank Mr. Freilischer, or I'll go and thank him myself."

"You're a good girl. I'm going to miss you." The old man's cloudy eyes were damp.

Aislynn threw her arms around him and said, "I'll miss you, too, but I won't ever forget you."

As the old man struggled up the stairs, she pulled up her skirt, stuffed the money in her pantalets and returned to Johnny. He asked several general questions about her visitor. Aislynn tried to be honest in her answers but the money, leaning against her leg, stole her focus. Pleading fatigue, she managed to convince Johnny to go home early.

Alone, she ran into her bedroom and extracted the bulging parcel. Loving the feel of the dollars in her hand, she counted them over and over. She knew she held enough money to live in New York for a full year, maybe two if she were exceptionally frugal. *By then, I might be able to find a job.* Aislynn placed the money back in the envelope and slipped it under her mattress. *But what if I can't?*

With uncertainty grating on her, Aislynn opened her dresser drawer and removed a box papered in a flowered print. A small stack of letters from Tim rested inside. Reverently, she opened each one and read them in chronological order.

The morning sun gave Aislynn clarity and strength. She walked into the office of Ben Holladay at 84 Broadway and caught the eye of a clerk seated at a cluttered desk.

He was a young man, in his twenties, she estimated, with greased dark hair and a serious look. As Aislynn approached, he puckered his mouth, as if sucking something sour.

When he failed to greet her, she asked, "Can you help me?"

"Don't know," he replied. "I'm very busy."

"Maybe I should speak to your employer?" she threatened, affecting an air of superiority.

The man huffed and told her to take a seat. "I'm jus' very busy."

"So you said. But I have business which I must take care of and if you can't help me, I'll have to find someone who can."

She started to rise, but he ordered, "Sit, sit."

He pushed some papers aside and asked what she needed.

"I'm going west and need to deposit some money. I want to carry letters of credit and be able to withdraw my money in Chicago, Cheyenne and Ogden."

"Where you going?" his interest piqued.

"My final destination is Ogden in the Utah Territory. I don't want to carry cash for the entire journey; I might lose it."

"More likely someone will take it from you. Who you travelin' with?"

Aislynn thought the question was terribly personal but she answered it anyway. "I'm traveling alone."

The young man let out a laugh. With sarcasm, he asked, "How you gonna get there alone?"

"Well," Aislynn hesitated. "I intend to take the train through to Cheyenne and the stage from there."

"And you intend to travel by yourself?" his critical eyes raked over her.

Aislynn straightened in her seat and looked at him hard, "Yes."

He leaned back in his chair and folded his arms over

64

his chest. "Well, now, I know it ain't none of my business but I jus' come back from a little trip west. I railroaded through to Cheyenne and took one of our stages through the Black Hills and I am grateful to be sittin' here to tell you it was the worst experience of my life. Now I ain't no sissy but you ain't never seen nothin' like Cheyenne. You know they got ten thousand railroad men sittin' there waitin' out the winter. They got nothin' to do but live wild. Why the newspaper has a daily column named 'Last Night's Shootin's.' Them men are drinkin', gamblin' and ... never you mind what else. They are the most unruly bunch. They're forever shootin' guns in the air and my theory is what goes up must come down. The whole time I was there I kept prayin' 'God don't let them bullets come down on me.'"

Aislynn knew the way west was difficult. Tim's letters told of the rough rail ride followed by long hours in an unfamiliar saddle. In school, she learned the search for an easy route west began with the discovery of the continent. However, it was not until the Civil War highlighted the growing need that the American imagination set out to build a passage, an iron road stretching from sea to sea. After the war, the progress of the transcontinental railroad progressed swiftly, but its westward branch only stretched into the Dakota Territory, 436 miles from Tim.

Aislynn devised a way to avoid the problem of being in such a dangerous environment. "I don't intend to stay in Cheyenne. I will board a stage and leave town immediately."

"A stage?" the man leaned closer to her, "Well, now I'd be glad to sell you passes to take you clear 'cross that Godforsaken country, but let me tell you about those coaches. First, they'll be overloaded. Every one of the occupants will stink more than any animal you've ever had contact with. Most will have lice and be happy to share them with you. Some will be drunk. Why, I seen one man kill another for jus' talkin' down the South. Everyone car-

65

ries a gun by the way; you better get you one or you'll be out of fashion."

"I don't need to hear all of this."

"I think you do." He paused and scrutinized her, "Why you goin' west alone anyway?"

Annoyed at his effrontery, Aislynn threw her nose in the air. She tried to ignore his prying but the young man stared her down.

Acquiescing, Aislynn replied, "I've recently been orphaned and my guardian is in Utah. I have to get there. And why are you trying to scare me?"

"I ain't trying to scare you; I'm trying to save your life. You look like a nice girl and nice girls don't travel on them stages by themselves. Why, the men I rode with were hard drinkin, killer types. And they were better than the ones who prey on the coaches from the outside. We were stopped by bandits twice. People think Indians are a problem, but it's them white outlaws who are the threat. I'd hate to think what they'd do to you."

"Perhaps I'll meet up with some other women on the stage, maybe a family."

"Oh, that'd be swell. First off, babies screamin' and spittin' up add a nice touch to the dust and the wind pourin' in the windows. I ain't never seen nothin' like the lightning out there. The weather comes in the coaches and this time of year it's a cold rain if it ain't snow. Snow will stop a coach dead."

The man paused to take a breath. Aislynn hoped he would stop talking but he continued. "Then you have to stay at a station. 'Cept don't get out at no station 'less you have to 'cause it don't matter if you're a girl; someone will snatch up your seat and you'll have to stay at the station 'til another coach comes by. Those stations ain't nothin' but sod over a sand floor. There's no place to sleep and even less place to wash. The food is miserable. I spent a gold dollar just for a hot potato. The water smells and it's thick with dirt. There ain't nothin could get me to go back

66

there. Why, they could fire me but I'm not runnin' any-thing out west for this company or anyone else again."

Aislynn leaned her elbows on the desk and sighed, "Well, how else can I get there?"

"I'd suggest a train full of decent families."

"But the train only runs through Cheyenne."

"I'm talkin' about a wagon train. They're better armed. They ain't carrying the gold or paper the outlaws want anyway. Indians don't bother trains passin' through. Trains got their problems but it's safer for women and children."

Aislynn looked at him with disbelief, "A wagon, I've never driven a wagon and I don't know anything about an-imals. I've lived on Worth Street my whole life."

"Well, you might be able to team up with someone. Trains will be leaving Cheyenne all spring. Be strangers but prob'ly decent family folks. Can you wait 'til next year? The railroad might be through by then."

A new fear rose, *I'll be eighteen by then and Tim won't be legally obligated.* She shook her head and declared, "No, I can't wait."

When the Nolans returned home, they found the Denehy apartment nearly empty. Aislynn showed them the thirty dollars she had earned with her furniture sale. She also announced she had been offered a cleaning job, which she told herself was not a true lie. The Nolans con-gratulated her and asked a few questions about her place-ment. Johnny's queries, however, seemed endless.

"Why are you interrogating me? I've told you every-thing there is to tell."

"I'm just interested." They were seated at the Nolan table, since her kitchen lacked furniture. Johnny rested his chin on his hands and stared at her silently.

Aislynn fidgeted in her seat. "It's a fine house."

Johnny nodded.

"They seem to be well-bred people."

67

He nodded again.

She fell back in her chair and said, "Stop staring."

He lifted his head and leaned back, folding his arms over his chest but his eyes stayed on her.

"Fine!" she shouted. "I'm going to Utah!"

His face remained static and he emitted no sound.

"Tim is my legal guardian. He'll have to take me in, and no one can object to it."

When Johnny made no response, she added, "There's plenty of work there. Lots of opportunities." She paused, thinking he was never going to speak to her again. She concluded with, "So I'm going."

Determined not to say another word, she waited, the silence thumping on her conscience. Johnny relented, "How are you gettin' there?"

"Train and stage."

"Where did you get the money?"

Aislynn explained how she had sold the silver.

"Do the Nolans know?"

"No," she snapped, "And you're not going to tell them. I have no home, no job. I have nothing to keep me here."

"I'm here."

Aislynn's heartfelt his words. For a moment, she felt sorry. "I know," she whispered, "but I can't get married just because I have no job, no..."

"You'd rather get yourself killed than stay here and marry me?"

"You don't understand." Her elbows fell on the table and she surrounded her face with her hands. "I don't want to live in a tenement and have a baby every year. We'd be stuck there forever."

"We'd get out."

"When? Two years? Five years? Never?"

"We'd be together."

Sympathy pulled at her heart, but she said, "It's not what I want."

Johnny reached for her hand and held it in both of

his, "I don't want you to leave."

"I know." She set her jaw and said, "I can't stay."

Johnny pulled her around the table until she stood before him. He squeezed her hand so her bones rubbed against each other. Looking down at their hands, he said harshly, "I could make you stay."

Aislynn's body sighed and she placed her free hand on his cheek, "No, you wouldn't. It's not in you."

He released her. Johnny glared at Aislynn while his tongue rubbed his back teeth. With bitterness, he asked, "So, you're goin' to Tim?"

"No, I'm going to get work."

"You don't need work, Aislynn. I'd support you."

Aislynn leaned toward him, her eyes narrowed, "And what if you can't? What if we have babies and you die like my Da? I can't support myself. How could I feed babies, too? I'd wind up in Five Points Slum, living on the street with nothing to eat."

"I'm not goin' to die."

"I'm sure your father didn't plan it any more than mine did. Go ask your mother how it's been for her. Ask her what kind of a life she's had, taking in strangers, washing and ironing 'til she can't stand straight anymore. It's not the life for me." Once she spoke the words, she realized why she was so drawn to the West. Of course she would be with Tim, but the West held the very thing Brendan longed for his whole life, the thing he had wanted for Aislynn and her children, the opportunity to be free and independent.

He stood and scowled at her. His face grew so red she thought it was expanding. Grabbing his cap and his jacket, he stomped out the door. She heard the street door slam and listened to his footsteps bang on the stairs. Aislynn thought she would feel freer when Johnny walked out of her life, relieved of the pressure to marry him, but she felt sad, sorry and empty.

She cared for Johnny and wished they had parted as

friends. Consolation came from believing she would soon be with Tim and all these bad feelings would be forgotten.

Papa Nolan gave her his bed and he slept in the parlor with the boys. With the different sounds, the strange bed and her thoughts tormenting her, she lay awake. The words of Tim's letters and those of the Wild West dime novels flit through her mind and she believed she could not make the trip alone. Unbidden, the advice of Holladay clerk came to her mind feeding her fear of the dangers. Following on its heels, the dogs of hell barked, "What if Tim can't take you in or won't?" Then, there was Johnny. The picture of his hurt face hung before her.

Aislynn invoked her father, begging for guidance or a sign. She lay still in the dark, waiting and listening with her eyes wide as the windows rattled and the men snored. Outside, she could hear the wind blowing off the Hudson River and coursing through Worth Street. Peeking through the curtain, she saw a funnel, full of ashes, dirt, bits of brightly colored paper and last autumn's leaves swirling until it exhausted itself and rested on the road. Aislynn woke to the sun and read the confident rays as a portent that anything was possible.

After the Nolans were sent off to work, she sat down to write them a letter of explanation. Aislynn wanted them to believe she was doing the right thing, but in writing, her reasoning seemed weak and she began to waver. She hung her head in her hands and told herself to decide, now, without equivocation, to go or to stay.

As she reached for a coin to toss, a soft knock landed on the door. She responded with, "Come in."

Johnny walked into the kitchen wearing a small grin.

Aislynn bounded out of her chair and grabbed his hands. "I'm glad you came. I didn't want us to part in anger."

"I don't want us to part at all." He leaned over her and whispered in her ear, "I love you."

70

Aislynn pulled back and smiled, "I know." She chewed her lip and squirmed in her place, "Do you want to kiss me goodbye?"

"I'd never pass up the chance to kiss you."

He pulled her close and placed one hand in her hair and the other low on her back. While he kissed her, his hand slid further down her back until it cupped her buttock. She began to feel a slight thrill until he pressed her forward and she felt his response to their proximity. Aislynn broke away from him and moved behind her chair. She admonished him, "It's a good thing I am leaving, Johnny Maher. You take too many liberties."

Johnny's eyes fixed on hers and he pulled the chair away. His hands shot out. With his fingers firmly encircling her arms, he pulled her to him saying, "Guess I'm goin' to keep takin' them because I'm not lettin' you leave me."

Chapter 7

Fear flowed through Aislynn. He tightened his grip and his breath brushed her face. Instinct ruled and she twisted away. Squaring off, she demanded, "What are you up to?"

"I'm goin' with you."

Aislynn vacillated, trying to decide if this was good news or bad news. As she searched for a response.

Johnny continued, "My mother says you're right; a woman should have a good job, be able to support herself and her family."

Aislynn was thrilled Mrs. Maher understood and sympathized with her position.

He explained, "She said for you to start a business and she and Kathleen will come and work for you when you need help."

Aislynn silently beamed under Mrs. Maher's approval.

Johnny stepped to her and touched her cheek. "I figured it must mean a lot if you're willin' to take such risks." Johnny shrugged, "If this is what you want, I should help you reach your goal. I want you to be happy, Angel."

Aislynn felt stunned. Guilt tingled through her nerves. She realized she did not deserve Johnny's adoration but could not let it go either.

Aislynn finished her letter and placed it on the kitchen table. Johnny dragged her trunk down the stairs while Aislynn gathered her valise and her carpetbag. She stood for a moment in front of her apartment door and said goodbye to the empty hall.

The drayman took them and their belongings to the Pavonia Ferry at the foot of Chambers Street. As they cruised to New Jersey, sunlit waves flashed like mirrors in their eyes. Aislynn had only been out of New York City once. On the first warm day following her eighth birthday, Tim took her to Brooklyn, to the end of the omnibus line. It stopped at a deserted wooden platform built along the road. They followed the boards until they ended in the sand. Removing their shoes, they climbed a small knoll. At the summit, Tim spread his arms and declared, "Aislynn Denehy, my ward and lady fair, I give you the Atlantic Ocean."

The memory made her smile. Johnny felt her mood. He took her hand and squeezed it. When she looked up at him wistfully, his eyes widened and his brows rose. He took her right hand and slid the Claddagh ring off her finger, turned it around and pushed it back into place with the heart pointing toward hers. "I'm givin' you a year. Whether you're successful or not, we're married in one year."

A subtle sinking feeling sat in her stomach. *I should have expected him to place conditions on me; men always do.* She looked at her hand and gave him a nod. *A great deal can happen in a year.*

The ferry bumped the pier and docked. They hurried off to the Long Dock Depot, a vast, vaulted structure open to the river on the east side and to the rails radiating on the west side. At the ticket counter, they purchased continuous emigrant passage to Cheyenne. Aislynn pressed the ticket to her breast and felt a rush of confidence. The clerk advised them to claim seats. He explained the Union Pacific Railroad was pushing westward and dozens of men were traveling to Cheyenne daily to sign on to the construction crews.

They captured a double, cane-covered seat. Johnny thrust their three bags onto the wrought iron shelves hanging from the row of sleeping berths situated over their heads. Aislynn sat next to the window and Johnny wedged in next to her, his broad body consuming more than his half of the bench. Happy to be on her way and feeling secure with Johnny present, she hugged his arm and rubbed her cheek against his shoulder. It was a shameless public display of affection, but she did not know any of her fellow passengers and looking at them, judged she would not care about their opinions. Aislynn knew the act would make him happy and she wanted to reward him for rescuing her from her fears. "You can still go home," she suggested.

He leaned his head toward hers, "Aislynn, I'm close enough to feel your heart beat; do you think there's any place in the world I'd rather be?"

The train full of excited people pulled out of Jersey City at 8:00 P.M. Children bounced in their seats and ran in the aisles while women chatted and the men roared. Smoke from the passengers' cigars and pipes filled the closed car and made the scene dreamlike as the train bumped and swayed to the grinding tune its wheels hummed.

At this hour, the window's view offered mostly darkness, with the exception of small pools of light distorted by the film of dirt coating the glass inside and out. Those lights soon faded as the train snaked south to Philadelphia. This leg of the trip would take five hours but Aislynn was determined to stay awake to see the city.

As the iron wheels rolled, she and Johnny planned their trip. They discussed their funds and found they had close to a thousand dollars. "With a thousand dollars, we could have stayed in New York and built a smithy and a house, or at least a part of one," he said.

Aislynn frowned, "What good is part of a house?" She shook her head. "I'd better handle the finances," she declared. They decided to travel as cheaply as possible, hoping to have money left when they arrived in Utah. Sleeping on the trains and on the stages, driving straight through would save time and money. Johnny's agreement with all of her suggestions satisfied Aislynn.

Philadelphia was a blur of dim lights. After fifteen minutes in the station, the train slid into the darkness of the Pennsylvania night. Johnny leaned his head back against the seat and started to snore. Aislynn studied her fellow emigrants and decided they were unsavory. Every time the man behind them exhaled, the smell of garlic drifted into Aislynn's nose. The thought of breathing his air made her cringe. She covered her nose with her silk handkerchief and slid closer to Johnny. Leaning against him she felt secure; she closed her eyes and thanked God for sending him to her.

Every stop and start jolted Aislynn. She fell into a deep sleep somewhere in the heart of Pennsylvania. When she woke the sun hung behind the train and the view outside their window hinted at a very un-New York City terrain. Budding bushes and branches reached toward the track. The train climbed hills and passed through tunnels of trees broken by cliffs of rock or bridges over rivers and streams. As the sun rose, they moved into flatter land, where brown fields stretched before them, long and undulating, meeting the sky. Farms flanked them into Ohio.

By evening, the odors exuded by the people in the car

76

were making Aislynn sick. She and Johnny bundled in their coats and walked to the sheltered platform between the cars. Johnny carried Aislynn's small valise and turning it on its side, created a seat for her. He leaned against the door while Aislynn sat. Steam, ash and rock dust billowed around them, but Aislynn preferred the debris and the cold to the smells in the car.

They passed the night in discomfort. Aislynn tried to sleep curled on the seat while Johnny squeezed onto the floor below. They ran out of the food Aislynn had packed at home and had to run off the train during one fifteen minute stop to grab coffee and sandwiches. The prices and the poor quality rankled Aislynn. She felt filthy and tired and hungry. By the time the train pulled into Chicago, she told Johnny she needed a real meal, hot bath and a night in a bed.

People swarmed through the vast Chicago station. It was massive stone building with a grand dome rising over a broad marble floor. The din was oppressive. Aislynn and Johnny discovered a quiet corner with a bench. Johnny left to find a room, while Aislynn sat and watched the luggage. She heard a clock strike six and watched passengers flow up and down the narrow staircase in front of her seat. Trying not to look anyone in the eye and thereby calling attention to herself, she watched their shoes, skirts and pants. During a lull in the rush, a lone man came into view. She noticed his boots were highly polished; his trousers were well cut and made of fine wool. Her eyes traveled up slightly to see a dark hat in one hand and a fine leather case in the other. She saw the feet stop abruptly, stand still for a moment then, descend the stairs and walk in her direction.

Aislynn trained her eyes on the floor. When the boots rested directly in front of her, she bit her lip and raised her head with trepidation and curiosity. The face resided somewhere in her memory; as she tried to retrieve it, he spoke. "Miss Denehy?"

When his dark head tilted and she saw narrow light blue eyes and a sly grin, she recalled his name, "Mr. Moran."

"What a surprise to find you so far from New York."

"What a surprise you recognized me."

His smile broadened, "You're quite memorable."

His gaze made Aislynn uncomfortable.

"So, what brings you to Chicago?" he asked.

Aislynn's spirit rose, "I'm going west."

"The West is a big place," he said as his eyes questioned her.

"I'm going to Ogden to join Tim."

"I just left him a few days ago; he didn't mention your arrival."

"I wrote, but the mail takes so long and I couldn't wait for a reply. But how is he?" The words jumped from her mouth. "How does he look?"

Moran chuckled and shook his head. "He's fine. Hairier than you remember him, I suspect, but he's doing very well. He's a bright young man, one I have plans for."

"Really?" Aislynn beamed to hear someone else appreciate Tim.

"Right now he's off in the mountains prospecting for me."

"Oh dear, is that dangerous?"

"He'll be fine. He's not alone. May I sit?"

"Of course," she waved toward the space next to her and returned her hands to her lap. "But if he's not at your ranch, how will I ever find him?"

"Leave word at the house. He'll be checking in." He leaned closer to her, his hard blue eyes piercing hers for a moment, trying to see through her, "You're undertaking a very strenuous trip, does your family know?"

Aislynn hesitated and looked at her hands. "My father died a month ago, I actually have no family."

"Who is your guardian?"

"Tim."

Moran straightened, "But he's in Utah. What did his family say about this trip?"

Aislynn felt uneasy with the direction of this conversation. "It was my decision. I'm an adult; I can make my own decisions."

"I believe you're just seventeen."

"How do you know?" she questioned.

"Utah winters are long. Men have lots of time to talk."

"Tim spoke about me?"

"Oh, yes; he regaled us with Aislynn Denehy stories."

"He told strangers about me?" For a moment she felt flattered, but her feelings fluctuated; she wished she knew what he had said.

"Don't be offended, Miss Denehy. A cowboy's life is full of loneliness. He was just giving them something to dream on." His face grew kinder. "They were decent tales. You don't have to worry; Mr. Nolan is one of the most upright men I've ever met."

Aislynn basked in his high opinion of Tim when he asked, "How are you planning on getting to Utah?"

Raising her head, she announced, "Rail and stage."

"Miss Denehy..." he faltered. "I don't believe Mr. Nolan would approve of this trip." He paused again, clearly considering his next words. "I do feel compelled to do something to return you to your family in New York."

"I have no family in New York, Mr. Moran. I only have my legal guardian, Tim."

"But his father and brothers?"

Hurt swelled in her heart when she thought of explaining her situation. Her eyes fell. "The priest wouldn't allow me to live with the Nolans. You see... we aren't truly family."

Moran watched her for a moment and added softly, "But you cannot travel alone."

"I'm not alone. I have a companion."

"Where is she?"

"He is looking for some suitable accommodations. He

is a young man from my parish who is very responsible and respectful."

"Johnny Maher?"

Astonished, Aislynn said, "Yes."

"You're a very smart little girl, Miss Denehy, but very naïve. I think you're wrong to believe Mr. Nolan would approve of such an arrangement."

"He's simply my escort. What could Tim object to?"

"That's between the three of you." He stood and bowed slightly, saying, "I wish you a safe trip."

Alone in the station, Aislynn's stomach grew nervous. She knew Tim had standards and traveling with Johnny might be stretching them too far. She worried he might think she was tainted by this trip.

"No," she told herself; she could trust Johnny and Tim trusted him, too. She assured herself that nothing improper would ever occur between her and Johnny and she could face Tim with a clear conscience.

When Johnny returned to the station, he found Aislynn hungry and anxious to get to their rooms. She mentioned meeting Moran and her concern about Tim's disapproval but Johnny said, "You worry about the wrong things. Tim loves you and he'll be happy to see you." Buoyed by his assessment, Aislynn enjoyed her first restaurant meal in peace.

They dragged their bags through the Chicago streets away from the station to a quiet, residential section of the city and a neat three-story frame. A refined-looking lady greeted them at the door and directed them to a room off the kitchen. Inside, Aislynn found a tub with steaming water occupying most of the floor space. She squeezed past the tub toward the bed standing against one wall. A small stove, its pipe pushing out through the room's only window glowed in the corner. The only other piece of furniture in the room, a chair, stood before the stove, with a chamber pot tactfully hidden underneath.

Aislynn place her valise on the chair and dropped her

carpetbag on the floor. She turned to find Johnny holding his large bag over the tub and trying to close the door behind him. Setting his bag on the floor, he leaned against door. "This is the best I could do."

"It's wonderful." Aislynn said with a smile. "It's warm and I have a hot bath. It's perfect for me."

" 'Cept it's for us."

"If I could reach you, I'd slap your face," she threatened.

"Aislynn, you're goin' to have to be a little flexible. There are hordes of people in this town lookin' for rooms. This one is clean; you can have a bath and a bed. I'll just wait outside while you bathe and you can turn your back when it's my turn."

"Oh, so simple. And where might you be sleeping?"

"I'll take a pillow and the quilt, and I'll use the floor."

Eying the limited floor space, she agreed, believing he deserved to be cramped for not getting them two rooms. "Fine," she said and ordered him out.

Aislynn sat in front of the stove drying her hair while she listened to Johnny bumping and splashing in the tiny tub. She giggled, imagining what he must look like. Fear suppressed her urge to peek. She heard him as he dressed and helped the proprietress empty the tub. When Johnny returned, Aislynn lay in the bed with the blankets pulled up to her chin.

"Give me the quilt and a pillow."

Aislynn surveyed him. "If you promise to stay outside the covers, you can have half the bed."

Johnny gave her a broad smile.

"I'm only offering half the bed," she said flatly. "Nothing more. And you better promise."

"Aislynn, do you think I'd ever make you do anything you didn't want to?"

"Promise."

"I promise."

Johnny settled himself on one side of the bed and

Aislynn curled up facing the wall. He said good night and Aislynn mumbled in return.

"Don't you want to kiss me good night?" he asked.

"No!"

"It's our first night alone. You could kiss me."

"No!" Her annoyance expanded.

Aislynn could not sleep listening to the silence hanging between them. Irritated, she turned abruptly and brushed his cheek with a kiss. "If you say one more word, I'll put you out of this room." She turned back to the wall, feeling his smile. Ignoring him, she began her prayers. When her devotions became personal and reached Tim, she whipped around to Johnny and sat upright. In a panic, Aislynn cried, "Johnny?"

Her call hauled him back from the edge of sleep. "What's wrong?"

"You won't tell anyone we're sharing a bed will you?"

"Aislynn?" Johnny questioned her distrust.

"You won't tell Tim? Especially Tim." She shook her head furiously. "He would never understand and he would never approve."

"Of course not."

"And we'll never do this again. We'll be traveling straight through from here on."

"Right."

Satisfied with Johnny's assurances and confident the arrogant Mr. Moran was wrong, Aislynn cuddled under the covers.

The train to Omaha was similar to the cars from the East, with rounded roofs housing tiny glass vents which allowed air to the passengers stuffed into the lofty sleeping berths. Large windows that could be opened in warmer weather paraded around the middle of the cars through the dark wainscoted walls. The passengers were more unruly, mostly men with aspirations of mining or railroading. The view of new grass and furrowed fields held no interest for her imagination and Aislynn grew bored. For amusement, Aislynn and Johnny etched tic-tac-toe games into the window's dusty film. Johnny told her tales of war, which extended from the streets of New York City to the fields of the South.

When Johnny rested, Aislynn listened to the secret conversations of her neighbors. They spoke of the West and the grand opportunities they sought, about living in a land without restrictions. It occurred to Aislynn she was like them, grabbing for a new life with both hands. She would not be confined by circumstance; she would live the dream that brought her father to these shores, partaking in the grand experiment her friends had fought and died to preserve.

Outside her window, like an invitation, lay the nation's virgin land yet to be inhabited and exploited by humans and their hopes. It stole her breath to think of the possibilities. She looked to Johnny, his head lolling against the back of the seat with his eyes closed and his mouth open, and decided her thoughts and her destiny were her own.

By Davenport, Aislynn had traveled enough for one day. Her body ached from hours of bone-rubbing bouncing and swaying. The sounds, the smells and the sight of her fellow passengers irritated her. Aislynn and Johnny disembarked at the station.

They found a family who took in boarders. The house appeared clean and they were promised beds although they would have to share them with the family's children. Aislynn agreed. She crawled into a soft, warm bed and was joined by three girls younger than herself. Two were small but the thirteen-year-old seemed nearly as large as Johnny. The younger ones passed the night kicking and throwing their limbs in every direction. One woke crying three times to no one's notice but Aislynn's. Between the child's sobs, she could hear the house sleeping. She pulled her pillow over her head, but it yielded no relief.

She lay wakeful and heard the clock in the parlor strike three. Exhaustion won out. However, with the morning, she woke weary.

The train pressed on another full day to Omaha, the Union Pacific's town. It was built for and around the railroad. Beyond the train cars and the rails radiating out from the station, a small clapboard city with dirt roads bloomed on the gently rolling plains. When their train pulled into the station complex, she pleaded for a meal and some sleep. They found lodging in two rooms behind a tavern. The larger room housed men, and women shared the smaller. There were two beds in the tiny women's room and Aislynn shared hers with a stranger. The woman spent the night squirming and scratching. Aislynn kept to one side of the bed with her shawl pulled over her head and her coat closed around her, hoping to ward off any loose bugs traveling her way. In the morning, while the others ate breakfast, Aislynn took two beakers of water and washed her hair and her body with brown lye soap. It left her skin dry and taut but she hoped it removed any critters before they took up residence.

The rail trip west from Omaha provided a train car with fewer amenities. Slats of wood served as seats. Windows were frozen in various levels of open. A stove sat untended and the lamps unlit. Passengers were more male and less civil. Scenery was extraordinary in its sameness. Huge fields with scatterings of small white or brown houses repeated themselves for miles.

As they neared North Platte, Johnny noticed Aislynn's discomfort and suggested they get off the train. She appreciated his offer and assured him they had enough money for the expenditure. Johnny shrugged and said the money did not matter.

While the train idled for fifteen minutes, they raced to the hotel. No rooms were available but a hotel worker referred them to a boarding house. There, the owner offered them accommodations behind the tavern. They would have to share their beds with one other person but Aislynn agreed. While Johnny went for a drink, Aislynn trotted off with the landlady.

In the log-walled, sod-roofed room, she found two shelves of bunks suspended between the wall and two posts of stripped tree trucks. Each bed stretched about four feet long but they held clean, white ticks stuffed with pine needles giving the room a fresh scent. These mattresses were topped with fluffy quilts in immaculate duvets. Aislynn crawled into her top bunk and fell into a deep sleep. Some time later, she awakened when a rough woman climbed onto her bed. The woman had no teeth and skin splotched with thick black patches. Her smell made Aislynn cringe. She hid her face in her pillow and tried to breathe. When the woman removed her old boots, the room reeked with an odor so offensive Aislynn could not catch her breath.

Grabbing her pillow, Aislynn jumped down from her bunk. Throwing on her clothes, she picked up her bags and walked to the tavern door.

Aislynn knocked until a disheveled man answered. Women were not allowed inside, so she stood in the doorway and asked for Johnny Maher. He appeared instantly.

"I can't sleep with these people; they're pigs."

Johnny's shoulders sagged. "Wait here."

He returned to the barroom and re-emerged with his bag and a lantern."Come on," he said.

"Where are we going?"

"To the stable."

As they walked away from the tavern through the numbing Nebraska night, Aislynn looked up at the navy sky. Through the brittle air, stars pierced the heavens and a huge slash of white glowed against the darkness. Aislynn stopped and pointed. "What's that?"

"A whole bunch of stars called the Milky Way."

"Why don't we see it in New York?"

"Too much light, not enough sky." Johnny answered.

Aislynn imagined the stars pointed west and viewed the phenomenon as a good omen. Johnny led her across the muddy yard through the broad bay doors of a barn built of raw wooden planks. Following, she struggled to keep her skirt up, but her shoes could not escape the damp. In the barn, the dirt floor was dry and swept and the stalls were clean. Johnny pointed to a loft with hay spilling over its lip. "We can sleep up there."

She started up the ladder and Johnny followed her carrying several horse blankets. He leveled the hay and covered it with the blankets. Then, he brought up their bags.

Motioning at the improvised bed, he said, "Sleep."

Aislynn threw down her pillow and lowered herself onto the blankets while Johnny dimmed the lantern and stretched out next to her. She found the hay comfortable but she shivered.

"Cold?" he asked.

Pulling her shawl over her head, she said, "Yes, mainly my feet."

Johnny rose and turned up the lamp. He fished around in his bag and pulled out a pair of large socks knit from thick grey wool. Kneeling at her feet, he untied one of her muddy shoes. He pushed the sock up her leg. She wondered if it was the sock or his hands under her skirt, but she felt warmer. Aislynn knew she should take charge of the job herself and reprimand his forwardness, but she did not want to. He took her shoes to the edge of the loft and slapped them together, knocking off the mud. "They should be dryer by morning." He lowered the lamp wick and lay next to her.

"Move closer and we can share my coat," Johnny offered.

Rolling to face him, she placed her hands on his chest and hid her face between them. He cocooned her in wool. She listened to his breathing, felt his heart and wondered at the mysterious workings of his body.

Aislynn knew she was a traitor to their plans but she thought it was a good time to ask, "Johnny?" she circled one of his shirt buttons with her finger.

She could feel him inhale, "What?"

"I don't think I can tolerate stage stations after the places we've slept. Do you think we could take a wagon instead?"

Although Johnny nodded, she continued her defense. "It will cost us close to three hundred dollars to take the stage and there's no telling how much lodging and food will run. If we wagon, I could do the cooking so we'd know what we were eating, and we'd know where we were sleeping. It's more expensive but we'd have a wagon and horses and lots of the things we'll need when we get to Utah."

"I was thinkin' the same thing."

"Why didn't you suggest it?"

"Because you did."

Aislynn wished he had said it first. She did not want him to think of her as weak and pampered. She knew they were beginning an arduous trip, one that required sacrifices, but she did have some needs. For a minute, she settled in her thoughts then asked, "Johnny?"

"Hmmm?"

"Cheyenne's a big town," she started. Aislynn felt Johnny nod. "I know we're trying to keep expenses down, but when we get there can we get two hotel rooms, real hotel rooms with hot baths?"

"No."

Aislynn thought she heard wrong. Johnny didn't say "no" to her. Astonished, she questioned him, "Why not?"

"Cheyenne is the roughest town in the West. There are thousands of men sittin' there with nothin' to do but get into trouble. You are not doin' anything alone."

Searching for a way to get what she wanted, she asked, "Can we stay together, like in Chicago?"

"Yes."

"You don't think I'm fast for making such a suggestion, do you?"

Johnny pulled his head back and looked down at her, "Fast? Aislynn, if you were in a race with a tortoise, the tortoise would win."

She pushed against his chest, "You don't want me to be fast, do you?"

"Only when you're lyin' next to me."

Chapter. 8

Aislynn and Johnny pulled into Cheyenne on April 5th. As their train rolled up to the railhead, they could see the army of the Union Pacific Railroad pulling out. Once on the street, they found the towns' people abuzz. All talk centered around surviving the ten thousand graders and track-layers who had been holed up against a cold, snowy winter waiting for spring to move out and complete the UP's transcontinental railroad. The workers had found plenty of diversions, losing their pay to the gangs of gamblers, saloonkeepers, whores and swindlers who followed the railhead on its westerly course. Cheyenne's sober, solid citizens, who stayed behind to maintain the roundhouse and repair shops, hoped they were gone for good. Johnny and Aislynn watched residents wave goodbye as a thousand horse and mule teams, groaning and swaying under the weight of camp equipment, dug in their hoofs and wagoned west toward Sherman Summit, the highest point on the rail line, 8,235 feet.

Aislynn and Johnny picked their way along the muddied, snow-lined boardwalks to 16th Street and the Ford Hotel. Two stoves and kerosene lamps wearing reflector shades lit the large dining room. Three well-dressed men were eating quietly at one table, while four others gambled boisterously in a corner. They were dressed in rough clothes and each had a gun resting on the table. Aislynn turned to Johnny, pleading to leave but Johnny pulled out her chair and said, "We'll be fine."

The first thing Aislynn noticed about the gambler facing her was how his eyes scanned the room like twin beacons searching for danger. They were pale eyes, frozen in a permanent squint and set in a face lined like a cobweb. He had a huge moustache hanging on his face. His hands were large and strong with veins protruding through the dark, weathered skin. He held cards in one hand while the fingers on his other twitched against the table. His long blond hair hung on the shoulders of his buckskin shirt.

Her eyes were drawn to him, and when he smiled at his companions' banter, she recognized he had been handsome in his youth. Her ears caught tales of scouting for the army, skirmishes with Injuns while erecting the telegraph lines, and riding shotgun on the Wells Fargo stages carrying payrolls. When her gambler spoke, his soft voice seemed to crawl over slivers of glass to escape his throat. Although his hushed words were as raw as his exterior, Aislynn found herself leaning across her table to eavesdrop on his comments.

"Aislynn?" Johnny recaptured her attention. "It seems to me in this company, it would be a good idea to mind your own business."

"I am."

"There's plenty of trouble available, let's not look for any."

Aislynn jumped out of sleep when something solid hit the wall next to their bed. The impact made the thin barrier shake, sending sawdust down on Aislynn's face. Johnny sat up holding Aislynn's small pistol in his big hand. Something bounced against the wall a second time and a woman's voice cried, "Please stop!"

Aislynn gasped, "We have to do something. He's going to kill her."

"If he were goin' to kill her, he'd shoot her."

"Do you think he has a gun?"

"Everyone here has a gun. Didn't you notice? We have to get one too, a real one," he said, displaying the toy-like pistol.

"What should we do?"

"Nothin'. I can't interfere; it's too dangerous."

Aislynn had witnessed the aftermath of husbands beating wives. She had seen blackened eyes, swollen lips, and cut faces hidden by veils in church and on the streets, yet she had never seen or heard fighting.

"Can't we get the police?" she asked.

Johnny blinked back his astonishment, "Aislynn, they don't have police in these territories; they have marshals who can't control the men killin' each other in the streets. Do you think one of them is gonna come runnin' because a woman is gettin' beat?"

The woman's cries grew louder. "Why is he beating her?" Aislynn whined.

"He's teachin' her a lesson."

"What lesson?"

"That he's in control; that he's the boss. He wants her to know she has to do what he wants." Disgust dripped from his words.

"If they're alone, well, shouldn't they be, shouldn't he love her?"

"Does it sound like love?"

The woman pleaded with her partner to stop. Johnny got out of the bed and pushed it to the opposite wall.

91

"Move over, I'll sleep on this side." He lay between her and the brutality.

The woman's crying seeped through the wall. They could hear the springs of the bed moan as someone's weight dropped down on them. "Please don't. You'll hurt me," she whimpered from the other side of the wall.

Johnny moved against Aislynn and placed his hand on her shoulder. With her mind tossing thoughts of dread and vulnerability, she squirmed away from his touch.

"Aislynn," he started. Johnny stroked her arm, "Don't blame me for what's goin' on in there. I'm no bully. You know I'd never hurt you."

"I know."

Each time their neighbor's bed hit the wall the woman's sobs followed. Tears slid from Aislynn's eyes and a circle of dampness silently swelled on her pillow.

Johnny whispered, "I love you,"

"I know," she replied. *I depend on it.*

The rooms quieted. Aislynn could hear the sound of a wagon moving down the street, with wheels rolling, hoofs slapping the mud. Johnny snored softly. She heard her neighbor sniffing her tears. Aislynn's heart sank and her resolve rose when she heard the woman whisper, "I'm sorry."

In the morning, Johnny led her out to 18th Street. At the Elkhorn Corral, he found Brother Morton, a Mormon freighter, readying a train to return to Salt Lake City. Johnny spoke to the man alone for a few moments while Aislynn watched. The short, stocky man wore an attitude of superiority. Aislynn disliked him on sight.

Johnny explained the terms. "His train is leavin' in three days, daybreak on the ninth. It's four freight wagons and five families, all Mormons. He plans on makin' twenty miles, maybe more, a day. Long days and hard wagonin' for families. We can join but they'll turn off at Echo Canyon for Salt Lake City. We'll have to get to Ogden on our own. It's about thirty miles, but he says the road is safe. The Mormons travel it regularly."

"I don't like him." Aislynn replied. She wanted to be open-minded, but she had read stories in the newspapers about Mormons and their religion. As a traditional Christian, or "Gentile" to the Mormons, she disagreed with the Mormons' heretical ideas about Christ, and their practice of polygyny. She recalled the sect wanted to establish an independent Mormon nation in the Utah Territory. Their separatist desires and their radical religious views had developed into conflicts with Gentile settlers and battles with federal troops. They were one more danger waiting in the West and she wanted to keep her distance from them.

Johnny stared at Morton, "I don't like him, either. But it's them or waitin' for someone else. The trains to California and Oregon tend to cut off west of South Pass City; if we join them, we'd be goin' almost two hundred miles alone."

"Then we don't have many choices." As she looked at the man, her face became pinched. "Well, I suppose if he were dangerous, he'd be in jail."

"I don't think you can make that assumption, but the clerk at the hotel said this man's been crossin' for years. I figure no matter who we go with we're takin' a risk."

They passed the morning shopping for mules and a wagon. The Great Western Corral had nearly two hundred animals. Aislynn thought they all looked exactly alike; yet, she waited while Johnny examined what seemed to be the entire herd. As he inspected, he explained the important features of each animal to an uninterested Aislynn. After he chose his animals, they moved on to the livery and shopped for a wagon. "The springs are important. You're going to have to ride most of the day; twenty miles is too far to walk." Walking twenty miles a day had not entered her mind. She planned to ride to Utah. She watched him crawling under each wagon until he found a suitable rig.

Hitched and harnessed, Johnny helped Aislynn into the wagon and jumped up beside her. He shook the reins and the mules stepped out. Happy to be free of the corral, they pranced up the street. The wagon bounced on the uneven road. Johnny's weight tilted the seat and she involuntarily slid against him.

Johnny leaned his head toward hers, bursting, "This is going to be more excitin' than the war."

"The war was not exciting," she stated flatly.

"It was; in some strange way, the danger was thrillin'. Of course, I didn't see much action," he added with disappointment.

She shook her head at his perception. Testy, she grumbled, "Thank goodness. It was bad enough I had to worry about the Nolans being killed any minute."

Johnny looked at her and smiled. "Well, this is much better; I get to be with you," and he patted her knee.

Aislynn picked up his hand and dropped it over his leg. "Just remember, Mr. Maher, you may be telling people we're married, but we're not. It's a public persona, and it doesn't come with any private privileges."

"Just enjoy the experience. It's somethin' we've heard about our whole lives, wagonin' west, the pioneers. We're goin' to be a part of it."

"Yes." She nodded at his childlike enthusiasm.

"It's somethin' we can tell our grandchildren."

Johnny pulled back on the reins. The mules and the wagon shuttered to a stop in front of Shackman Brothers Outfitting. "Grandchildren?" she asked with sarcasm.

"It doesn't hurt to have a plan."

No, it doesn't hurt to have a plan.

Shackman's appealed to Aislynn because they advertised reduced prices. With the absence of the rail workers, deflation set in quickly and Aislynn felt lucky for it. Captain Morton estimated the trip at one month. Aislynn stocked two months of supplies, knowing Johnny's appetite and not knowing what they would find when they arrived in Utah. Eggs, hams, bacon, smoked meat and dried fish. Flour, rice, coffee. Potatoes, carrots, onions, beets and turnips. Canned fruits and vegetables. Cookware, laundry essentials, bedding and bath necessities. Johnny bought tools, knee-high boots for both of them, a Winchester repeater and a .44 Colt Army revolver. Everything went into the wagon.

On the east side of town, adjacent to Crow Creek, waiting wagons camped. They pulled next to a schooner housing another young couple. Before they had climbed down from their wagon, a blowzy woman, breasts flapping, rushed forward to meet them. A scarecrow of a man with a long, sad face followed her.

"Hey, ya'll. I'm Maybelle; this here's Zach. Ya'll need help? Zach help him get wood. I can tell you anything you need to know 'bout this here camp. We been here for days."

With a Missouri drawl, Zach told Johnny where he could find wood. Aislynn stood on the back of the wagon, fishing out what she needed to prepare their evening meal with Maybelle ceaselessly chatting.

Starting a fire proved difficult. The wind took the spark. Johnny dug a hole and stacked the kindling in it. As soon as the flames rose, Aislynn's skirt blew into the blaze. Still on the ground, Johnny clapped his hands over the flaming fabric. He stood and moved her upwind.

While Aislynn cooked, she, Johnny and Zach listened to Maybelle prattle. She explained they met in St. Joe. After three days they realized they were in love and got married. Aislynn could feel Johnny's reaction. When she turned to him, she found his eyes narrowed, his face hard and critical. Maybelle talked on about their overland trip to Cheyenne and emphasized the humorous aspects. She bounced around the camp as she spoke, prancing between the men and the fire, revealing a shadow show of her legs through the thin fabric of her skirt.

Johnny laid boards between the walls of the wagon and Aislynn arranged their featherbed, sheets and quilts.

As they lay in their new bed, Johnny attempted to make the most of their privacy. Lying on his side, he stretched an arm around her and pulled her toward him, searching for her lips.

Aislynn protested, "We're not actually married, you know."

"How many times are you goin' to remind me? Besides, we could be. It sure didn't take much for Maybelle to marry Zach."

"We are not them."

"No, ma'am." Johnny shook his head, "We are not."

"You don't like them?"

"He's a fool and she's a whore."

Aislynn was astonished. She did not think Zach was very bright. Maybelle talked too much and dressed poorly, but she reasoned they were from Missouri. Aislynn did not know if backwoods people knew about corsets and petticoats or if they could afford them. She did not agree with Johnny's assessment.

"You're awfully harsh," she reprimanded.

"You asked; I told you."

"They're poor."

"I don't want to argue about them. I think we should use this time to practice kissin'."

Johnny leaned toward her again and gently brushed his lips against hers. With his hand in her hair, he angled her head and pressed closer for a deeper kiss. She fell back onto her pillow and Johnny's mouth moved to her ear and down her neck. Aislynn could feel her heart rate quicken and began to feel warm and uncomfortable. Johnny's hand wandered from her head to her shoulder and began migrating over the front of her coat, Aislynn sat up and announced, "I think it's time for us to go to sleep." She moved to one side of the bed and turned her back on him.

Johnny muttered, "Why do you always get to say when enough is enough?"

Aislynn thought about her answer for a moment. She did not really know why but Johnny was like her father and most of the Nolans. They generally let her make choices about certain things, like their home, meals, and womanly things. Only Tim would tell her how to behave, what not to wear, where she could or could not go. "It's just the way it is," she announced. "I, well, women make certain decisions; men make others."

"And I guess you'll let me know when I can make some."

Aislynn lay back and listened to the sounds of the night. Sleeping outside on this wide-open prairie with no walls or locked doors gave her a nervous feeling in her stomach. Aislynn sighed, "We're sleeping outside."

Johnny's eyes flew open. "I thought this was what you wanted."

"I did, but I've never slept outside."

"We're not outside; we're in our... home. It's just not like the homes you're used to. It's got a roof and walls. We'll be fine." He pulled her close, kissed her cheek, and holding her hand, commenced patting it. "We'll be fine."

Aislynn lay awake straining her senses in the darkness. Above the repetitive splashing of the creek, Maybelle's wagon squeaked on its springs and she could hear Maybelle moaning and gasping. Aislynn pitied her and cursed Zach's abuse. In the distance, she could hear the howling of some unidentifiable animals and the popping of guns. All the while, the continuous buzzing of life close to the ground reached her ears. Aislynn could not name the critters, nor could she conjure their shapes, but she could hear them and imagined them scheming as they slithered, squirmed and crawled in the grass.

Trying to absorb some of Johnny's confidence, Aislynn moved under her covers until her leg rested against Johnny's. She knew the rifle reclining at his side and the revolver poised over his pillow gave Johnny strength. Taking a deep breath, Aislynn filled herself with the western wind and fell asleep.

The 3:15 train whistle woke Aislynn. She tossed about until the grey light of dawn filled the wagon. Quietly, she climbed off the bed and peered through the puckering string. Wisps of fog, pushed off the creek by the ever-present wind, hung among the wagons. Ghostly over-landers were stumbling out of the draught of sleep and crunching the lace of frozen grass and the patches of snow.

Aislynn slipped down to the floor of the wagon bed. Concealed under her coat and nightgown, she pulled on her clothes, wandered to the creek for water. Johnny was waiting with a mouthful of warnings when she returned. "I don't like you goin' off alone." She soothed him with a hearty breakfast and turned her attention to chores. The wagon had to be repacked for economy of space and efficiency of use.

Maybelle appeared close to noon. She watched as Aislynn carted and boiled water to wash clothes. Although she offered no assistance, Maybelle hurried Aislynn along, wanting her company on a walk to the general store.

The day was growing old when Aislynn approached Johnny with Maybelle's request. Johnny was adjusting the springs on the wagon and explained to Aislynn that he had no time to go to the store. "But, Maybelle will be with me." Johnny crawled out from under the wagon and stood before her, wearing a skeptical face. She continued, "The store is at the end of the boardwalk. You'll be able to see us from here."

Johnny did not look convinced. Aislynn cocked her head, "I'm not going to spend any money. I'm just going to take another look, in case there's anything we've forgotten. I won't even take any money, so I won't buy anything impulsively."

He shook his head at her, "Aislynn, you don't do anything impulsively, 'though I wish you would." She gave him a puzzled look and he added, "You know I don't worry about money. It's her. I don't like her. She's loose."

"I think you're wrong. I think she just seems flighty, but I'm sure she's trying to be a good wife. I think Zach is a beast," and she explained the sounds she heard from their wagon.

Johnny laughed out loud. "I'm sure she enjoyed every minute of it. Does she look unhappy?" Maybelle stood by her wagon humming and swaying.

"No; I suppose not."

Johnny shook his head, "Go but be very careful. Don't talk to anyone. Don't even look at anyone."

With their eyes adjusted to the bright sun, Aislynn and Maybelle stepped up on the store's shaded porch in a state of blindness.

"Well, what we got here?" reached Aislynn's ears as her eyes squinted to see the source of the coarse comment.

Three men were lounging on a bench in front of the store. Aislynn walked past them and had her hand on the doorknob when she heard Maybelle reply, "That depends on what your lookin' for."

One of the men rose and reached toward Maybelle but she wiggled away. "Maybelle, you get in here," Aislynn commanded. Bells tinkled as she pushed the door. She held it open while her eyes pierced Maybelle's with disapproval.

Maybelle trotted up to the door and said, "Aislynn, you're too stiff."

"How could you speak to those men? They're strangers, and they're rude."

"You sound like my sermonizin' ol' granny."

"Don't you care what I think? What Zach would think?"

"I don't care! I wuz just havin' some fun. 'Sides, Zach ain't gonna know 'less you tell him."

Maybelle flounced past her and sidled up to the counter greeting the shopkeeper with a long "Howdy."

Agape, Aislynn turned slowly to follow Maybelle but her eyes caught two men lounging in the middle of the store, feet propped up on the cold stove. The man on the left was old, round, and balding with vacant eyes and a limp arm hanging in his lap. In the light hair, pale eyes, large moustache, and skin like a road map, Aislynn recognized her gambler. Her eyes ran down the long, muscular legs resting on the stove and she cowered for a moment, noticing the huge hunting knife strapped to his ankle. Swallowing her fear, she apologized softly for interrupting their peace.

Display cases topped with wooden counters ran around three sides of the store. Barrels filled with pickled vegetables and dried foods stood in the front windows. Two oil lamps hanging from the rafters provided the meager lighting. Aislynn was examining the stock on the floor to ceiling shelves that rose behind the cases when the clerk approached. They exchanged pleasantries and he asked if she were new in town. Aislynn explained she was traveling west. "With your friend here?" he queried.

"No," Aislynn hesitated. In a deep blush, she managed the lie, "With my husband."

He introduced himself and she hesitantly stated her name as Mrs. Maher.

Aislynn explained she was looking for books, and they exchanged the titles they enjoyed. Maybelle, jealous of the attention Aislynn was earning, called to the man. Aislynn realized Johnny was right about Maybelle being loose. It annoyed her that he could assess people and situations so quickly. Aislynn eventually came to the same conclusions, but she always needed more time. A former conversation surfaced in her memory. Johnny had said, "You'd be better off traveling with a man like me." She laughed to herself, admitting he was right and recognizing her growing appreciation of him.

Aislynn noticed the lengthening shadows, "Maybelle, we'd better start back."

"You go. I'm gonna socialize a piece."

"It's getting late."

"Are you a 'fraidy cat? Go alone."

Fear churned in Aislynn gut. "I can't go back alone. Johnny will be furious if I'm walking the street by myself." She could feel her voice and her anxiety rising. "Maybelle, you have to come back with me."

"No. I wanna stay."

A loud bang rang through the store. The gambler had slammed the wooden heels of his boots on the wooden floor. His action shook the flimsy frame building and all its contents. He pulled himself to his full height, which was exceptional, and glared at Aislynn. She looked at the guns hanging from his sides and the huge knife strapped to his leg and winced. He growled at the clerk, "Make the introductions, Mack."

The clerk's voice cracked, "Missus Maher, this here's Orrin Sage."

Glowering at her, he asked, "Where's your man?"

Aislynn pulled herself up, trying to be tall, and announced, "At the wagon camp."

"Let's go talk to him."

Aislynn chewed her lip and begged God to keep this hulking horror from hurting her.

He banged his way to the door and threw it open. The bells knocked about in chaotic clanging. Aislynn stepped out onto the porch alone and the three men rose from their seats, whooping and whistling. One said, "So you decided to join us?"

Sage stepped behind Aislynn and took her arm. In a breath, each man backed away from them. "Orrin," the leader began, "I didn't know you was in there."

"I ain't," the gravel in Sage's throat ground. "I'm out here."

"Why, I can see that, Orrin, and it is nice to see you. Step back, boys. Let Orrin and this purdy little piece get through."

"Shut your mouth, Clem."

The man grew mute. Sage's hand gripped her elbow tightly as he guided her into the street. His strides were long and he seemed to expect her to keep up.

"How come your man let you go with that trash?"

"Well," she hesitated, "he didn't want me to. He doesn't have a high opinion of her."

"Why didn't you listen?"

"I thought she was nice."

"Men know whores when they see 'em. How long you married?"

"Just a short time." Aislynn winced at the lie.

"Youngins?"

"Oh, no." she replied, embarrassed by his personal questions.

"You probably ain't workin' at it neither."

Aislynn missed a step in her shock. She decided not to answer him for fear he would ask her for details she could not furnish.

"Gotta gun?"

"Oh yes, I do," she replied, pleased to change the subject.

His long legs stopped, "Let me see it."

"It's in the wagon."

"You think a man's gonna wait for you to fetch it out the wagon?" he barked.

"Aislynn?" Johnny stood in the road, wiping his hands on a rag watching the exchange. He started to walk toward them when Aislynn broke into a run. When she reached him, she maneuvered behind his back, finally grateful for his bulk.

"Johnny, this is Mr. Orrin Sage. He was kind enough to walk me home."

Johnny extended his hand and said, "I'm grateful, Mr. Sage." He turned to Aislynn, eyes wide and brows high, "Where's Maybelle?"

Positioned next to his wagon, Zach sauntered into

the street at the mention of Maybelle's name.

"She's probably pokin' Clem by now." Sage offered.

Aislynn did not understand his phrase but Zach approached ready to fight. "Wha'd you say 'bout my wife?"

"Your wife's a whore," Sage casually commented.

Anger strangled Zach speechless.

Aislynn broke in, "Oh, Zach, she acted shamelessly. She actually flirted with a group of men, and then, she refused to come back with me. She wanted to stay with them."

"I'll kill 'em."

Orrin's calm, raw voice rose again, "There's three of them an' she ain't worth gettin' killed for. 'Sides, there's real shortage of women out here. You might wanna keep what you got, just keep her real busy so she ain't got no need to go elsewhere."

A small, shocked "Oh" escaped from Aislynn and the men turned their eyes on her. "Now her," Sage looked at Aislynn, and her insides turned, "she just needs a stronger hand." She watched him closely, afraid this undisciplined creature might provide the stronger hand. "I know it's hard when she looks at you with them green eyes, but we ain't got but a few laws an' a passel of men ready to break all of 'em. Married or not, don't matter to them."

Johnny thanked Sage for his advice and invited him to share their dinner. Seated around the fire, they watched in silence as Maybelle returned. Zach walked her down to the creek and they disappeared for a short time. When they returned, Maybelle limped into the wagon; Zach sat alone by his fire. Sage shared his hard-gained lessons on wagoning with Johnny, as Aislynn served them the potted roast she had steamed in low coals all day. When Sage asked them why they were attempting the journey, Johnny explained their desire for better jobs and better pay. Aislynn explained that Tim was in Utah. She gushed about him and his accomplishments for a moment but Sage's hard eyes stopped her. She busied herself preparing a plate for Zach and handed it to Johnny.

In Johnny's absence, Sage made conversation with Aislynn. "You got what you need for this trip?"

"I think so."

"You got your medicines?"

"We have chamomile tea and laudanum, some castor oil, paregoric, ipecac and Epsom Salts."

"You're facin' mountain fever, dysentery, cholera, snake bites, broken bones, scurvy, parched skin an' God only knows what. You best get yourself a pencil, an' I'll tell you what you need."

He reeled off a list that included camphor for cholera, hartshorne for snakebites, glycerin for alkali burns and quinine for malaria. Instructions followed the list. When Johnny returned, Sage was telling Aislynn, "This ain't no picnic you're goin' on; it's a dangerous trip. The ways still difficult, even for experienced drivers. Wagon's break-down, people get hurt an' drown. Animals die."

Aislynn looked at Johnny and bit her lip. "Aislynn, Mr. Sage isn't tryin' to scare us; he's tryin' to help us."

"Don't never go near no animals; assume they all bite. An' the biggest danger of all is men. Injuns won't tend to bother you none; it's whites, outlaws." Sage turned to Aislynn, "Let's see this gun you got in your wagon."

Aislynn proudly produced her father's revolver. Sage turned to Johnny and said, "Hope you got better than this."

Johnny described his guns and Sage said, "Get her the same."

"You don't honestly think anyone is going to shoot at us?" Her question came in the shape of a plea.

"Yep."

"But she doesn't know how to shoot." Johnny interjected.

"Teach her."

"I don't have time before we leave. I'm makin' changes

to the wagon." He looked at Aislynn. "I suppose we should buy the guns here and I'll teach you en route."

"You buy the guns. I'll come by for supper tomorrow an' take her out on the prairie. I ain't got much to do 'til the railroad's money comes through."

The thought of being alone on the prairie with him, was not to her liking.

"Do you shoot well, Mr. Sage?" she ventured.

"It's what I do, ma'am."

"What you do?"

"Yes, ma'am. I'm a gun. I'm hired to shoot people who can't follow them laws I mentioned 'fore."

His words took her breath, "People?" she asked, her hand leaping to her throat.

Sensing her distress, Johnny chuckled. "Outlaws, Aislynn. He doesn't kill women and children."

Aislynn looked into Sage's pale eyes. In his unblinking stare, she saw sorrow. Recognition passed into curiosity until it stopped at sympathy. Aislynn wondered about Sage. There seemed to be sadness in the man, something that touched her and made her trust him.

"I ain't gonna hurt you ma'am."

Remembering his advice and counsel, she felt awe in the way that grace is granted. She said, "Fine, Mr. Sage. I'll fix you a nice supper."

Chapter 9

Aislynn trudged alongside Sage, stumbling painfully in her unfamiliar, uncomfortable boots. The prairie welcomed them with its green-brown swells of grass and brush against a sky unbroken with clouds. Pushing up like whitecaps, shards of pale rock broke the smooth, soft lines of the plains.

Sage set a can on a stout rock and handed her the tiny pistol. "Shoot," was all he said. Aislynn held the gun in front of her, looked away and pulled the trigger. The pistol jumped from her hand and landed on the ground. Frowning, he asked, "Ain't you never seen no one shoot a gun 'fore?"

"No! I ain't never seen no one shoot a gun 'fore!" she retorted.

"You gotta aim, for land sakes. Use your eyes." Sage looked for the gun in the grass. "What kinda place is this here New York? Ain't they got no guns?"

"Of course, people have guns, but they certainly don't brandish them in public, nor do they shoot them in my neighborhood. Someone could get hurt."

"Ain't that the idea?" Sage picked up the pistol, slapped it into her hand and said, "This time look at the target."

Aislynn tried to aim with both eyes but the barrel appeared to double. She closed her left eye and the barrel moved to the left. She tried closing her right eye but found the barrel moved right. "It keeps moving."

"Well, hold it still."

Puzzled, Aislynn held the gun in her right hand and aimed with her left eye. She missed the target, but she held on to the gun.

"Gimme that," Sage ordered, shaking his head. Grabbing the weapon from her hand, he reloaded and said, "Watch. You can't use your left eye with your right hand."

Two bullets burned through the can. Sage pushed two bullets into the barrels and slapped the pistol back in her hand, "Now you do it just like that."

Aislynn stretched her arm, pointed the gun toward the target and pulled the trigger.

"Raise it, aim it and shoot it." Sage commanded.

Again she tried, stretching her arm, bringing the gun up to face the can and pulling the trigger. She hit the ground; she hit the brush and she hit the rock with the can. She came near the target but never reached it. "Let's move on," he suggested.

They worked with the Colt. "Raise it, aim it en squeeze it." Aislynn needed two hands to hold the gun and the full strength of both arms to keep it steady when she pulled the trigger. She gripped it with each bang, straining to contain the animated metal. After an hour of trying to tame the wild bucking beast, Aislynn's arms shook with fatigue.

"I need to rest," she pleaded.

A piece of rock offered them a seat. Aislynn opened a basket holding a jar of lemonade and a leftover piece of cake. She shook the jar and filled two tin cups. He smiled when she handed him the cake and the cup. "Tell me 'bout this New York that's such a peaceful place nobody's shootin' it up."

Aislynn threw her head back to the endless blue sky and took a breath. "Well, the streets are straight and paved with grey cobble stones stretching north and south and they intersect with other streets stretching east and west. The streets are lined with sidewalks of brick or stone." She held her hands together and spread them wider and wider apart as she spoke. "Lining the sidewalks are buildings: brick buildings, stone buildings, wooden buildings of all shapes and sizes. Some are huge buildings covering an entire block and rise five or six stories." Aislynn's hands went up over her head and came down again. "Some are low and narrow, and some are tiny and a hundred years old. Some look like castles and fortresses. There are even tenements with a hundred people crammed inside."

"How'd they all get in?" Sage asked, incredulous.

"They walk through a door." Aislynn laughed. Her tone changed as she continued, "But inside, they're terrible, dirty, dark, and cramped. Some people have no choice but to live there. The poor just can't afford anything else. It's live there or in the streets."

"Can't they make a camp?"

"There isn't any space; it's all streets, buildings and lots of people. And the people, why there are all different types of people: brown people, black people, yellow people, and white people all from different parts of the world. They speak all kinds of languages. Sounds like gibberish sometimes with so many sounds, but they understand each other. You can pass a building and smell cooking from the far corners of Europe and from the deepest, darkest places in Africa. Some people cook right on the streets and sell what they cook. Then there are the stores. Why you can buy anything you've ever wanted in New York City."

Aislynn straightened, her eyes grew wide, and she waved her hands in excitement. "Oh and once, we went to the ocean. Mr. Sage, you should see the ocean. If I ever return to New York, I'll take you with me and show you the ocean. It's so vast, wider than the prairie. It never ends. It's alive, in constant motion." She swayed like the waves. "When the surf rolls into the shore, it rises. Then, as it crashes in a roar of thunder and it bursts into white foam that rushes along the entire beach." Her arms stretched wide. "It only lives a short time because the sand swallows it. But you don't miss it because just as one dies, another rises right behind it, and the whole drama repeats on a stage as big as the sky." Sage seemed to enjoy her presentation, until she said, "Tim took me to see it once. It was wonderful."

His face turned hard and he took a breath, "What's Johnny think a this Tim?"

"He admires him."

"Not as much as you, I'd wager."

Sensing his disapproval, Aislynn twisted her face into a pout.

"You seem mighty partial to him."

She stiffened under his accusation and defended herself, "I am fond of him."

Sage's eyes bore into hers. She pressed on, "I try to be good to Johnny, but I can't help what I feel." She felt sorry for her admission the minute it fell from her mouth. Guilt ate at her; she had wanted to confess her feelings to somebody and, in a fashion, gain expiation. She thought Sage, old and scarred, could carry the burden of her secret.

"Yep, you can. It's all in how you choose to look at someone. Sometimes younguns get ideas an' they get bigger than what's real." He shook his head at her, "Jes be careful. Mistakes can't always be corrected."

110

Aislynn chewed her lip and Sage said, "You think on it." He handed her the cup and picked up the Winchester rifle. "Let's go."

Aislynn followed his instructions and held the cumbersome piece against her shoulder. When she pulled the trigger, the buck sent her stumbling backwards. Tripping in her boots, she fell on her buttocks. Sage laughed and said, "That's God tryin' to knock some sense into you."

They toiled with the rifle until Aislynn complained of being tired, hungry and nearly blind. Sage took the gun from her hands and placed it on the ground. "Set down," he commanded, motioning toward the rock. They faced the western sky where the land seemed to be swallowing the sun. Storm clouds suffocated the peak on Sherman Summit. The wind, so welcome while the sun burned, turned cold as the sky darkened. He eased his bulk down next to her and Aislynn waited impatiently for a lecture on her poor target practice.

"You gotta good man."

"Yes, he's a good man."

"You should 'preciate what you got."

Aislynn sat quietly looking west. The sun tipped over the edge of the earth and left the sky orange, pink and purple, as a reminder of its power. Facing Sage, she tried to think of something to say, something to justify her feelings. She took a breath with the intention of explaining herself.

"I was married once." Sage said. The revelation shocked Aislynn. Sage seemed almost superhuman to her, like a character in a dime novel, out of place in a domestic scene. "A girl come into Fort Laramie 'bout fourteen years back. It was Fort John, then. She was a green-eyed thing, blonde, like my Ma. My Ma was daughter to the first missionaries. They come out here to convert Injuns: Cheyenne, Sioux, Osage. They'd preach to any who'd listen. They was all gone when I come along, my Pa included. Ma did laundry an' cookin' at the fort 'til she

111

died. I was young, four, five maybe. Soldiers took me in."

Sage's grey eyes never wavered from the horizon. His face fell expressionless, blank and remote. "So, one day this gal pulled into Laramie with a train. Her family stayed four days to rest an' supply. When it come time to go, I wouldn't let her leave, I just held on to her. Her folks left. After a time, she had a child."

He stopped speaking. Aislynn knew the child and its mother were dead. Death was the end of many stories she had heard about the West. He sat stone still, his long blond hair blowing under his hat in the stiff wind. He unclenched his teeth and continued, "The baby looked like an Injun. Black hair, black eyes, deep skin. She swore 'twas mine, but I couldn't make no sense of it, neither could no one else. There was plenty a Injuns about, at the fort, on the trail. I'd left her alone some, scoutin', huntin', but she seemed such a good gal. I just couldn't believe she'd done it, but there it was atauntin' me. I coulda took 'em an' left, just gone into the mountains, made the best of it but 'stead I believed the worst, told her to go. She took that baby, walked out onto that prairie an' did never look back."

Aislynn's heart hurt. She watched him staring; he was looking for them. Searching for some way to comfort him, she looked at his hard face and raised her hand to touch his arm. It seemed he had stopped breathing, then he inhaled and continued. "A few years later, a old Osage woman come into the fort with a bunch of Injuns. She heard my name an' said 'Your pa was my brother. He took a white wife an' that Christian name.' Ain't no one never told me I was half-breed, no one 'cept that ol' woman... an' that baby." He spit the last words from his mouth and did not utter another sound. Aislynn hugged his arm as tears streamed from her eyes. She noticed the sky was a dark navy; the stars were becoming faintly visible when she felt him release the rigid tension he held inside.

"Sage?" she ventured.

He looked down at her as though he had just discovered her sitting there. She placed her free hand on his stubbled cheek and said, "I think tomorrow is more important than yesterday."

In the darkness, she could feel his intense, penetrating eyes. "Well, gal, you got lots of tomorrows."

Chapter 10

The bugle sounded wake up with the first hint of
light. They were granted an hour to eat and break camp.
The sun showed full on the eastern horizon when Captain
Morton yelled, "Ho for Utah!"

Johnny shook the reins, the mules leaned northward
and the wooden wheels turned. They were traveling the
Black Hills/Cheyenne Road. At Fort Laramie, they would
reach the Overland Trail and put the east at their backs
to drive west toward the sunset.

The Mormon train formed around four, wide supply
wagons. They stood more than three times the size of
Aislynn's wagon, packed with wares to sell in Salt Lake
City. The four lugubrious schooners lumbered like white
elephants leading the pack. A scout road ahead and another outrider trailed behind.

The family wagons now counted six with the addition

of Zach's. Each man signed an agreement to accept Brother Morton as their captain and to follow his rules and directions. Aislynn thought him crude and low class, with a critical eye toward everything. He made her uncomfortable; she did not trust him.

Once they started to roll, dust engulfed their wagon. Aislynn and Johnny pulled their bandanas over their faces. Sage had warned them about dust so full of alkali powder it could sear human skin. He had given Aislynn an old buckskin shirt. It hung down to her knees but the dust did not penetrate its leather. Under the shirt, she clung to her wide-skirted dress, shunning the pantaloons some women adopted for the trip. Aislynn felt the skirt would afford more privacy when a lady needed to relieve herself on the barren plain. She maintained convention with her corset, underwaists, camisole, chemise and petticoats. A sunbonnet drooped to her shoulders topping the cumbersome costume.

The wagons jolted and jumped at every small rock and rut. Aislynn's body wobbled with each bump. Johnny's weight tilted the seat and despite her efforts to stay on her side, she slid along the rough wood until they were hip to hip. Aislynn tried bracing herself on the footboards in the front of the wagon, but the rope brake lay there, and each time Johnny pushed on it, she would have to snatch her feet up or get tangled in it. Without her feet on the floor, she nearly bounced out of the wagon. Johnny grabbed her and held her to his side saying, "Just stay here and hold on to me."

At first glance, the prairie seemed monotonous to Aislynn with its endless brownish-green landscape. Hours of staring brought the view into clearer focus. As she studied it like a piece of art, she discovered the colors were intense. The green-brown waves were frozen in an endless variety of contours. Frequently, the waves were sliced, revealing striated earth in delicate tones ranging from brown to white. As the wagon rolled and their perspectives changed, so did the shapes and the colors of the protuberances. Indiscernible distances obscured proportion. Light varied with the hour, changing the picture. Within the composition, everything seemed to be moving toward the horizon. Silvery-green brush huddled in small troops. Along the banks of the streams, stunted trees marched shoulder to shoulder. Where it appeared barren, prickled plants and tiny yellow flowers charged out of the ground.

The sky seemed higher here than in New York. Devoid of clouds, the relentless blue encircled them. As the day wore on, they witnessed wisps of light blue become white and grow into clouds.

With an amazing twenty-three miles behind them, they halted for the night. Lying in bed, Aislynn decided nature was noisy, loud and strange. Sage had said, "Look, listen, smell and feel. That'll keep you alive." She focused all her senses and felt anxiety pluming in her belly.

Aislynn lay alone. Johnny stood the first watch from nine o'clock to midnight. Sage had warned Johnny to stay close to her. He had explained most western men were respectful to women, but like anywhere else, there were some who could not be trusted. "She don't git water, pick flowers or take a shit without you an' your gun." Sage had a few words for her when they parted as well, "En you don't go doin' nothin' stupid. You do what your told." She listened to his harsh words, but she heard the concern in his voice. Remembering how her father and the Nolans obliquely express their love, she said, "You must have some Irish in you. I'm going to miss you, too." And she kissed the top of his head.

On the second day, Aislynn's buttocks were too sore for wagoning. She opted to walk through morning. Her boots were overlarge and rubbed her feet sore. Trying to avoid the puddles and flop left on the trail by the animals, she stumbled through the sage and new grass. Maybelle jumped down to join her and attempted to make conversation. Aislynn only returned silence but Maybelle continued to try to explain her behavior.

After they nooned, Aislynn joined Johnny in the wagon. They bumped along until the trail met Chugwater Creek, their first water crossing. As they descended the bank, the wagon groaned forward and nearly ran up the mules' rumps. Johnny stood on the brake to hold their load back and maneuvered into the water. Aislynn's insides churned. She did not know how to swim and she did not like watching the water swirl under the wagon through the wheels. Johnny pointed out it was shallow enough for her to stand but she felt relieved when they climbed out of the creek and emerged safely on the other side.

With Johnny's night watch scheduled between midnight and 3:00 AM, they settled in early. The Mormons chose to sleep in tents and erected them in the center of the corralled wagons each night. The children cause plenty of commotion as they packed into their cots. While they quieted, one of the men played a harmonica and another fiddled. The Mormons loved music and danced freely. Aislynn and Johnny were not asked to join, nor did they presume they would be welcome, as the Mormons seemed to shun their company. They tried to sleep through the racket and were grateful for the peace when it came.

In her sleep, Aislynn heard the popping of bullets. She felt Johnny dragging her under the wagon cover and over the wooden sidewall. She tumbled into his arms. When she hit the ground, Johnny handed her the Colts. He pulled the two metal milk cans he had filled with extra feed and water for the mules off the side of the wagon and threw them down. They dove behind them. The captain ordered, "Shoot at anyone you see." Aislynn raised a gun, aimed into the dark and squeezed the trigger. After several volleys were exchanged, the attackers' guns quieted.

A voice rose over the wagons saying, "We come for them Gentile women."

Aislynn looked around the corral. The women, two who were huge with pregnancy, gathered their children in their arms, and crouched beside their tents. Her eyes caught someone standing; it was Maybelle. Aislynn heard her cry, "Clem!" and everything became clear.

"I'm comin'!" Maybelle called with excitement. She scampered to her wagon and collected her things. When Zach recovered from his shock, he pleaded with her to stay. She turned on him, "Trash. You ain't got nothin' to offer me."

Aislynn and Johnny rose to their feet and watched the pitiful exchange. When Maybelle finished with Zach, she turned to Aislynn, "Ain't this romantic?"

The captain shouted, "She's comin an' you can have her."

Another voice rang out, "We want both women."

Maybelle flushed with excitement, "Oh, Aislynn, come on."

Aislynn looked at the cowering Mormon women and children. She raised her hand and it fell sharply on Maybelle's face. The taller woman rocked back two steps. Redness bloomed on Maybelle's cheek as she spat at Aislynn, who jumped out of the way.

"I'm comin' alone," she shouted.

Some loud discussion ensued among the outlaws as Maybelle exited the corral. Johnny was watching Zach. When he raised his gun, Johnny took a swipe at Zach's arm. The shot exploded in the air. An uncommon coldness rose in Johnny's voice, "She's not worth the bullet."

Aislynn found the medicinal whiskey. The three of them sat by a low fire while Johnny and Zach pulled on the bottle. Zach insisted on rescuing Maybelle. Johnny tried to convince him his pride was talking, not his common sense. Nevertheless, Zach chose to leave with the morning.

Johnny sat his watch from the wagon seat. Aislynn lay trying to quietly cry out her fears. She had heard tales of women who been kidnapped, abused and murdered by outlaws. Johnny leaned through the puckerstring, "I would never have let them take you."

"What could you have done?"

"There's no reason to even think about it, Angel. They won't be back."

Aislynn closed her eyes and squeezed out her remaining tears.

Fort Laramie sat on a stark treeless plain in a curve of the Laramie River. The fort, devoid of palisades, exposed on all sides, looked more like a town than a military post. Approaching from the south, they encountered a small city of Indian teepees standing pristine white against the golden-brown terrain.

Aislynn had read about Chief Red Cloud and the war he was waging to retain the Sioux's sacred hunting grounds. Since the early 1860s, wagons of overlanders traveled the Bozeman Trail, which cut through hallowed hills, and spurred attacks on settlers and soldiers. The Sioux chief refused to participate in a peace conference or consider moving to reservations until all the forts along the trail were abandoned. In April of 1868, the government agreed to close the forts, and the Sioux contemplated a restricted life. However, when Red Cloud entered negotiations to end the war, he discovered deceit; their sacred hunting grounds had been excluded from the proposed reservation. While their chief worked out a compromise, the Sioux waited peacefully at Fort Laramie.

Aislynn, a fan of dime novels, feared and distrusted Indians. When she shopped at the sutler's store, she watched the Sioux women and their wide-eyed, shy children. She was surprised to find them so similar to whites. Although she knew female tribal elders were involved in decisions and even included in treaty negotiations, Aislynn decided the men were responsible for all the violence against settlers and railroad workers. Women were not to be feared; it was the men who were dangerous.

Johnny puzzled over the Indian problem and said, "With so much land, why do we keep bumpin' into each other?"

"Once they're restricted to a reservation, we will all be safer," Aislynn asserted.

"I'm not sure that's fair; even the newspaper says they were more sinned against than sinners."

Aislynn frowned at him. "They want to be left alone. We're giving them land where they can be alone."

"I wonder if they'll be left alone," Johnny pondered.

"I don't care," Aislynn dismissed his concern, "as long as they leave us alone."

Just north of Fort Laramie, they met the Overland Trail. The prairie stretched behind them and the mountains lay ahead. The stark white ruts cut into the solid rock promised a rougher road and increased grades. Their wagon pitched along the trail and Aislynn complained about her discomfort and nausea.

"Why don't you take a nap?" Johnny suggested.

"I'm not tired."

Johnny shook his head, "You're certainly out of sorts."

"I am not," she said shortly. "Why don't you just stop finding fault?"

He looked her over and asked, "Are you like this every month?"

Furious at his intimate question, Aislynn slapped his arm, "I am going to take a nap just so I can get away from you."

While Johnny enjoyed their close quarters, Aislynn chafed at the lack of privacy the wagon afforded. Thinking on it, she had to admit he was very considerate of her, but this was one of the things she wanted to keep hidden. It was her private business.

That is what Sean had said the day he came home and found her sobbing on her bed. She had returned from school and discovered the blood staining her underdraw-

121

ers. When she could not stem the flow, she knew she was dying. Aislynn took to her bed and Sean found her there, terrified and tearful. He explained it was her body's way of preparing her for having babies.

This information was not a relief. "I can't have a baby! I'm twelve."

He pulled her into his arms and stroked her hair and said, "You're just getting ready. It'll take years."

"Then what?" she asked.

Sean looked bewildered, "Then what?"

"How do I get a baby?"

Sean pulled his head back and looked down at her, "Damn, doesn't anyone talk to you girls?"

"We'd get slapped for asking at school."

"Tim?" he pleaded. "Your Da?"

Aislynn shook her head.

"Well, that's something your husband will explain."

Aislynn started to cry again, "It's so awful you can't tell me?"

"It's not my place."

"Why can you know?"

"You see that's why no one tells you girls anything. You ask too many damn questions." Aislynn pouted on her bed. Sean stood up and leaned over her, "Listen, just don't lay naked with a man 'til you're married."

She crinkled her nose, "Why would I want to?"

"Just don't, no matter who asks. Understand?"

"No."

"Well, remember your body is your own personal business. You don't have to share it with anyone. Now, stuff a rag in your underdrawers and start dinner."

As Aislynn lay on the featherbed, her feelings wavered between anger and guilt. However, she decided she did not have to apologize to Johnny; he was prying. When the wagon corralled for the night, the noise and activity woke Aislynn. She cooked dinner in silence, hanging on to her exasperation. For Johnny's dessert, she opened a jar of cherry preserves and prepared a small pie. At Laramie, Aislynn had purchased some milk and skimmed off the cream. She knew he liked it poured over his pie. With the remainder, she flavored his coffee.

"Aren't you havin' any?" Johnny asked.

"No," she replied, "It's all for you."

He chuckled softly and whispered, "I accept your apology."

"I didn't apologize."

Johnny just smiled and nodded. Aislynn let the matter rest as she became distracted by one of the Mormons. Mr. Smith removed a rocking chair from his wagon, placed it by the Mormons' fire and gathered his children around it. He entered their tent and emerged with a small bundle in one arm and his wife leaning on the other. Mr. Smith invited everyone to meet the new member of the train.

Aislynn presented a jar of quince preserves to the pale, nearly gray, Mrs. Smith, who seemed barely able to lift her hollow eyes to meet Aislynn's. The baby was silent, purple-faced and wrinkled. Aislynn admired Mrs. Smith's noble dignity. Under primitive circumstances, she had given birth on the trail, quietly and privately. It amazed Aislynn how frontier women accepted major life changes calmly and without fanfare.

After standing the late watch, Johnny crawled into bed. The light of day showed softly. Aislynn started to rise but he pulled her down. "You can sleep in. We're not leavin' for a few hours."

When Aislynn asked why, Johnny put his hand on her cheek and looked at her silently for a moment. "We have to have a funeral first."

The baby and its mother were wrapped in a quilt tied with a string. Several crates were fashioned into a coffin while Aislynn and the children gathered rocks. The two were put down in an unmarked grave and the rocks were piled on the loose dirt to deter wolves. Words were said. Tears were shed. The train moved on.

Like most travelers on the Overland Trail, Aislynn discovered boredom presented the greatest challenge. She started the mornings fidgeting next to Johnny in the wagon seat. When the tedium overwhelmed her, she jumped down and walked. She exchanged words with some of the women and children who also chafed at the dullness of the tiresome trip. She watched the mothers struggle with children who kept themselves occupied by finding trouble and felt grateful she did not have children to entertain.

Walking was difficult. The way was slowly ascending, rocky and tangled. The unending wind blew unending dust. Yucca plants, with their sharp stiff leaves, were unbending. Sagebrush and prickly cactus tugged at her skirt. Aislynn had to wear Johnny's socks over her own stockings to keep her feet from blistering in her loose boots. In contrast with the chilly nights, they had been blessed with a few unseasonably warm days. Aislynn abandoned her excess underclothing and wore her mourning dress under Sage's shirt. She hoped the Dakota Territory, unlike some states, did not have laws requiring women to be corseted. Even if it did, she did not think anyone would suspect her lawlessness.

After the noon stop, she would join Johnny in the wagon. She preferred to endure the sour smells of the mules and their various excretions to walking in the afternoon heat. The unfamiliar, fascinating topography had become commonplace. The head snapping motion of the wagon made her teeth clatter and her eyes bounce in her head, rendering reading or writing impossibility. She chatted with Johnny to occupy her mind and while away the time.

They passed other trains trailing livestock. Aislynn thought they might find friends among those emigrants, but their caravan moved quickly and none kept their pace. Aislynn found comfort in the fact they were rapidly progressing through the foothills.

Once they were beyond Ayres Natural Bridge, they rode within sight of the North Platte River. At first, Aislynn thought the North Platte impassable. So wide and blue, it seemed a piece of the sky had fallen. Its water rushed through the grass. The bottom appeared a soft, sandy tangle. Aislynn began to dread crossing.

They were four days outside of Fort Laramie, when the weather changed. Dark clouds puffed out of the horizon like smoke. A cold wind blew in light snows. They sheltered at old Fort Casper, abandoned the previous year by the army but occupied by traders. When the sun emerged and the melting commenced, they took to the slushy trail. To Aislynn's relief, the Fort's bridge remained intact and allowed them to cross the Platte easily. For two days, they pushed through cold wind and heavy mud until they approached their first Sweetwater River crossing.

Unlike the wide, shallow Platte, the Sweetwater roared with icy snowmelt. Narrower but deeper, it rushed downhill. Lined along the bank, the wagons waited for their turn to ford. They watched as the first, big supply wagon mired in the sandy bottom and came dangerously close to tipping. Extra horses were hitched to pull it from the Sweetwater's hold. The captain moved the train northward a few hundred feet, and the trial began with another supply wagon. They continued to move up river slightly until they found a spot with a firmer, rockier floor.

Johnny tied one end of a rope around Aislynn's waist and circled himself with the other end. He made her stand in the wagon bed behind him as he eased their wagon down the slight slope. Aislynn clutched his shoulders and kept her eyes on Independence Rock, the huge, granite monolith resting on the plain directly opposite them. She tried to visualize them reaching this landmark, climbing to the top and standing on firm, unmoving stone. The sounds of the wheels grinding on the rocky riverbed and the stream thrashing under them rose to her ears. Icy water splashed on to her hands and face. The wagon rocked and Johnny shouted at his mules. He shook the reins hard, slapping their rumps. They jumped and the wagon jerked forward. He smacked them hard once more and they sprang up the south bank.

Their train passed the night with several other trains camped around Independence Rock. Like the hundreds of Argonauts who had come before them, Aislynn and Johnny engraved their names in the huge turtle-shaped granite. They climbed to the top and squinting into the constant wind, they surveyed the inconceivably vast land. A deceptive flatness spread before them edged by jagged, gray-blue hills. Traveling distances were indiscernible for they had learned there were hundreds of ups and downs hidden in the grass.

Looking down at the camps surrounding the rock, they noticed the corral next to theirs had excluded one wagon from its ring. Johnny concluded its occupants must have a contagion. They decided to avoid this wagon for fear of illness.

While mounting the tailgate steps, Aislynn stopped and studied the couple in the isolated wagon. She did not think they moved like the infirmed. The woman progressed around a small table lighting candles while the man stood mumbling into his open hands. Aislynn noticed he had a shawl over his shoulders. "Johnny," she called. He looked up from his book. "They're not contagious, they're Jewish."

The following day, the trains moved past Devil's Gate, a huge cleavage in a granite ridge cut over thousands of years by the Sweetwater. At its base, the river ran thirty feet wide but the chasm rose almost 400 feet and gaped 300 feet across at the top. Their wagons did not stop at the phenomenon; they rolled on simply counting it as one more signpost of progress. Ahead stood Split Rock; it had been in their view for a full day. Like the sight of a gun, this cleft in a stark, granite hill aimed their vision west to the mountains looming darkly on the horizon. Atop this harsh stone, as on many other outcroppings, Aislynn noticed a solitary tree, pushing up through the raw rock, green against the blue sky, beaten by the wind, bent by the snow, sustained by the rain, growing and surviving alone.

After dinner, Aislynn handed Johnny a plate and turned a cherry upside-down cake out of her skillet. A smile crossed his face, "You are the best cook."

"It's not for you," she announced. She watched his face fall, "We're going visiting."

They approached the exiled pair and introduced themselves. Aislynn held out the cake and said, "This is for you."

The young woman burst into tears. Aislynn's eyes darted between Johnny and the woman's husband. She considered leaving when the woman collected herself and sniffled, "It's been so long since anyone has extended us any kindness."

California bound, Sophia and David Rabinowitz were from the Lower East Side and they knew Mr. Freilischer. Like Aislynn and Johnny, they traveled with a freight train; it seemed no other trains would take Jews. They shared the cake, coffee and stories of home until the wind grew cold. Clouds expanded heavily in the darkened sky. Great spears of lightning stabbed the earth and thunder vibrated the thin air.

Retreating to their wagon, Aislynn and Johnny readied for bed by dressing in coats and quilts. She pulled the puckerstring closed and crawled into bed. Rain bounced off the wagon cover which had been soaked in beeswax and linseed oil to prevent leakage. The pinging of hail could be heard between the roars of thunder. Although her eyes were tightly closed, flashes of lightning could still be seen. Pulling the quilts over her head, she remembered reading nothing was as fearsome as a ship tossed in an ocean with gale force winds batting at it. But here, on this sea of grass, with the wagon bobbing and swaying, the wind howling, the lightning flaring, and the thunder shaking the very ground she relied on for stability, this seemed more fearsome than anything she could imagine.

Burrowed under the quilts together, Johnny pulled her close. "This would be a very good time for us to practice kissin'."

"How can you think of that when we could die any minute?"

"We're not goin' to die. Besides, if we were, at least we'd be havin' fun."

The wagon shook with the thunder. "I'm too scared to do anything."

"You can lie here and worry, believin' catastrophe is going to strike or you can enjoy the time we have." One thing Aislynn had to admit about Johnny, he was distracting. As he kissed her, his hands started to wander over her back and slipped down her buttocks but she did not protest. Although she remembered Sean's warning, she knew they were far from naked and he was keeping her warm.

Johnny's breathing became labored, and he pulled away from her. "I'm goin' to go check the mules," he said as he scrambled to leave the wagon.

Aislynn bolted upright, astonished at the interruption. "It's storming!"

"You might use this time to take care of your personal business," he told her as he climbed over the tailgate.

When she finished her toilette, she peered through the puckerstring and saw him washing his hands in the snow the storm was tossing at them. He reentered the wagon and said, "Let's get some sleep." In the face of the continuing turmoil, Johnny snored, while Aislynn tried to understand his behavior.

On Sunday, Sophia and David's train kept pace with theirs. They drove through the shallow snow and arrived at Three Crossings. Despite the cold and the stress of crossing the river three times, Aislynn's day flew. She spent a good part of it with Sophia. In the evening, they shared a fire, cooked and ate together.

Early the next morning, they again traversed the river. The sun broke through the heavy sky and the snow melted. As the wagons rolled through the fresh mud, they passed the Ice Slough, a boggy marsh, which by some natural phenomenon, held ice through the middle of summer. As the sun warmed them, Sophia and Aislynn chatted through the afternoon while sharing the wagon seat with David.

In the evening, the trains camped near the final Sweetwater Crossing. Aislynn invited the Rabinowitzs to join their camp. After dinner, David offered to play his violin with the Mormon fiddler. To Aislynn's surprise, the Mormon accepted his offer. David explained Mormons viewed Jews with empathy, believing they were brothers in opposition to Christian oppression. On the soggy grass, they laid a piece of canvas and Aislynn and Johnny attempted to teach Sophia to step dance.

The morning dawned bright in the east but dark clouds moved from the west. Aislynn and Johnny sat poised in their wagon waiting for their train's turn to cross. From their vantage, they could look over the washboard terrain and the Sweetwater as it showed itself between two gently rising hills. Their unwelcome companion, the bitter wind, blew around them.

Sophia and David's wagon stood in line at the end of their train. The river ran fast and high. A lumbering supply wagon descended the bank and slipped like a ship from dry dock into the water. Huge horses dragged it across guided by outriders. The second supply wagon caught its wheels in the ruts of the first and started to tip. The riders pulled on the ropes tied to the bed and easily righted it.

The third and fourth supply wagons crossed and were followed by the train's family wagons. Last to take their turn were David and Sophia. Aislynn and Johnny watched them pull up to the bank and descend. David had his foot on the brake as they slipped down into the torrent. The Rabinowitzs' wheels sank; the wagon stalled. The current collided with the wooden wagon bed and slowly pushed it over. The cover billowed in the stream. When Sophia slipped into the water, her skirt blossomed like a flower. The bloom closed over her head like a morning glory in the evening as she disappeared in the abyss. David slapped at the water until the wagon floated over him.

Johnny shouted, "Where are the guides?" The outriders were on the opposite shore moving the wagons along and riding away. Aislynn jumped from the wagon and ran to her captain and his men. She stood on the edge of the river screaming at the riders. "Help them! They're drowning!"

The outriders galloped downstream and pulled the limp pair from the water. Drenched in death, the bodies were laid on the opposite shore. Captain Morton started across.

Aislynn called to him, "Tell them not to touch them. We'll bury them."

Morton sneered at her, "I'll tell 'em. Not for you, for them." He turned his horse and splashed away.

After a hasty burial, the Mormon train moved on. They camped five miles east of South Pass, the gentlest ascent of all the Rocky Mountain passes and the easiest crossing of the Continental Divide. Aislynn woke in the darkness with pain gripping her middle. Attempting to be quiet and trying to maintain her modesty, she stumbled to the chamber pot. Evacuation was fierce. She rested her chin on her knees, moaning as her body tried to turn itself inside out.

She could hear Johnny patting her side of the bed, "Aislynn?"

He crawled to the end of the bed and found her balanced limply on the chamber pot, steadying herself against the tailgate.

"What did you have to eat today that I didn't?" Johnny investigated.

"The Johnson children gave me some lemonade after the funeral."

Johnny moved to light the lantern.

Aislynn screamed, "No!" With her propriety under attack, she insisted she would be fine. "Just leave me be."

She heard him pull on his boots. He climbed out over the wagon seat. Aislynn peeked under the cover. She saw a fire burning by the Johnson tent and watched Johnny starting one of his own. She felt weak and wanted to crawl into the bed, but she knew she could not be separated from her new partner.

Johnny climbed back into the wagon with the skillet in his hand. She squinted in the dark. He arranged the pillows around the bed and covered them with a sheet. In the center, he rested the skillet and surrounded it with a towel. "Come up here," he ordered.

Aislynn grabbed his hand and he pulled her onto the bed. He said, "Put your rump in the pan and get comfortable. You're gonna to be here for a while."

She moved to the pan and lifted her nightgown. Johnny grabbed it by the hem and said, "This is only gonna be in the way." He began lifting it over her head.

"Close your eyes," she demanded.

Johnny shook his head. "It's dark."

He covered her with the quilts and blankets. She felt grateful to be lying down. She experienced constant pain and a rising fever. With some clanging and crashing, she heard Johnny searching through the wagon.

When he returned, he had chamomile tea and laudanum. "You have to drink; get fluid in your body. That will flush you out."

Aislynn said, "I'm already flushed." Johnny held her head and poured the tea and medicine into her. She apologized, "I'm sorry you have to witness this."

"Aislynn, this is nothin'. You should see a whole troop of men get the flux at the same time."

The wagons rolled and she refused to stay behind. Despite her churning belly and the discomfort of the ride, she chose to pass the day pounding against the iron skillet rather than be left behind to the outlaws and Indians. Under the wagon cover, heat was her intense companion. After Johnny rolled up the sides to give her air, the dust joined her. Johnny had taken the last position in line so he could stop throughout the day and help Aislynn drink the tea, which sat in a kettle under his seat. He dosed her with laudanum and it helped her doze. By evening, she felt well enough to wash her raw body parts.

While she washed, Johnny attended the burial of the youngest Johnson boy. He had been a frail child. Small bodies dehydrated quickly and frequently succumbed to diarrhea. In the morning, still weak, Aislynn mounted the wagon seat and balanced her soreness on two pillows. Her heart ached with the thought of putting a child in the ground and leaving him alone against the elements in this wild place.

Along the rough road running parallel to the Big Sandy River, the wagons climbed. Trees gave shade; however, they blocked the expansive view to the south. To the north, the gentle Rocky Mountain passes rippled into heavy peaks that seemed to weigh down the earth in the thin air, keeping it from floating into the sky. A warm, morning rain subdued the dust. The altitude made her head spin and her heart race. She felt feverish and weak, but kept her place leaning against Johnny.

By afternoon, the clear air and strong sun intensified eyesight. Scanning the horizons, a group of riders became visible on a northern ridge. The Indians sprang from the earth like ships bobbing out of the waves.

Chapter 11

The train's trumpet called them to corral. With their wagon in position, they jumped from the seat. Johnny threw the milk cans to the ground and they lay behind them. Aislynn gripped the two Colts while the little pistol waited in her pocket. Johnny held the rifles.

A dozen braves galloped toward the train, leaving a large contingent on the rise. It was difficult to gauge their distance where shadow and shape distorted space. She could hear their thunder and felt the earth respond to some forty-eight hooves pounding it. The Captain told them to hold their fire and he walked out of the corral with his hands held high.

When he returned, he announced, "They just wanna trade for money, silver and gold."

Five braves entered the arena. The two approaching Aislynn and Johnny carried brown leather bundles stained red. The shorter man spoke to Johnny in scattered English. The taller crouched and laid his package at Aislynn's feet. He opened it, exposing chunks of meat soaked in blood.

He was dressed in tight, buckskin pants flapped in the front with a piece of red cloth. His long, glossy black hair hung down his brown, naked back. When he stood before her, she stared into his bare chest. Half-naked men did not figure into Aislynn's experience. She rarely saw her father or any of the Nolans without their shirts. Johnny washed out of her view and when they were together, he was covered. Her eyes followed the lines of muscles running through the Indian's chest until he pushed a ragged hunk of buffalo meat at her. Startled, she looked into his face. It was smooth, shiny and sharply carved, like those she had seen on the statutes at the New York museum she had visited with Tim. Within the striking face, two cold eyes scrutinized. They held hers as she reached out for the meat.

Still queasy from her illness, the smell of the meat took her breath. "Thank you," she murmured and curtsied casually.

He flashed an unexpected smile, elaborately bowed to her and laughed a comment to his companion. She turned to get a bucket and dropped the meat in it. Facing him again, she shot him a stern look and reprimanded, "I don't know what you said but by your tone, I'm sure I take exception to it."

Johnny exchanged some words with the English speaker and handed him a coin. They moved on. Johnny asked, "Do you still think they're all dangerous?"

"Of course, and insolent, too."

"You don't even know what he said."

"Do you?"

"Yes, I asked." He raised his brows and sent her a smirk. "He said, 'She's civil. Maybe she doesn't know we're Indians.' "

"You're telling me Indians have a sense of humor?"

"They're human, aren't they?"

Aislynn knew she was being admonished, "I suppose so."

The Green River ran in a torrent, spasming against its banks, threatening to overflow. It was wide, deep and terrifying. Johnny paid a ferryman to sail them across on a flat, wooden raft. They poled through the choppy waves and disembarked in canyon country. Here, the road rose through barren, rock walls. The wagon brushed against soaring buttes furrowed by wind and water, layered in shades of red, yellow and brown as it climbed to sage-covered knolls rolling toward Fort Bridger.

Aislynn was cleaning up after their noontime supper when she heard Johnny's howl. He was washing his hands in the Hams Ford River and she dropped the plates to run to him.

"Stay there!" he called. "It's a rattlesnake. Don't know if there are any others."

Johnny limped back to the wagon. Aislynn could see two small dots of blood seeping onto his pants above his knee. "Get into the wagon, take off those pants, and I'll get help."

She found the Captain and his outriders mounted and ready to break camp. "Captain Morton!" she placed her hand on his horse's neck, "Johnny's been bitten by a rattler. Please come and help him."

Morton looked down at her with scorn, "You take care of him." He pulled back on his reins and his horse took a step away from Aislynn.

"I need help."

"It's my job to get you to Utah. It's your job to keep up."

Aislynn's eyes scanned the two outriders, hoping to find support. Disappointed, she returned to Morton, "What do I do?"

135

One of the scraggly haired, brown-toothed trail hands replied, "Cut him and suck him."

The Captain shouted orders to the train as he circled her with his horse. She turned, following Morton and trying to regain his attention. "But I don't know how."

The trail hand interjected, "I could stay and teach her to suck a man." He laughed and wore a look that made Aislynn shiver.

"Blow the horn," the Captain ordered.

Morton halted his horse and Aislynn touched his stirrup, "You have to help."

"No, ma'am, I have to drive this here train and we're movin'."

Jesting, the trail hand added, "Just suck him 'til it tastes like him. You do know what your man tastes like, don't you?"

Aislynn did not understand the humor. She ignored the repulsive man and addressed the Captain, "You can't leave us."

He raised his hand, signaling the train to roll.

With her full weight, she grabbed his rein and pulled it down. Taken unaware by her attack, she nearly unseated him. She held fast and sneered, "Your God or mine, Morton, you'll have a hell of a time getting absolution for this."

He straightened in his saddle. Aislynn saw his foot move; she released the rein. With the kick, the horse bolted forward. She raised her skirt to her knees and ran to Johnny through the blossoming dust.

Aislynn climbed on the bed and gave him a quick kiss. "Where's Morton?" Johnny questioned.

Tilting her head, she smiled at him, "I'm going to take care of you."

She saw the fear in his dilated eyes. "They're leavin'."

"They're busy," she lied.

"I can hear, Aislynn."

She collected a bucket of water, a basin, and clean

rags. Then she stropped his razor. Kneeling beside his wound, she took a deep breath and pushed the edge of the razor into his white flesh. Blood flowed from the incision. Aislynn dropped the razor. She pulled up the wagon cover, leaned over the side and expelled her supper.

Sweat formed on his brow and upper lip. Breathing hard, Johnny suggested, "Maybe you shouldn't?"

Aislynn took a few deep breaths and murmuring positive words continued slicing. She placed her lips around the cuts and pulled his blood into her mouth. She spat into the basin and rinsed with water. She sucked and spat until she thought the bitterness was gone. She wiped the wound and covered it with a rag.

Outside the wagon, she stirred the fire and heated the kettle. She made some mild tea and gave him the hartshorne Sage had prescribed. She rolled up the sides of the cover. Leaving the wagon, she suggested, "Rest for awhile."

She sat by the fire and her body started to shiver. Sweating, she felt cold. Tiny dots of light danced in her eyes. She vomited again. Her head fell on her knees and she gasped for air.

Fear for Johnny gave way to fear for herself. She remembered the Indians were close, hidden in the crevices of foothills. Outlaws. They had not encountered any since the Black Hills/Cheyenne Road, but she suspected they were about. And animals: wild, ferocious, 'assume they all bite' animals.

She tried to distract herself by cooking ham and bean soup for Johnny's dinner. She wanted to have a fire in the daylight so she would not be alerting any enemies to their vulnerability in the dark. She stood over the flaming sage, waving at the smoke, attempting to void its signal. Every time she checked on Johnny, he reported his pain seemed to be increasing and a different part of his body felt numb.

She let the mules lead her to the river, hoping they would scare any snakes away. Before she knelt down, she beat the grass with a stick. Then, she filled her buckets with cold water and returned to the wagon.

Johnny was cold and sweating. She did not know if she should keep him cool or warm. She wiped him with the cold water and he shivered. She covered him with the quilts and he complained of the heat. She fed him soup when he asked for food and tea when he asked for drink. It was beyond her. She had no experience with a rattlesnake bite. She strained to remember the things Sage had told her but in her preoccupation, little would come.

Aislynn fell to her knees and prayed to her father, her mother and all her ancestors. She petitioned Johnny's grandmother and his father for help. Kneeling in the hot sun, Aislynn could feel the rivulets of sweat dripping down her back. She could not tell if they were from fear or heat.

As the sun set, she watered the mules back at the river, then tied them to the wagon on a long rope. She fed them and tried to feed Johnny. His breathing became slow and shallow. His strength weakened and he did not want to eat. He felt nauseated and vomited. She spoke to him softly and ran cool cloths over his warm upper body. When he fell asleep, she put her hands on his chest to check his heartbeat. It was imperceptible. She held her ear to it. She did not hear much, but her knowledge of heartbeats was limited. She decided discerning the state of his heart did not matter; she had no means to give him additional assistance. She climbed up to the wagon seat and remembered what Sage had said, "Look, listen, smell and feel. That'll keep you alive."

Darkness stalked her from the east. The foothills were deep in shadows by the time the moon, the size of a lemon zest, showed in the navy sky. She was disappointed in the amount of light but assumed if she could not see neither could anyone else. She listened for danger. The wind blew under the stars, whooshing past her ears. The river droned. The trees next to their wagon moved. Creatures scampered, insects whirred, birds called, owls hooted, animals howled. She remembered hearing that the spirits residing in all living things come out at night and express themselves. With every nerve standing at attention, she listened for their messages. In her lap, the two Colts lay like talismans.

Aislynn rested her head against the wagon bow. Her eyes strained through the darkness toward the faded light over the foothills. Atop a barren ridge, she saw the silhouette of a woman, walking slowly and holding a child close to her heart. Aislynn felt herself falling. Her eyes flew open and her leg shot forward to bring her into balance. She jumped up and checked the mules. She climbed into the wagon bed and listened for Johnny's breath. She held his head and poured cool water into him. Believing she had done all she could do, she returned to the wagon seat and looked out at the darkness. The woman was gone.

Aislynn resumed her sentry duty. The darkness hurt her eyes. She tried singing herself calm, but no music flourished in her mind.

Johnny's raspy breaths struck her silent. She scrambled to him. She poured more hartshorne down his throat. Aislynn cradled his head, placed her hand over his subdued heart and began talking to him, promising him she would try harder. Vowing to be very good to him, she swore she would do whatever he wanted if he would just live. Recognition hit her. She was not pleading with Johnny; she was trying to bargain with God, an act forbidden by the nuns. Fear struck her and apologies fell from her lips.

She began a novena, repeating over and over, "Saint Jude, patron of hopeless causes, have mercy on us. May the sacred heart of Jesus be adored, gloried and preserved through the world, now and forever. May the Sacred Heart of Jesus have mercy on us. St. Jude pray for us."

The mules bawled and pushed against the wagon. Aislynn woke to their cries. She crept over the seat, lifted a gun and squinted. Tension hung heavy in the air. As she scanned the darkness, she could feel it. She could hear it in the mules' pawing and braying. She could smell its gamy odor rising on the breeze. It was moving. Its low growling rose to where she stood. It was not one but several, a pack, a black phalanx creeping through the grass.

Aislynn aimed a Colt in direction of the wolves. She held her breath. "I can kill you!" she threatened. "I can kill anything, anyone!" She heard herself shouting as the gun bucked in her hands. Tears poured down her cheeks as she emptied the cylinder. The wolves yelped and scurried off as she shot the bullets of the second revolver into her fears.

She sat with the hot guns in her lap, fumbling bullets into the chambers. Quiet settled around her. Only the river, the wind and the leaves were still speaking to her. Aislynn checked Johnny. The shots had not stirred him. The darkness pressed loneliness and guilt down on her, heavy as the mountains accusing her from the north. It was her fault; she knew it. Johnny had come for her and she had come for Tim. But she had no Tim, no Da, no Nolans, and now, possibly no Johnny. She cared, truly cared for him and admonished herself for not seeing it sooner. Aislynn knelt on the floorboards and steepled her hands on the seat, praying to every saint she could recall, in alphabetical order, for Johnny and forgiveness.

Aislynn heard Johnny calling her awake. The sun was giving the earth back its colors. She felt safer in the light. Straightening from her joint-stiffened position, she leaned over the seat. "What are you doing?" she asked.

"How many times do I have to tell you I don't like you goin' about by yourself?"

She climbed into the wagon bed, knelt beside him and said, "I'm right here."

Johnny placed a hand on her cheek. Aislynn leaned over him and kissed his mouth. He was still in pain and his breathing was strained. She dosed him with more hartshorne and made a light breakfast. By noon, Johnny's suffering had eased and he wanted to be moving. "If we leave now and ride straight through we might make Fort Bridger by evening."

Aislynn worried about his breathing in the dust. "How much dust can there be?" he asked. "We're only one wagon."

The mules presented a struggle. They did not respond to her commands as they did to Johnny's. She called them every bad name she could think of while trying to move them up to the wagon tongue and into their harnesses. "Miss Denehy," she heard Johnny call from the wagon, "where did you learn such language?"

"Quiet in there or I'll turn my anger on you!"

With the mules finally hitched, the wagon rolled. At the first small creek, the animals balked under her hand. Aislynn jumped down and picked up a long switch. She soon discovered they understood her whip better than her words. Night fell near six o'clock. From the top of a ridge, Aislynn spied the lights of Bridger, but in this land there was no telling its distance by the road. Johnny told her to feed the mules and let them drink. He instructed her to tie a burning lantern on the chains between the mules and keep moving.

In the darkness, they approached Fort Bridger. Like Laramie, Bridger lay on a flat plain without palisades surrounded by an Indian camp. The trail ran through dozens of teepees with Indians huddled around sagebrush fires. With their gaunt faces and bony bodies, they looked like ghouls in the shadowy light.

Aislynn drove the wagon past a stable and some log and adobe buildings. She could see tents and wagons scattered to the north on the other side of a creek, but she turned left toward a neat row of buildings. A distinguished-looking young couple strolled along the road. Aislynn stopped the wagon and the woman asked if she could help.

"You're a New Yorker," Aislynn cried.

141

"Yes," the woman said. "How did you know?"

"It's in your voice and it's wonderful. I'm Aislynn... Maher." She started to tell the couple about Johnny and begged them for help.

"James, put the man in our bed and then go for the doctor," the woman ordered her companion. "You come with me, dear," and Aislynn fell into the woman's arms.

The young couple, James and Abigail Gordon, generously opened their home to Johnny and Aislynn. The doctor pronounced Johnny well on the mend and sleeping soundly. Abigail prepared a bath for Aislynn in front of the large stone fireplace standing in the Gordon's kitchen. While Aislynn soaked away her anxiety, the two women conversed. "What do you miss most about New York City?" Aislynn asked.

"Stewart's Dry Goods Palace, of course."

"Just before we left, I discovered you can buy most everything at Stewart's for half price on Orchard Street."

"Isn't it always the way?" They chatted and laughed until a knock came to the door. "Do you mind if Lillian comes in?" Abigail asked.

Aislynn emerged from the tub and covered herself before the door opened and the commander's wife entered. As the wife of Lieutenant Colonel Henry Morrow, Lillian watched over everyone in the camp. "James has gone to bed at my house, Abigail and he does not seem happy to be without you."

"Oh, he'll sleep just fine."

"I don't think it's the sleep he's missing." Sarcasm fell from Lillian's lips and they both laughed at what Aislynn assumed was a private joke.

While Aislynn dried her hair by the fire, fatigue crept over her. "I'm sorry to end this lovely and oh, so enjoyable discussion, but I am exhausted."

Lillian agreed, "Yes, dear. The overland trip is bad enough, but you have had quite an ordeal. Well, don't fret. Women will bring civility to the West."

Chapter 12

Aislynn woke with a heavy weight on her chest. In the process of becoming conscious, she discovered her protective shield, the quilt, lying on the floor. Her nightdress was pushed up to her hips and untied to her waist. Johnny, clad only in cut-off long johns, had one leg flung between hers and his face snuggled between her breasts. In a panic of ignorance, she pushed him awake. As Johnny opened his eyes and discerned his position, a grin spread across his face. His hand slid over her soft flesh. Aislynn screamed, "Johnny!"

He bolted upright alert to danger. He scanned the room and asked, "What are you doin'?"

Aislynn curled up into the corner of the bed repairing her disheveled state. As she tied her gown, she said, "I could ask you the same thing. You promised!" Aislynn reached for the quilt and covered herself.

"Promised what?"

"You wouldn't do anything to get me pregnant," Aislynn snarled.

Johnny laughed, "Damn, Aislynn, even I wouldn't sleep through that."

Aislynn scowled and studied him for a lie. Johnny leaned against the scrolled iron footboard and folded his arms. His eyes flew open. "You don't know. Good God, Aislynn, you've been denyin' me the slightest touch because you don't know."

"I do." She explained Sean's warning.

"You don't know. I should have realized." Johnny shook his head. "You lying naked with me isn't goin' to get you pregnant. Me touchin' your breast isn't goin' do it either." As he explained the facts, Aislynn recoiled further from him with every word.

"How revolting. Decent people would never," she replied while she pulled a blanket up to her chin.

"Ask Tim."

Insulted, Aislynn said, "Don't drag Tim down to such a level."

"He's a man, Aislynn; every man wants to do it."

She could not put Tim and this behavior together. "Why?"

"Because it makes you feel like your body's gone to heaven."

Aislynn's face twisted in disgust. "I can't imagine any one behaving like that and getting anywhere near heaven." She drew her knees up to her chin and wrapped her arms around her legs.

"Hey, I didn't make things this way; He did." Pointing upward. "If you would just let me show you, you'd see."

Aislynn lowered her head and asked, "Is that what you did with Patty and Linda?"

Johnny's tongue rubbed his back teeth. He reluctantly nodded, "Yes, and they enjoyed it."

Aislynn hugged her legs tighter, "I'm not like them."

"Which is why I've followed you for 2,000 miles."

Aislynn stared at the covers trying to absorb the information. Johnny reached out and gently stroked her exposed toes. Pouting, Aislynn stammered, "I don't want to."

Johnny exhaled a long frustrated breath, "I know." Johnny rose and pulled on his clothes. "I'll accept that for now, but things will change, Aislynn."

Fort Bridger was a low, orderly arrangement of adobe, log and plank buildings surrounding a green parade ground. Tall cottonwoods with leaves rattling in the perpetual wind stood sentinel around the camp. Groshen Creek separated the enlisted men's barracks from the neat row of officers' quarters. Abigail held Aislynn's arm while they strolled around the camp. Aislynn tried to be attentive to Abigail's chatter, but her mind wandered back to her morning tutorial.

"Abigail," she started, "do you like being married?"

"Being out here isn't like being at a big exciting post. I have some duties, but mostly, I just have to behave properly." Abigail stopped walking and looked at Aislynn. "You're not talking about official duties. You mean the other part."

Aislynn could feel her face go red and her nose curl. She looked at the ground and nodded.

"Sometimes it's enjoyable, and sometimes it's the last thing I want to do. But it's so important to men, isn't it? I always begin by telling myself, 'This time it might be satisfying.' It's always such a pleasant surprise when it is." Abigail grabbed her arm again and propelled her forward. "Of course," Abigail continued, "James isn't nearly the size of your husband."

Aislynn missed a step. She had not considered a size factor. She took a breath and walked along thinking the entire idea so repulsive she would not consider intercourse with anyone, not even with Tim.

They ambled to Lillian's house and found her sitting in the shade of a pine. "Hallo, my dears!" she exclaimed.

"You look rested, Aislynn. I hope you're recovering." Old enough to be their mother, Lillian seemed to adopt a maternal air with everyone under her husband's command. Aislynn assured her she felt fine.

Lillian invited them into the dining room for lemonade. She explained they would have to be quiet as her husband and some of his officers were in the parlor encouraging the Bannock and Shoshoni Indians to settle on reservations. After an 1867 gold strike on the Indians' lands in the Wind River Mountains, the government wanted to make the area safe for the prospectors thronging into the region. This meant confining the tribes.

With the coming railroad, the tribes recognized they were losing their native ground and their supply of life-sustaining buffalo. The Western Shoshonis had the added threat of their traditional enemies, the Sioux, the Cheyenne and the Arapaho, invading their allocated lands. Before they settled on reservations and adopted farming, the tribes wanted assurance from the government they would be protected. Henry was conducting the preliminary negotiations with the chiefs so all would be ready for General William Tecumseh Sherman to formalize the treaty when he arrived.

The ladies climbed the stairs to the porch and Aislynn held the door as Lillian and Abigail entered the dimly lit hall. She heard Lillian say, "Oh my, isn't he splendid?" Abigail giggled and they turned into the dining room. Aislynn quietly pulled the door closed and started down the hall. Her eye caught a tall, well-built Indian leaning against the parlor's wooden archway. His white, woolen shirt hung open to his waist, exposing his muscular chest. Her eyes were drawn to the red fabric flap hanging over his tight, buckskin pants. The handsome profile had the striking, carved features of a statue. He turned slightly and gave her a sullen, sideways glance. Abruptly, his head whipped around and she could see his skin darken as recognition and embarrassment spread over his face.

Aislynn tugged at the sides of her skirt, bowed her head and dipped into a low curtsy. With suspicion in his eyes, he bowed to her. She tilted her head and sent him a reassuring smile as she entered the dining room. Although she sat facing the kitchen, she could see the hall and its occupant in her peripheral vision. He stood arrow straight. His face held taut muscles and clenched teeth. He appeared to be wound as tight as a clock.

While Aislynn carried on a light conversation with the ladies, the discussion coming from the parlor drew her attention. Chief Washakie's voice was dignified and solemn. The Indian's language became English and English became Shoshoni, as words filtered through an interpreter with a French accent. The Chief was asking for a guarantee from the white men not to trespass on the reservation. The Indian's repeated requests to be unmolested in their own country resonated with familiarity for Aislynn.

"And if gold is discovered on our land, what will the white father do?" Washakie asked.

"Well," Henry began, "we cannot promise..."

"Aislynn, are you all right?" Lillian interrupted her eavesdropping.

The back door slammed. Aislynn looked up and discovered her Indian gone.

"I do need to excuse myself," she said as she rose and went out the back door in the direction of the latrine.

She found him standing beneath a tall cottonwood, looking up at its leaves clattering like bones in the wind. As she approached, she could feel the space between them vibrating with his anger. She stepped into the dark, shaded circle. "I'm sorry," she began, "We've come to find our place and we're taking yours."

He raised his hand, encircled her neck and pulled her toward him. Reflexively, her hands shot up and landed on his bare chest. The smell of burning sagebrush surrounded his body and tobacco smoke hung on his breath.

147

His thumb ran down her throat and pressed into the soft tissue above her breastbone. She trembled under his hand but she did not feel fear. "It's wrong, backwards. We take your land and we give you back tiny pieces to live on." Aislynn shook her head. Remembering her father's plight in Ireland, tears rose in her eyes, "We've become the English."

His eyes softened as he visibly passed from anger into grief. She felt the chasm of their differences narrowing, but she felt the tension between them expanding. He moved his thumb to her mouth. Slowly, he slid it over her top lip then pressed it across the wet inside of her bottom lip. Aislynn felt his touch deep inside her body. For a moment, the taboo against white women with Indian men vanished. Her breathing faltered and she could feel what Johnny had told that morning was true.

His language spilled from the top of the steps. Startled, they turned to find his English-speaking friend. The distraction allowed her to catch her breath. Her Indian gave her a slight, spiritless smile. He placed his hand on her shoulder and nodded toward the house. As she walked past the English speaker, she whispered, "Tell him I'm sorry."

Aislynn prepared dinner for Abigail and James to thank them for their kindness. As the discussion progressed around the table, Johnny announced, "The blacksmith offered me a job here on the post."

Fear dashed through Aislynn.

"Oh Aislynn," Abigail cried, "you could stay. You could buy land and build a house. We could be together every day."

Aislynn struggled for a polite refusal. "But you'll be restationed soon and we would be here alone."

"We're hoping James will be appointed commander. Then, we could both have big houses and we could decorate together. We would have such fun, Aislynn. Please stay."

Aislynn's heart raced. "We can't," she nearly exploded, "Tim is counting on us. He has no one." She looked at Johnny and pleaded, "We have to go on."

Aislynn held her breath watching Johnny for a response. He rubbed his tongue on his back teeth and nodded, "She's right. We promised Tim. It wouldn't be fair to stop 135 miles short of him."

Aislynn relaxed with relief. James interjected in his formal manner, "Well, if you're set on going to the Utah Territory, we're dispatching a patrol to relieve the men from Fort Russell who have been escorting some Union Pacific directors and inspectors along the proposed rail line. I'd be glad to add you to their detail. I can guarantee you safe passage as far as Echo Canyon. They'll go on the Salt Lake City and you'll have to travel alone to Ogden, but those last thirty miles are reportedly well settled."

An acceptance burst from Aislynn.

The Union Pacific's wagon road was poorly cut and followed the surveyors' line. It wound through canyons of rock and over streams full from snowmelt. Everyone followed Chief Engineer Samuel Reed's commands. Although they frequently stopped to examine the route, Johnny's mules were pressed to keep pace with the mounted men and their supply wagons teamed with muscular horses.

Neither the railroad men nor the soldiers paid particular attention to Aislynn; however, she felt intimidated by her status as the lone female. Her days were spent riding next to Johnny, only speaking to him. She prepared their meals at the tailgate and sat in the wagon while Johnny cooked it over their fire within the corral. Not wanting to create a shadow show for the men, she washed in the dark of the wagon. It was a lonely journey, but they made Echo Canyon in five days.

Like most Americans, Aislynn and Johnny followed the progress of the transcontinental railroad with great interest. The press had reported that the preliminary survey designated the transcontinental railroad route would run through the center of the Mormon world, Salt Lake City. Brigham Young, President of the Latter Day Saints, who ruled the Mormon's secular and sectarian community, favored the Union Pacific's project. Although he worried about the impact the inevitable outsiders would have on his saintly followers, he welcomed the economic benefits the Mormon capital would reap by being the terminus of the line. At Echo Canyon, where all believed the line would turn to Salt Lake City, the soldiers went south and the Union Pacific workers veered north to Ogden.

For Aislynn, Ogden was a milestone, the town closest to Moran's ranch and Tim. Pulling into the small Mormon community, they found a wide, dirt road stretching through the center of the town with several tributaries running perpendicular and parallel; all were flanked by log and false fronted wooden buildings. Residents glared as they passed, riding under the American flag. Mormon ideas of separatism and their practice of polygyny frequently strained relations between them and the Unites States government.

The group leader directed Aislynn and Johnny to the telegraph office. They walked by the furtive eyes of the onlookers to a small shack radiating wires and waving the Stars and Stripes.

"How much for five words?" Johnny asked the thin man.

The operator squinted at the couple, "You Gentiles?"

Aislynn, remembering Morton, steeled herself for a difficult time. "Yes," Johnny answered.

"Good, we need more of us 'round here. Five words for a dollar. Where's it goin?"

Johnny answered, "New York City. We want it to say, 'We are safe in Utah.' "

"Don't you want to identify yourselves?"

"How much for two names?"

"I'll give 'em to you."

150

"Thank you. It's Aislynn and Johnny."
"You Aislynn?"
She nodded.
"I got a letter here for you."

CHAPTER 13

Tim's short letter read:

Aislynn,

I have trusted Mr. Wall with this letter and pray you will arrive safely to receive it. I am not at the ranch. Mr. Moran has honored me with a more suitable position. I will tell you about it when I see you. I am in the mountains just four miles north of the ranch. Enclosed is a map.

I suggest you buy whatever supplies you need as it takes nearly four hours to reach Ogden by wagon.

Come quickly and come safely. You are forever in my prayers.

Tim

Mr. Reed entered the office to inform them the train

would be leaving and continuing north in one hour. Aislynn pulled Johnny to the nearest general store. Determined to reach Tim's heart, even if she had to get there through his stomach, Aislynn whirled through the shop buying food.

In a hushed tone, she asked the clerk for two cots and turned her attention toward a cast iron stove. She listed reasons why she needed the expensive item to Johnny.

"Aislynn, I only had four hundred dollars when we started. The money we have left is yours. Do what you want with it."

"You don't think it's extravagant?"

"When it comes to spendin' money, I trust your judgment."

They set out north toward Promontory Point with the stove anchored in the wagon bed. The road cut through acres of farmland, irrigated by the massive system of ditches the Mormons had trenched. In the east, the steep hills were topped with bald, rocky peaks. On certain rises in the road, the Great Salt Lake could be seen in the west, a huge, blue mirage dropped in the dusty desert.

Just beyond the tiny settlement of Brigham City, they passed a ranch distinguished by its long log stables and high barns. A huge wood and adobe lodge rose from the sandy earth. An archway of whitewashed adobe stood at the entrance of the long dusty drive. Chiseled into its peak were the initials L. M. While Johnny marveled at the size of the house, Aislynn was thinking four more miles.

Excitement fluttered in her stomach, and she attempted to suppress a broad smile. She wiggled closer to Johnny and hugged his arm. Unable to contain herself, "Thank you for bringing me," spilled over her lips.

Johnny looked down at her with a tolerant smile and said, "I love you."

"I know," she replied and bounced up and pecked his cheek.

They could see the cut-off nearly a mile before they reached it, slashing wide through the thick pines and climbing to the edge of the barren rock. Among the trees, small squares of white tents dotted the hillside, looking like tombstones from a distance. Thin strands of smoke, signs of life, swirled among the trees.

Johnny waved to the soldiers. Then, for the first time in a month, they turned their wagon east toward home. The road was steep and newly cut. Stumps and brush that had been blocking the way lay strewn on the sides of the wide trail, damp and still clinging to clumps of the earth. Rock and rubble filled the voids they left behind. All the underbrush was cleared, and an open roadway remained.

They rolled through a flat lined with brooks, willows and aspens, then climbed through tall cottonwoods, until the trail rose among pines, cedars, mountain ferns and wild rose bushes. The smell of decaying foliage and damp undergrowth filled the air. The steep incline, thinning air and heavy load strained the mules and Aislynn's impatience.

At the top of the trail, they could see a clearing. Piles of timber and rocks were scattered among tents and wagons. The road rose to the mouth of a mine, a dark hole in the face of the rock. They could see a log cabin below the mine, encircled by a spur road. A large wagon stood at the far end of this drive. Men pushed carts piled with broken rocks out of the mouth of the mine and dumped them into the wagon waiting on the circular drive below.

Through the crashing rocks and the whacking of axes, the humming of an engine could be heard. Men called to each other as they hauled timber and split logs. The smoke of wood burning fires added substance to the thin air. The energetic activity of the camp enhanced Aislynn's excitement. Her pulse raced. She gripped the wagon seat. Aislynn found herself holding her breath until she remembered to take in more air. Her eyes grew wide as she tried to search each face for the one she longed to find.

Two men on the step of the log cabin caught her eyes. They stood facing each other, their profiles clear. Both wore overalls covered in gray dust. Under a dingy hat, the taller man's tawny hair hung shoulder-length and a full beard covered his face.

Aislynn's hand went to her breast. Her heart seemed to swell, crowding her lungs so no air could enter. "Tim!" she shouted.

Johnny pulled back the reins. She jumped down to the footboard and swung her legs over the side. She pushed off the wagon, gathered her skirt and ran. The taller man turned and their eyes met. He pushed his partner aside and stumbled down the path, his hairy face changed from surprise, to relief, to joy.

Aislynn buried her face in his chest and melted into tears. His hands grabbed her face, and he kissed the top of her head. She felt his whole body sob. He took a ragged breath and said, "I was so worried."

She looked up at him and wept, "It's been so long."

Tim looked over her head, "Now I know how she got here." He moved away, extending his hand to Johnny. Tim pulled him close and hugged him, clapping him on the back, repeating, "Thank you, thank you."

Johnny said, "She wanted to come, and you know how she is when she gets an idea in her head."

Tim laughed, "I know." He looked at her sternly. Aislynn smiled up at him and hugged him again. Tim lifted her off the ground and spun around.

Three men emerged from the cabin clapping and waving. They all spoke at once. "She made it," "He vas so vorried," and "She's lookin' fine," all blended into one sound.

Tim introduced the men. Mr. Spittlehouse, the assayer, analyzed the ore. Mr. Frank was the surveyor and engineer. Murphy managed the mine and acted as Moran's surrogate. "And me, I'm everyone's lackey," Tim said with pride.

"Assistant," Mr. Murphy corrected.

Aislynn curtsied to each man while she held fast to Tim's hand like a lifeline, afraid to let go. She gazed at him. He looked dreadful and smelled worse, but for her, nothing could obscure his beauty.

Johnny shook hands, asking, "So you've got yourselves a mine?"

"We're workin' on one," Murphy replied.

"Expectin' a boom?"

Tim answered, "Yes and no. Men are pouring in but we'll see how many stay. This land belongs to Moran. It's his mine. A lot of them will come to prospect and be disappointed. They can stay and work for Moran if they want. Murphy thinks we'll have a hundred miners by the end of the year, maybe more."

Wanting to be involved in Tim's conversation, Aislynn asked, "With all this space, how is Moran going to keep prospectors out?"

"Don't worry about Moran; he finds a way to control everything he owns," Murphy answered.

Tim's tent was pitched near the mine, close to his co-workers; however, he felt Aislynn should not be too close to the operation. Miners were a superstitious lot and believed women were bad luck in a mine. A half-mile down the hill, Johnny had spied a level area with few trees. To Aislynn's delight, they established their own private camp. A spring bubbled through the rocks on the far end of their clearing, and here, Aislynn had Tim and Johnny set up her stove.

She had come to camp prepared. For dinner, Aislynn made a potted roast with carrots, onions, and potatoes swimming in a tomato base. She baked gingerbread with a lemon-flavored sugar sauce. They were Tim's favorites. He invited his three friends to dinner, and they confirmed her suspicion. Murphy said, "This here's a real treat for us, Miss. We haven't had nothin' but beans and bacon for nearly two months." Aislynn smiled, content her stomach strategy had promise.

While they ate, Mr. Spittlehouse, a serious-faced German, spoke about the difference between silver and gold mining. "Let me tell it simply. Gold stays on the surface and vashes down the mountains into streams or sits there right vhere prospectors can just pluck it up. Silver it's different. You see vater will take silver and carry it downvard into the earth and deposit it vhere the vater decides to stop. Silver sinks deep to the vater level. Could be two, tree, five hundred feets down. It takes thousands, maybe fifty thousands of dollars to reach it."

"How do you know it's there?" Aislynn asked. She was engaged by Spittlehouse but glanced at Tim every few moments as if to assure herself he was real.

"Good question. I tests the surface ore. Ve dig down. I tests more. As ve go down I see the rock is richer in silver."

"With all this land, why did you pick this spot?"

Tim interjected. "There is an old Ute Indian on the ranch. Mr. Moran took him in last winter when it was brutally cold. We had very little work to do, so we did a lot of talking. The old man said he had seen a cave that shone in the dark. So here we are."

"Fifty thousand dollars, where'd Moran get so much money?" Johnny asked.

Murphy explained he had known Moran for years; they had met during the gold rush days in California. Moran was very young but very smart. He had a talent for making money.

Aislynn leaned against Tim while she listened to the man spin his tale. Murphy was a product of the West. He appeared to be in his fifties. Round and soft, he had a face like a ball of bread dough with holes poked in the appropriate places. Friendly, voluble and funny, Aislynn liked him instantly.

"During the rush, Moran became an outfitter and a

grubstaker in Sacramento. When the gold washed out, he continued to sell goods and bought up some timberland and a ranch. Then, round about '60, this guy they called 'Crazy Judah,' he 'pproached Moran and some big mon- eyed men with a scheme. You see, Judah'd spent the summer trekking through the Sierra Nevada Mountains. He had this idea about cutting a rail route straight through 'em, connectin' the U. S. from east to west. Well, these four millionaires got in it and formed the Central Pacific Railroad, so Moran threw in some money of his own. Now, you'll know what happened. The United States government itself gave the CP money and the authority to build eastward, while the Union Pacific is buildin' west- ward. So Moran's makin' money off the railroad 'fore it's even built." Murphy slapped his thigh and continued, "Now, them roads have to meet. Most folks are figurin' they're gonna meet in Salt Lake, 'specially since ol' Brother Brigham is runnin' the show hereabouts. 'Cept, seems Moran gets wind the line ain't goin' through Salt Lake, it might be goin' through Ogden. So, he takes a chance. He buys up this here land we're sittin on for near nothin' and starts up a ranch. Now, there's always money in foodstuff so 'gardless of where the line runs, his horses and cattle ain't gonna be too far from the rail or the mar- ket. But, he's bettin' it's comin' this way and the value of this land will go sky high."

"Well," Johnny interrupted, "I believe Moran wins his bet. The men we traveled with are plannin' to grade through Ogden to Promontory Point. Mr. Reed is goin' to Salt Lake City in a couple of weeks to get Young to help with the work."

"Damn!" Murphy shot a look at Aislynn and Tim. "Oh, sorry, Miss. Don't you know it went his way again? He is one of the luckiest rascals I know. He takes risks, but he does seem to hit those safe bets."

All the men nodded in agreement. Murphy con- cluded, "Now the son of a gun has hit silver. Can you beat

159

that? Well, money makes money, don't it?"

Johnny offered to sleep under the wagon to protect Aislynn but Tim insisted they could fit three cots in the tent. They pinned a sheet to the roof of the tent allowing Aislynn some privacy. She lay listening to Johnny's familiar snore and strained to hear Tim's breathing. She peeked around her cloth barrier and found his bed empty.

Aislynn slipped on her shoes, huddled down in her heavy coat, and she stepped through the tent's flaps. Tim sat on a log among the moon's shadows facing the fading fire. He seemed to glow like a wakened dream. Aislynn silently padded through the soft pine needles.

Coming up behind him, she wrapped her arms around his neck and rested her cheek on his hair. His hands reached up and held hers. They were silent. The woods' wild noises seemed subdued and the still air bordered on the soft side of frost. Aislynn felt his warm body rise with every breath; she relished the vital and stable feeling of him. Holding him in her arms, she felt all the pieces of her life pulling together. For the first time since her father's death, she began to feel whole.

Tim broke the silence. "You should be in bed."

Aislynn moved around the log and settled herself against him. "I'd rather be with you," she whispered, taking his hand in hers. It was golden in the fire light and rougher than she remembered.

"I missed you," Tim said, "and I'm so proud of you. Look at you. You're so strong and independent. It makes my heart proud." Aislynn beamed in his approval. "Of course, I take credit for the way you've turned out." He laughed quietly and nuzzled his chin into her head.

"Of course." She closed her eyes and felt the strength of her love.

"I'm sorry things became so difficult for you." He paused and sighed, "You know life won't be easy here."

"I know, but we'll be together."

She felt him nod in agreement.

After a few moments, he smiled down at her. "I'm very happy about you and Johnny."

Aislynn pulled away and looked at him in disbelief. "What?"

"You and Johnny?" he asked.

"Johnny? I'm here because I love you. I came two thousand miles, a quarter of which I walked, to be with you!" As her excitement rose, so did the pitch of her voice.

"You are with me, but you're promised to Johnny."

Aislynn shook her head. "No!"

"You made a promise to him before you left New York and you reaffirmed it every night you lay next to him."

Aislynn felt her heart stop. "He promised not to tell you."

"He didn't," Tim smiled, "but you just did."

Angry tears were rising to her eyes. "Nothing happened."

"I know. If I had any doubt, you'd be married tomorrow." Tim frowned, brushing a loose hair from her face. "Johnny's a decent man, a fine choice."

"He's not my choice and you know that."

"I know that now we're both promised."

Aislynn sat back and glared at him. "I don't care about those promises."

"Yes, you do. You're an honorable young woman, it's part of the reason I love and admire you so much."

Aislynn's mind raced. She had dreamed this moment thousands of times, from beginning to end. Her fantasies had been so real, so sure, she never imagined they could not come true. Not once had she thought of him accepting her engagement to Johnny. It was intolerable. He had to want her. She felt the need to act. She threw her arms around him and kissed him like Johnny had taught her. Tim leaned into her. She knew she had done it right when she felt his mouth move on hers. She waited for his reaction to stir her.

Tim jerked his head back. He grabbed her by the shoulders and held her at arm's length. "Don't," he ordered. "I am not going to act on my loneliness and take advantage of you. Nor will I allow you to make such a huge mistake. It would be wrong."

"Not if you love me," she entreated, squirming under his hold.

In the dim light of the fire, she could see sadness in his face. He relaxed his grip. Slowly, a small indulgent smile came to his lips. He bent his head and rested his forehead on hers. "Now that you have Johnny, I'd hoped you could understand the difference between my love for you and the feelings I hold for Emma."

Emma, the name made her furious and her anger fed her resolve. Aislynn huffed. She stood and pulled her coat around her like a knight girding for battle. She leaned over him, her eyes blazing with a challenge, "The biggest difference is I'm here and she's not."

Chapter 14

At sunup, Aislynn brought Tim back to a civilized
state with a haircut and a shave. She sent him off to work
with a full stomach and a warm kiss. Then, she and
Johnny turned their attention to setting up their home.

With a two-man saw, they pushed and pulled until
three obstructive trees were felled. While Johnny and the
mules dragged the trees and began pulling stumps,
Aislynn boiled water to soak laundry and started to prepare suppertime pasties from the leftover potted roast.
With extra pastry dough, she made a pie from dried apples
for dinner.

When they finished supper, Aislynn promised Tim
ham and potatoes for dinner. He told Aislynn to expect his
co-workers; he did not feel comfortable eating so grandly
while they suffered with beans. Aislynn sighed in agreement. She did not like the idea of his friends eating up her

costly rations, but she wanted to please Tim.

Aislynn removed the pie from the oven and placed it on the stove's shelf to cool while she brought her buckets to the spring to collect more water for more laundry. When she returned, she discovered a strange creature leaning over her pie. It was covered in fur from top to bottom with an incomplete, hairy face. She stared at it for a moment in horror.

"This your pie?" it asked.

Aislynn nodded.

"Ain't et no pie for years. Spare a piece?"

Afraid to get too close, she waved toward the pie and said, "Have some," while her eyes searched for Johnny. He was on the far side of the clearing, behind the mules, dragging a stump. She started to call but thinking escape, she picked up her skirt and ran until she stood next to him.

"There's a thing, a hairy thing by the stove," she stammered, holding one hand to her throat and waving in the direction of the beast with the other.

Johnny's eyes flew in the direction of the intruder who had his hands in the pie. "Did he scare you?"

"Yes."

"Do you have your gun?"

"Yes." She patted the apron pocket where her little pistol resided.

"Why didn't you shoot it?"

"I was afraid I might hit it."

"Not likely," Johnny said with a half smile. He brushed his hands on his pants, pulled his Colt from its holster and took her arm. "Come on. Let's see what this thing is."

As they approached, the man was shoveling pie into his hairy face. He looked up and with a full mouth, he asked, "This here your gal?"

Johnny grinned at Aislynn and answered, "I like to think so."

"Good cook."

"You look hungry."

"Yep. I ain't et in days. Some men stole my gear: knife, gun and all. Down to bugs and grubs."

Johnny looked back at Aislynn with a question in his eyes. He returned his gun to his holster and said, "He seems harmless." Addressing the man, Johnny introduced himself and Aislynn.

"I'm No Nose Goodman."

They looked through the tangle of facial hair and found a stub of flesh hanging over two dark holes.

"Appropriate," Johnny said. "How'd you lose your nose?"

"Mountains, frost. Ain't got much toes nor fingers neither." The man held up his pie-covered hands and displayed thumbs, partial indexes and stubs where his other fingers had been.

Aislynn bit her lip as her repulsion turned to pity.

Johnny turned to Aislynn and asked her to give him a proper meal.

"He's filthy," she protested.

"I can warsh me hands," No Nose offered.

Johnny walked away as Aislynn shook her head. She made the old man bathe in steaming water with lye soap. After she shaved him and cut his hair to the scalp, she made him bathe a second time to ensure death to any bugs remaining on his body. The furry clothes were burned. By dinnertime, No Nose sat at the table Johnny had built from their bed boards with his hobbled hands folded before him. He was drowning in Johnny's shirt and pants, but he was clean.

During dinner, No Nose introduced himself to the group. He had been born during the War of 1812. When the war was over, his parents joined the Great Migration and started west to the Indiana Territory, looking for cheap farmland. After his mother died and the farm failed, he and his father continued to move farther west. They became trappers, hunting for pelts, living off the abundance of nature. Thirty years passed and the fur trade faded, as did the abundance of animals. His father died, and No Nose tried prospecting. Like most adventurers, he said he had never found more than a pocketful of dust at any one time. Life in the mountains was hard, with winters cold enough to freeze a man to death. The winter of 1867-68 had been one of the worst he had ever seen. He decided it was time to give up the mountain life and move into the big city and find work.

Aislynn laughed, "This is not a city."

"You got jobs, ain't you?"

Everyone looked to Murphy for an assessment of the employment situation. "Right now I have more men than I can use. In awhile, we'll need more, but we're just gettin' started at the mine."

Aislynn's face fell and she looked at the old man. He seemed like a dog beaten so many times he just crawled through life, hanging on until his next beating. She frowned at Murphy who was leaning over his plate to raise another forkful of ham to his mouth. Sensing her displeasure, Murphy dropped his fork and added, "I'm sure there'll be plenty of jobs once people set up businesses in camp."

Trying to soothe the old man, she stated, "Johnny is starting a business."

Johnny's brows darted up and his eyes searched Aislynn's for an explanation.

Angry he had not taken his cue, she glared at him, eyes wide, mouth pinched.

Johnny's tongue rubbed his teeth and he nodded at Aislynn. "Fine, No Nose can help me until he finds some work."

Aislynn smiled her approval of Johnny's generosity around the table.

"You been right kind, feedin' me and all. I'm gonna repay you 'fore I starts a job." No Nose offered.

166

Mr. Frank added, "You have been very generous with all of us, Miss Denehy."

"You oughtta be chargin' us," Murphy laughed.

"It's settled," No Nose declared, slapping his partial hand on the table. All eyes fell on the old man. "We gonna build you a cabin."

In the lantern's light, she could see the various levels of surprise registering on the faces of the men.

"You boys and me starts tomorrow."

"I have to work tomorrow, but I'm off on Sunday," Tim offered.

"Ve all help on Sunday," Spittlehouse suggested.

Aislynn lay in bed reviewing her day. *For all the miles I've come, I'm still doing laundry, mending and again, cooking for five, no, six men. Men, would starve, stink, do anything to avoid chores they deemed women's work.* Her lot in Utah seemed very much like life on Worth Street.

But now, I'm going to have my own house. She kept herself awake building the cabin in her mind: how big she wanted it, where the windows would go, and how she would arrange their things. She recalled the prints she had seen in Godey's Ladies Book. *I'm going to need curtains and carpets and furniture.* Then, she decided how to pay for them.

Aislynn sacrificed one of her chickens and fried it for supper. She made biscuits with honey and vanilla cake and served some to Johnny and No Nose. She packed the remaining food in a basket and walked up to the mine office. Tim was in Ogden with Frank and Spittlehouse, but she found Mr. Murphy seated at one of the five cluttered desks. The office smelled of chemicals and hard-working men. In one corner, a large table with bottles, tools and a scale anticipated Mr. Spittlehouse's ore tests. Mr. Frank's maps, charts and memos, tacked on the log walls, watched over the sunlit room.

"Good afternoon," she said sweetly. "We just finished

our supper and I remembered you up here, alone and hungry. I said to myself, 'Aislynn, go invite Mr. Murphy to have a picnic with you.' "

Murphy's face showed his great surprise, and he smiled at the idea.

"Look what I have for you." Aislynn brought the basket up to his face and slipped off the cloth. The smell of the chicken rose in the room.

"Goodness, Miss Denehy, this may be the nicest offer any lady has ever made me. I don't recall the last time I picnicked."

Aislynn tugged his sleeve and said, "Well, then, let's go."

"Well, you see. I got work to do."

Aislynn pulled the basket away and pouted, "Are you turning me down?"

Watching the basket disappear behind her hip, Murphy panicked, "No, Ma'am." He grabbed his hat and took her arm.

"I'm sure you know some nice quiet place nearby where we can talk while you eat."

"Well, yeah. Follow me."

They climbed up the mountain through the forest. The ground was scattered with hardy understory, dead branches and needles. Murphy struggled with the climb, but he took her arm, helping her over the debris. They halted over a slight ridge that stifled the noise from the mine. The air rang with birds calling, and sunlight cracked through the trees, painting bright golden shapes on the dark forest floor. Aislynn spread the cloth on the ground. Murphy lowered his great weight with a thud. Finding a comfortable position for his cumbersome body took a great many movements. He came to rest on his side, propped up on an arm. Aislynn opened the basket and presented him with a chicken wing.

While Murphy chewed on the wing, Aislynn spoke. "You know, Mr. Murphy, I must thank you and your friends for the lovely offer to help build a cabin for me. But I was wondering," she hesitated for a moment and cocked her head to the side. "You see," she continued, "I don't know anything about property and money and such. I am uncertain, who would actually own the cabin if we build it on Mr. Moran's land?"

"Well, I s'ppose Moran."

"Oh dear. What a shock. I do need to purchase the land then, don't I?"

"I s'ppose you do."

"I am willing to make you an offer of eighty dollars."

"I believe Moran 'spects more than that. He thinks minin' camp land oughta go for $250 a lot, with no mineral rights, of course. And them lots are half the size of the one you're on."

"But we need the room. Johnny has to build his forge. Mr. Moran has seven thousand acres; do you think him so selfish as to begrudge me one?"

"No. Well, he shouldn't. But he might. And he wants $250."

"But I only have eighty dollars." Aislynn frowned and hugged the basket in her lap. "Let me ask you this, has anyone else made an offer to buy land?"

"No, Miss, not a one, yet."

"Well, there you have it." Aislynn reached into the basket and extracted a biscuit and a jar of honey. "It's obvious. Mine is the best offer you've received." She started to spoon honey onto the biscuit. It formed a soft, golden mound with a tiny point on the top. "You're Moran's agent. He expects you to make independent decisions for him. He trusts you to do what's right, or he would never have put you into such an important post. Why, you're like the captain of a ship, out on the waves, making choices for the owner, steering it on the right course." She slowly lifted the biscuit near his lips, asking, "Now, don't you think Mr. Moran would rather have eighty dollars over nothing?"

Murphy nodded slowly. His eyes were fixed on the honey dripping down her fingers. Tiny beads of sweat were forming on his forehead, and his breathing seemed short. "Yes," he stammered. Aislynn slipped the biscuit into his mouth.

"Thank you. It is such a relief. I knew you would understand me. Well, I suppose," she whispered leaning close to him, "you understand women. Homes are so precious to us. I would have been so worried if I did not know for sure I owned my cabin." Aislynn stuck her fingers in her mouth and sucked the honey off of them.

She handed him a chicken leg and began to tell him about her cabin and how she was going to pay for all the things she wanted. "I am opening a restaurant. Of course, it was your idea. You suggested paying me for cooking meals. I'm planning on using the tent once the cabin is built. But I will need about $150.00 to get started, for pots, pans, chairs and china."

"That's a heap a money. Where are you gonna to get it?"

Aislynn held a full chicken breast before him. He grabbed it and brought it right to his mouth. "When we go into Ogden to file the deed, I'm going to ask for a loan at the bank."

"You might have trouble gettin' money there. Mormon's don't like doin' business with Gentiles."

"But I have to have the money or I have no way to make money. Even you said, 'money makes money.' "

Murphy sent her a sympathetic smile. He swallowed and said, "I'd lend it to you if I had it."

Aislynn shoulders slumped. She took a wide wedge of cake from the basket and a small jar of strawberry preserves. As she piled the jam on the cake, she spoke, "What a terrible disappointment. I thought this would be a way to feed you and the others every single night. I could make all your favorite things. All you'd have to do is ask and I'd give you anything you want." The cake lay in Aislynn's lap as she licked the spoon. She sighed, her chest heaving. Sweat poured down Murphy's face and he wiped it with the back of his hand. His breathing grew rapid and hard as he stared at the cake resting on her thighs.

"Well, I guess..." he stalled and nodded.

"Yes?" Aislynn lifted the dessert.

Breathless, he whispered hoarsely, "I suppose the mine wouldn't miss $150.00 if you promise to pay it back right quick."

Aislynn handed him the cake. While he frantically forced forkfuls into his mouth, barely pausing to chew, she leaned toward him with her hands crossed over her breasts and cried, "Yes, Mr. Murphy! Yes!"

Chapter 15

By June's end, the landscape from Ogden to the Treasure Mountain camp had visually altered. Beyond the Mormon farms that supplied the miners with fresh produce and meat and Moran's wide ranch, Aislynn could see the change. On the plain below the heaving mountain, a stamp mill processing ore had been erected. Tents and shacks dotted the level ground around the mill. Further along the dusty road, a crude sawmill sat close to the base of the hill. The camp road began its ascent through a canyon then cut up into a broad cleavage on the southern face of the mountain. Crowded against the road were tents, shacks of whipsawed boards and log cabins serving as saloons, gambling dens, shops and stores. Their density increased as the road rose closer to the mine. Behind the Main Street buildings, brush-covered dugouts, tents and lean-tos were scattered on the freshly timbered slopes of the mountain.

On the day Moran arrived, nearly seventy miners were picking, drilling, blasting and shoveling rock. In the tradition of most new camps, for every miner, four jobs were created in the community. The camp hummed with over 250 people engaged in a variety of occupations and Aislynn was happy to serve meals to any and all.

Hanging wash on the line Johnny had strung between the cabin and a tree made Aislynn sweat. She returned to the washtub, sitting in the shade, full of cool rinse water. She furtively searched the yard for prying eyes. On the front side of the lot, Johnny banged at his forge; on the backside, over the brook, No Nose was digging a root cellar deep in the earth.

Slipping off her shoes, Aislynn raised her skirt and dipped her feet into the water. Balanced on the edge of the tub, she swirled her legs and some coolness splashed up on her thighs. With a wet rag, she wiped her face and neck. She unbuttoned her shirtwaist and ran the rag over her chest. The water and the shade offered relief from the heat.

Aislynn picked up the bar of soap she used on their clothes and dipped it into the water. She rubbed it with her fingers until it was sudsy and slowly blew across the lather. After several tries, a renegade bubble broke away from the thick foam, sliding off the edge of the soap, and taking flight on a slight current of air. Aislynn's eyes followed as it rose. The bubble drifted into the harsh sunlight and popped. Its abrupt demise was expected but disappointing. As she pouted, she thought she heard someone laugh. While she scanned the area, she scrambled out of the tub, slipped on her shoes and lowered her skirt. She saw no one.

Aislynn called to No Nose explaining she was going to the cabin and would be returning to the restaurant. She stepped up on the porch and entered the cabin.

Inside, the cabin stood dark and warm, holding the fresh smell of pine sap. Through the darkness, she could discern a figure of a man silhouetted in the open front doorway. Aislynn was blinking him into focus when she heard him query, "Miss Denehy?"

She recognized the voice before she could clearly see him in the dim light. "Mr. Moran, welcome. Do come in." He removed his hat, bowed slightly and entered the single room. In a few suspended seconds, his eyes ran over everything there was to see. She followed his gaze as it swept the pump standing in the corner next to the door. His eyes traveled to the table with its four mismatched chairs. The back wall was decorated with shelves. Keeping with the fashion of the day, Aislynn had lined them with lace. They displayed their meager treasures: books, a china cup and a vase. Johnny's trunk and a stove sat under the shelves. A small glass window, also dressed in lace, hung in the west wall opposite its twin in the east wall. Beyond the window, a ladder rose to the loft where Johnny, Tim and No Nose slept. Aislynn's cot lay tucked in the corner, surrounded by an old, crocheted bedspread hanging from the rafters. For a moment, she tried to assess their home through his eyes but decided she did not value his perspective.

"This is cozy," he offered.

"We think it's wonderful," she replied, sure his comment reflected his manners not his true opinion.

"It feels like a home."

Bewildered, Aislynn answered, "It is."

They stood silent while he appraised her. Uncomfortable, Aislynn offered him a seat and coffee. "I have sugar and skimmed milk," she said. "I save the cream for Johnny."

He seemed surprised by her comment. His eyes met hers directly, searching. Moran smiled in his offhanded way and said, "Anyway is fine, thank you."

He seated himself in one of the mismatched chairs and placed his hat on another. Moran examined the faded photos tacked on the wall over the table while Aislynn placed their china cup before him and took the opposite seat.

Moran pointed to the largest picture, "Who are these people?"

"Johnny's parents. This one is my mother and father."

"They're a very handsome couple."

"Thank you. I didn't really know her. Tim has shared so many stories of her; I think I have memories, but I'm never sure if they're mine or his."

Moran's eyes softened and he sipped his coffee. "Let me guess who these fine fellows are." The photo portrayed five boys and one baby girl. The girl was perched on the smallest boy's lap. Apparently struggling to keep her pointed at the camera, the boy held the baby's face in both his hands. "They must be the Nolan boys. But who is this baby who does not seem to be obliging the photographer?"

Aislynn could feel her face growing red. "Who do you think it is?"

"Some very headstrong little girl."

"No," Aislynn objected. "A determined one."

"Disobedient," he countered.

"Independent."

"Well, it seems little has changed. Mr. Nolan still has his hands full."

Aislynn giggled at the truth. Smiling, Moran leaned toward her. She could feel he had something to say but he pulled back and let it go. His eyes narrowed and the air filled with accusation. "I was just at the mine office reviewing the books."

Aislynn decided on innocence. "Were you?"

"Yes. I noticed some interesting entries."

She smiled, her eyes wide, her voice silent.

Scrutinizing her, he added, "I thought we might clear up a few things."

Aislynn weakened under his hard gaze. She looked away and casually offered, "If you're here for the licensing fee you're charging everyone running a decent business, I am planning on paying it."

"No. Actually I am not here to dun you, but now that you've made the offer, I would be happy to accept it." As she exhaled her frustration and annoyance, he added, "Let that be a lesson in business, Miss Denehy. Never make the first concession."

She frowned, angrier with herself than with him. Biting her lip, Aislynn attempted to keep choleric words from shooting out.

He placed his arm on the table and leaned closer to her. "You swindled me out of my property."

Aislynn took on the air of righteousness. "I made an offer to Mr. Murphy and he accepted it."

"According to Murphy, a very low offer and under some, shall I say, persuasive circumstances."

"If you have a problem with the agreement, you should take it up with Mr. Murphy."

"Such treachery," he charged. "I just did."

"He was just trying to be helpful."

"With my land and my money, $150.00 to be exact."

His tone was demeaning and Aislynn was indignant. "It's a loan and I am paying it back."

"I understand it's a loan, but he lent you my money."

"He's your agent. There can't be anything wrong with him making decisions for you." Aislynn stiffened.

"No, not unless you look at it for what it might be considered, perhaps embezzling?" He seemed to be amused with his comments.

"Good God, it was just a loan," she declared.

"Simply a loan?" Moran smiled as she squirmed in her seat.

"What are you going to do? You can't fire him. Oh, you'd be just mean enough to do such a thing!"

His smile disappeared. He looked at her without expression, "What have I done to make you believe I'm mean?"

Aislynn wanted to reel off a list of outrages; however she only had her prejudices.

She took a deep breath and sighed, "Nothing, except all these threats you've come here with."

"Threats?"

"Yes!"

"Hardly. I want you to be aware that you are a landowner and a restaurateur because of me. And the next time you need a favor, I want you to come to me directly. After all, I'd enjoy a picnic alone in the woods with you myself."

Aislynn could feel her face burning with embarrassment. Unable to accept defeat, she rallied, "I won't be needing any more favors."

"We'll see." He slid the cup and saucer to the middle of the table and reached for his hat. He rose and bowed slightly, "Thank you for the coffee. I'll be coming by the restaurant this evening. I do hope you're serving fried chicken; I understand it's positively spellbinding." He laughed out loud as he turned toward the door. Aislynn opened her mouth to admonish him, when he spun to face her. "By the way, I suggest you button up your bodice before you go over to the restaurant. I can only hope you don't display yourself for other men."

Aislynn stomach churned. She looked down and found her shirt open to her camisole. "Why didn't you say something?"

"And spoil my view? You spend far too much time with the virtuous Mr. Nolan."

"Oh, go you ... you rat."

He backed out the door, but through his laughter Moran said, "I look forward to seeing more of you in the future."

Chapter 16

Fourth of July had special significance in the West. Although many men ventured into the frontier for fortune, they also sought to escape the bonds of civility with its rules, restrictions and restraints. In the West, freedom was attainable. It was the land of rugged independence and July the Fourth celebrated the ideal.

Aislynn, Johnny, Tim and No Nose arrived at Moran's celebration in time to watch the wranglers demonstrate the skills they used herding cattle: riding, roping, tackling and tying calves and steers. Not special enough to sit in the grandstand Moran had erected for guests like Brigham Young, President of the Mormon Church, and Leland Stanford, President of the Central Pacific Railroad, Aislynn and her friends stood at the fence with the other commoners. Dust puffed up from the riding and wrestling, coating Aislynn's uniform of mourning: her white shirtwaist with a black armband, black skirt and wide-brimmed straw hat tied with a black ribbon. Following the show, four filthy wranglers raced to greet Tim and meet Aislynn.

Spurs clanged, chaps flopped and gloves flailed at their clothes as the men approached. Tim had wintered with the men. As she watched them approach, Aislynn was astonished to discover Tim had lived with a Negro. "In New York, everyone we know thinks Negroes are people who take jobs from white folks. That's not true, Aislynn. They're just like the rest of us, people trying to get by. Besides, not all are former slaves. They've been here as long as whites; some came with the explorers. Negroes have done the same things as whites, good and bad." Tim cautioned her. "I expect you to behave; he's my friend."

The black man was named Buck; he was tall, powerfully built, a quiet man in his late twenties. Jeb was shorter, sweet-faced, equally reticent and near Tim's age, twenty-two-years-old. Dollar Bill was older, perhaps thirty. He had a nose that appeared to have been broken several times, many absent teeth and a name reflecting his poor luck at gambling. Lank was tall, thin and talkative. When Tim introduced the wranglers to his friends, he drew a moan from the men when he explained Johnny was Aislynn's fiancé.

"You din have to bring your own man. Din Tim tell you we was all waitin' here for you?" Lank demanded.

"It must have been an oversight." Tim apologized.

The guests were swarming toward tables set up under the few trees where lemonade and cookies were being served. Lank led them to the back porch of the house, offering Aislynn the only seat and some shade. To the group's amusement, he rushed to get her refreshments. Looking directly at No Nose, Tim and Johnny, she said, "I could get used to such treatment."

"We'll see you don't," Tim countered.

Lank told Aislynn amusing stories about tenderfoot

Tim. Not to be outdone, Tim had plenty to say about Lank and the others. Amid the laughter, Moran emerged from the back door of the house. "I knew there was someone special back here. I could hear the chatter throughout the house. Miss Denehy," he bowed toward her and faced the men. "Boys." He turned back to Aislynn. "You attract these men like bees to honey. Have I ever mentioned to you that I, too, like honey?" A wicked smile spread across his face. "Especially on fresh baked biscuits."

Aislynn took a deep breath and suppressed the harsh words pressing against her lips. She raised her eyes and took a hard bite from her cookie.

Moran addressed the wranglers. "Do you boys think Miss Denehy might be interested in the little thing we have in our stable?"

"You like horses, Miss?" Lank asked.

"Yes, I do." She gave Lank her sweetest smile.

Moran's arm stood waiting in front of her face, "Allow me escort you."

Slowly rising, she lowered her eyes as she took his arm. Moran led her across the yard toward the stable and the men followed.

Aislynn had seen Moran with a big-breasted, broad-hipped blonde dressed in a fine blue gown, sporting a wide blue hat decked with red and white feathers. To Aislynn, the woman who spent the afternoon hanging from Moran's arm looked like a schooner under full sail. "Thank you for inviting us to your celebration. We are having a lovely time." Aislynn hesitated for a moment before prying, "Did you plan this entire affair yourself?"

"No, one of my guests made the arrangements."

"Which guest?"

Moran looked down at her with the suspicious half-smile he frequently sent her. "Miss Fairbanks. You may have noticed her. She is in the blue gown."

Aislynn tossed her nose in the air and lied, "No, but I will look for her and let her know what a fine job she's done."

Moran cleared his throat, "I'm sure she will appreciate your comments."

"Why aren't you bringing her to the stable?"

"Miss Fairbanks is not interested in anything residing in a stable," Moran laughed.

They entered the stable and Aislynn wondered if Moran had just insulted her. The stable exhaled heat and the smell of hay and horses. Moran led her through the dimness. As her eyes adjusted, she saw him open the gate of one stall and sweep his hand before her. On a bed of fresh hay, a tiny colt lay nestled against his mother.

A smile burst across her face and Aislynn sank to her knees. "Can I pet him?"

Crouching next to her, Moran's knee brushed her arm, "Of course." He reached down and stroked the colt's neck. Aislynn touched his nose and he lifted his head and dropped it in her lap.

Aislynn glowed, "He likes me."

"He's a smart horse, a thoroughbred. In a few years, I'll take him east and race him."

"What's his name?"

Moran looked to the wranglers. Lank answered for them, "He ain't got one."

Moran shrugged, "Why don't you name him for me?"

"Can I?"

He nodded.

"Well, my father's horse was named Cuchulainn."

Moran gave her a curious look, "What a strange name."

"Don't you know Cuchulainn?" She surveyed the group. Except for Johnny and Tim, the men looked at her with curiosity. "Well, Cuchulainn was a mythical Irish hero. He was a shape changer. When he went into battle, the shape of his body altered. He became one being with his horse, a monstrous thing." She raised her arms wide. "He was never defeated."

Her enthusiasm gained their attention. "When my father was a young man in County Galway, he would go to the beach and watch the wild ponies run. One day, a very special horse appeared. He was bigger, stronger and more beautiful than any other. My father decided to tame the horse and make it his own. Every day he brought a treat to the beach to entice the horse closer and closer." She beckoned them with her hand. "Finally, the horse came close enough for Da to grab his mane and hoist himself up on the horse's back. Once mounted, Da said he felt magic flow through him; he and the horse became one."

The men murmured their amazement. Aislynn leaned closer to the men and continued to spin her tale. "Well, he raced the horse all over Ireland, from county to county, never losing a race. They were undefeated just like the original Cuchulainn. Then, an evil landlord accused Da of stealing the horse and put out a warrant. Da set Cuchulainn free and he escaped to America." She straightened and took a breath. "Da's mother wrote to him and finished Cuchulainn's story. It seems the landlord's men nearly captured the horse in a fenced field, but as they approached, Cuchulainn ran and ran, so fast he flew away."

Lank cut in, "You sayin' horses can fly?"

Aislynn's eyes raked over the men. "Perhaps."

Buck leaned toward her and whispered, "Maybe a magic horse?"

Warming to the dark man, Aislynn nodded. "Maybe a magic horse." She looked at Moran and tilted her head to catch his admiring eyes. "That's the tale that's told."

Moran beamed at her, "And a fine tale it is." He stroked the horse and addressed it, "So, Cuchulainn, let's hope you are undefeated, as well." He stood and brushed off his trousers, saying, "Perhaps you can ride him next year, Miss Denehy."

He extended his hand to her. Rising, she said, "Thank you, Mr. Moran, but I don't know how to ride."

Moran shook his head, "I'm sure you'll find no short-age of instructors." He bowed to Aislynn and added, "I must return to my other guests. Enjoy the remaining events." Aislynn bit her lip, her eyes danced with excitement as she watched him leave the stable until she caught Johnny's frown.

She approached Johnny. "What have I done?"

"Nothing. Except we'll be married by next year."

Aislynn scowled, "Don't you think about anything else?"

"Don't you think of it at all? Married women should-n't ride horses, Aislynn. Why you could lose a baby before you even know you're having one."

Her cheeks flashed red, "Don't speak of such things, especially in public!"

"Nobody's listening," Johnny groused.

Aislynn knew he included her in his statement. "And nobody wants to discuss such a thing either!"

The afternoon continued with horse races. Moran invited everyone in the area to compete on his track. It made for several heated races. The horses ran at speeds that made her believe, quite possibly, they could fly. Aislynn declared she had never seen anything as exciting. She understood why her father remembered his years as a jockey so fondly.

A western bar-be-que and dance followed. Aislynn busied herself trying to dance with each of the men in her group. While she was spinning on the floor with No Nose, Moran approached her companions with his lady friend on his arm. All the other introductions had been completed when Aislynn and No Nose arrived. Breathless, they greeted Moran.

"Miss Fairbanks, this is No Nose Goodman."

Her reply was unexpected. "My goodness," she cried, her hand rushing to her throat, "you truly are shocking."

Angry, Aislynn stepped between No Nose and the re-pulsive woman. Moran made an obvious attempt to ignore the offense. "And this lovely lady is Aislynn Denehy."

Aislynn eyes narrowed. She stood stiff and erect, waiting.

"Oh, you're the little thing who crawled across the country in a wagon. I would never. It's so primitive." The woman pointed her nose in the air and looked down at Aislynn, "And you're so ... tiny. However did you endure such filthy, uncivilized conditions?"

Aislynn cracked her whip, "Sometimes pups are stronger than bitches."

Miss Fairbanks glared at Aislynn, her mouth hanging open. Moran's eyes flew wide and he stammered, "Let's go see Leland for a moment. He's been wanting..." His voice died away as he led her onto the crowded dance floor.

When she turned to face her friends, she found them in a variety of contortions attempting to stifle their laughter until Moran walked out of earshot. She took No Nose's face in her hands and placed a kiss on his cheek.

Lank spoke first, "That a gal, Miss Denehy. Doan let that ol' buzzard get the best of you." Congratulations spilled from everyone but Tim.

When the laughter died, Tim asked her to dance. Aislynn had waited all day to be in his arms. She could tell from his grip he was not proud or amused by her response. Waltzing across the canvas floor rolled out over the dusty yard, Tim began his lecture. "Aislynn, you do realize we all owe Mr. Moran a great deal. He's my employer, he gives Johnny work, and you know he could put you out of business."

He had her attention. "How?"

"If he were spiteful, he could open a mess hall and feed his miners for free. As you've seen today, he can afford to give away food."

Aislynn sniffed, "Miners aren't my only customers."

"Are you listening?"

"Yes, I understand. I just don't like it."

"What is it between you two? You usually make

185

friends so easily. Tonight notwithstanding, it seems an effort for you to simply be polite to him."

"There's something about him." Aislynn shook her head, wanting to shake off the subject.

"What is it?"

Aislynn squirmed, "He just makes me uncomfortable."

Tim stopped dancing, "Has he done... something to you?"

She understood his meaning. "Heavens, no." Aislynn smiled at his concern and pulled him back into the dance. "I don't even know why." She leaned closer to him and whispered, "If you want, I'll try harder."

"That's my girl."

His handsome face glowed in the light of the torches surrounding the dance floor. Under the deep navy sky, the smell of burning pine floated through the air. The music of guitars, fiddles and horns drifted past their ears. As she moved in step with Tim, she forgot about Moran. She closed her eyes and felt him solidly in her grasp. *This is why I came here, to be with Tim and to enjoy his love.*

With a pause in the music, they edged off the dance floor. Tim placed his hands on her shoulders and spun her around. "There," he said. Aislynn could see Moran speaking to a short, round man in a wrinkled suit. As the man drifted away, Tim gave her a push.

"Why, Miss Denehy, are you without a partner?" Moran wore his mocking half smile as he tilted his head toward her.

"No, sir." The "sir" brought him up straight. "I just wanted to ask you to apologize to Miss Fairbanks for me."

"Apologize? She was the rude one." His eyes reached over her head and rested on the spot where she had left Tim. "You know, Miss Denehy, you will never be happy if you do things just because someone else wants you to do them."

186

Aislynn turned and caught Tim smiling his approval. Inching away from Moran, she, "Well, I guess it depends on what makes you happy."

Chapter 17

"Sunday morning is hardly the time for whores to be parading up Main Street," Aislynn mumbled. She watched Madame Stella and four of her girls with their flashy dresses and highly furbelowed hats huff up to the mine office. In Aislynn's mind, they were five hot air balloons spewing gas.

Throughout the day, Aislynn's customers buzzed with the story. One of the whores had turned up dead, and the others wanted Moran to deliver justice in his camp. Moran asked two Wells Fargo men, dozing at the Express Office, to investigate the murder and if possible, locate the culprit. By late afternoon, Jake Johnson, one of the mine's timbermen, quaked in the Express Office while a gang of men planned a hanging outside.

Moran stood behind the bar of The Claimjumper Saloon, banging a tin cup on the hard wood, calling the general meeting to order. When the crowd quieted, he began, "As you know, Mattie is dead. Jake Johnson stands accused of this very serious crime. Now, I don't want any miscarriage of justice in my camp. You're goin' to vote to elect a council of men who will decide how to proceed and henceforth, they'll serve as your representatives in our community matters. We're goin' do this all democratic and orderly. Any questions?"

Between Johnny and Tim, Aislynn's hand rose. Moran's brows arched. "Miss Denehy?"

Aislynn stood between her surprised companions. "I was wondering; do I get to vote?"

The gathering gasped. She could feel Tim and Johnny exchanging looks behind her as she studied Moran's amused bewilderment. "Well, Miss, I don't rightly know."

"It's your camp," she pressed.

"Yes, but you know women aren't enfranchised."

"They have been in some local elections, and this is just a camp vote." Moran shook his head, but she added, "Wyoming is considering allowing women to vote in territorial elections, and Brigham Young has said he may allow women the vote here in Utah."

Moran sighed, "Let's consider the question."

Comments were shouted out. "You can't give women the vote, just ain't proper." "Why women ain't capable of votin', don't got the brain for such things." "Gives 'em too many ideas. Then they wants to change things, no drinkin', no gamblin', no…" "Votin' ain't what women are good at."

The dissent grew loud. Aislynn bit her lip and started to tremble under the force of the objection.

Tim pulled her down into her seat and stood. He turned and addressed the crowd, "If we are to allow fifteen-year-old muckers to vote, I do not see why Miss Denehy should be disqualified simply by virtue of her sex. She owns land, a traditional qualification for voting, while most of the men in this room don't. She can read and write; most of these men can't. She has completed the full seven-year course of schooling required by the great City of New York. And I believe if you asked any man in this room to recite the Bill of Rights, he would be hard pressed to do so, yet Miss Denehy knows all thirteen amendments and the two which are pending." Tim paused and looked over the frowning men. "I do not believe the democratic process will be threatened by allowing her to vote. In fact, I believe it will be enhanced."

A rumpled man stood in the back of the barroom and stated, "It ain't right, look at the Bible. Woman are 'pose to follow their men, be submissive, 'cept seems to me like she's leadin' you."

"Well, sir, I wouldn't say she leads but she has her own opinions, her own thoughts. She has a mind and she is capable of using it. Right now, she's simply asking to vote in a camp election, not run for president." Most of the men laughed, but the man would not be silenced.

"Yeah, well we been wonderin' 'bout your sitcheation. Three men living with one woman, and she ain't related to one of youse."

Johnny rose to his feet, seething. "What are you sayin'?" he hissed at the man.

Tim and Aislynn grabbed him, trying to coax him down. Moran banged his cup hard. "I will not allow you to besmirch Miss Denehy." Clearly angry, he spoke with vehemence. "We all know she is an orphan. Mr. Nolan is Miss Denehy's guardian and Mr. Maher is her intended. She was kind enough to take in poor Mr. Goodman. No one can question the morality of these people." Moran's voice grew stronger, "I will not permit you to sully her reputation simply because she has asked to vote." The cup loudly met the boards again. He took a breath, and, in a calmer voice, stated, "Now, the question is political not personal. If you cannot address the issue, keep your comments to yourself."

A man leaning against the sidewall raised his hand. "I think we need to ask why women are not given the right to vote. I believe it is because they are not physically

191

equipped to do such things. I have read that using their brains too much causes women to lose certain attributes...abilities." He paused and gestured with his hands, "You know what I mean; procreation, that which makes them women."

Flashing above the male heads, a red-gloved hand waved. Moran acknowledged Stella, who rose and nodded at the men. Holding her head erect, she said, "Me and the girls wanna vote. We ain't got her egication," Stella motioned toward Aislynn, who turned bright red and diverted her eyes into her lap. Aislynn believed the nuns when they said, "If you look at a whore, you'll become one." Stella continued, "But we work and we contribute," she emphasized the word, "to the community. Let us vote, or we'll see who loses certain attributes."

"Well," Moran laughed and looked at Tim and Aislynn, "politics really does make strange bedfellows." The men roared. Aislynn sneaked a grin at Stella. Moran suggested, "Let's take a vote."

Stella interjected, "Ask 'em to raise their hands, I wanna see who votes against me."

"Let's make it easy." Moran said, "Anyone opposed, please stand." A few men rose to their feet to the hoots of the others. "All in favor say aye."

Aislynn beamed as the collective "Aye" rang through the room. Moran hit the bar with his cup. "Now let's elect a council." The historic vote elected Al Bowman, the newspaper editor, Fred Schmidt, the butcher, D. Clark, owner of the Claimjumper, and Tim. Moran would preside and break tie votes.

With a nod from Moran, the accused was dragged through the gauntlet of jeering men and brought before the bar to stand in front of the assembled council. The Wells Fargo men explained the reasons for his apprehension. They were few. Johnson was Mattie's last known customer, and he had blood on his clothes when they found him drunk on the floor of his lean-to. Johnson claimed the blood belong to a rabbit he had killed and cleaned. Closer examination revealed a freshly killed rabbit strung up in the dwelling.

Questions and answers volleyed between the council and the accused, who remained persistent in his denial. The crowd howled its disbelief and cried for a hanging. Moran polled the council for direction. Tim stated there was not enough evidence to keep Johnson in custody and the entire matter should be referred to the federal marshal in Salt Lake. Bowman agreed. Clark and Schmidt felt someone had to pay for the crime. They thought Johnson capable of the crime and recommended a quick hanging. The crowd cheered and the defendant seemed to shrink in size.

Moran's turn had come. His gaze traveled over the audience and they fell silent. His narrow, pale blue eyes scoured Johnson's face. Heat and tension pressed in on the room while the split-timbered walls and roof creaked with the weight of the decision at hand. Johnson stood, eyes wild. His dry mouth opened and closed as he searched for words to exonerate himself.

Moran banged his cup. "The case and Johnson go to Salt Lake." Johnson fell to his knees and sagged against the bar. Moran was not distracted. "But, let me warn everyone in this room, and you tell those who are absent, this is my camp. It's not Virginia City; it's not San Francisco. I'll not tolerate vigilantism. You've heard the decision. Anyone who touches this man, I'll see out of a job, out of my camp and out of this territory." Moran surveyed the crowd and asked, "Is there any other business?"

Aislynn pushed No Nose to his feet. He stammered, "I, we, uh, we think we need firemen in this camp." He bent down and pulled Aislynn to her feet. "You tell 'em, yourself."

Looking at the bar rather than the men, Aislynn tentatively stood. "Well, we are all aware in the past three months there have been numerous fires. Two men have lost their lives and several others have lost all their belongings. I think all the wooden buildings and tents are very vulnerable to fire, especially when winter comes. Why, a fire could rip through this camp in a flash. I was just thinking the camp should have equipment for fighting fires and some fellows who know how to use it."

Moran nodded. "Thank you, Miss Denehy. That is actually a very good idea. As you may know the mine is getting fire equipment, a water truck, a pumper, and I agree the camp should be protected, as well. I would be willing to provide the equipment but we need a group of men who would be willing to learn how to use it and someone willing to organize and lead a fire brigade." Moran's eyes searched the gathering for volunteers.

"Johnny could do it." She offered without asking him. Johnny was popular with the men and agreement could be heard from the crowd as he tugged his objection on her sleeve. "He doesn't know anything about fire-fighting but when you train the miners, he and his volunteers could learn, too."

"Do you have volunteers?" Moran asked Johnny.

"No, sir," he replied while rising, "This is the first I'm hearin' about it. This is totally unexpected."

"You're a trusted, responsible young man, Johnny. I am sure I speak for everyone when I say there are few men in camp more capable of leading. You get some volunteers and we'll talk about the training."

Johnny scowled at Aislynn who beamed her pride at him.

Moran asked, "Anything else?"

Still standing Aislynn said, "Yes."

The men moaned. With one hand on her hip, she sniped, "This is for the benefit of everyone."

"Please continue, Miss Denehy; you seem to have the camp's welfare in mind."

A rough miner added, "She wants to turn this into a decent place."

"Well, Carter, as long as you're in camp, we don't have to be concerned about getting respectable, do we?" Moran tipped his cup at the man. "Now, Miss Denehy, please."

"I think we need to clean up the trash and ashes and the animal droppings. Not only is it becoming impossible to walk on the boardwalks, you cannot cross the street without stepping in filth. And we have to consider that we're going to have an epidemic in this heat if things are not cleaned up and carted away somewhere."

Moran gave her a hard, unreadable look. He turned to the council. "What do you think?"

"Dis street ees filty. Eet come een my shop." Schmidt offered.

Bowman said, "She could be right about sickness. I was in a city when the cholera spread."

Stella's hand shot up. "I think she's right," she declared as she rose. "We pay 'lot a money for our clothes and they're always gettin' messed. You know, I like to run a clean place an' these here men are forever traipsin' filth into the girls' cribs. I'd like to see the street clean 'fore my new place is open."

While Aislynn listened to her new ally's support, she searched Tim's face for any indication he knew Stella ran a clean place. "No," she told herself. "Tim would never." Unbidden, the question of Johnny's knowledge surfaced in her mind along with an unexpected twinge of jealousy. She looked down and his round, innocent face smiled at her. She could feel her anger rising and her stomach sinking at the thought of him with one of the whores. Just because she did not want to be intimate with Johnny did not mean she wanted anyone else to be.

"Fine," Moran agreed. "I'll hire two men and give them a wagon. Bowman, you get word out that ashes and trash must be out front to be picked up. The men will take care of the street." He nodded at Stella and then at Aislynn, who, careful to avoid Stella's eyes, sent a satisfied smile in the scarlet woman's direction. Moran continued, "Before these women think of other ways for me to spend my money, I am closing this meeting and offering every man here a drink."

195

Aislynn turned to Johnny and said, "I can't wait to write home and tell everyone you are the chief of the fire brigade."

"Chief? Aislynn, I don't know anything about fightin' fires."

"Well, you'll learn." She brushed his cheek with fingertips. "And you'll be good at it. I know you will." Tim approached and she opened her arms to him. "I'm so proud of you, two government officials."

"Hardly," he smirked.

"You're always so critical."

"No, Aislynn, realistic." Tim corrected.

Moran came toward them and extended his hand to Johnny and Tim.

"Aren't they wonderful?" she gushed.

"Yes," he joked, "they're wonderful."

"I think so." She tossed her head at his mocking laughter.

"I was actually more impressed with you. I didn't realize how civic-minded you were."

Touched by the serious admiration of his tone, she smiled. "Thank you, Mr. Moran. I think a public spirit is important."

The crowd of men, trying to reach the bar, pushed around them. She was jostled and separated from Tim and Johnny. Moran's arm circled her shoulders; he protected her from the crush by pressing his body against hers. "Public spirit? Is it one of those 'female attributes'?" His breath on her ear warmed the room. "Now that you have the vote, I am going to make a personal effort to keep an eye on your 'attributes,' Miss Denehy. Just in case you consider losing some."

Chapter 18

In October, Aislynn secured a loan from the Express Office and a simple one-room building with a false front was mail ordered. Now, its proud face watched Main Street while its body balanced on the stone foundation she and her men had dug and stacked. With the cold, hard winter moving in, many of her customers remained at their tables long after meals were eaten, warmed by her large cook stoves.

Tim, Johnny, No Nose and Murphy were sharing a table with Moran and the two men who regularly rode with him, Buck and Jeb. The talk of the evening buzzed around the traveling show driving into camp the next night. When Aislynn approached, all lips came together. She slammed the pot of coffee on the table and said, "You can serve yourselves."

Johnny tried to reason with her, "It's not our fault."

"If this show is so indecent I can't see it, why are you three going?" Aislynn aimed her question at No Nose, Tim and Johnny.

Glances were exchanged among the faces that wore redness or hid amusement or looked away from her to be excluded from the fray.

"It's what men do." Johnny grinned and reached for her hip. His hand was swatted away. "Every man in camp will be there; how can we stay home?"

Moran broke in, "You know, it might not be wise to leave her alone."

The lightheartedness dissipated. Knowing looks traveled around the table. Tim offered his sacrifice, "She's my responsibility; I'll stay."

"No, I'll stay." Johnny waved away Tim's generosity.

"I can take care of myself." Aislynn patted the pocket where her tiny revolver resided.

Tim shook his head at Johnny, refuting her claim. Aislynn scoffed and turned toward a pile of dirty dishes. She stopped mid-step when Moran spoke. "You two go. I've seen the show."

Aislynn turned abruptly. From behind Moran's back, she shot a look at Tim; he stiffened under her fire. "Thanks, Mr. Moran, but we couldn't ask you."

"You're not askin', I'm offerin'."

The men shuffled around the cabin, trying to appear too occupied to address Aislynn's tirade. "So now I'm to be doubly punished just for being female?"

Tim relented, "What could we say?"

"You could have said no!" she shouted. "You should have insisted!"

"Don't raise your voice. It's not ladylike."

Aislynn stamped her foot. Johnny calmly joined the discussion, "You know, maybe an evening together would be good. You might discover he's not a bad sort."

"He's arrogant, self-centered and proud."

Johnny reached for her shoulders and pulled her close. "Angel, be Christian. Maybe he hasn't had the advantages we've had."

Aislynn shook him off. "He has everything, including you two kowtowing to him."

"That's not what I mean. He's alone, always has been from what I hear. When a man always has to look out for himself, he can get hard."

"Such wisdom from a man who talks to his mules."

Johnny put his arms around her waist and placed a peck on her hair saying, "I talk to you, too."

Tim and No Nose laughed at the comparison while Aislynn elbowed Johnny in the side.

Aislynn cleaned the empty restaurant as Moran pretended to read a newspaper. She could feel him watching her. She turned and looked at him, "Yes?"

"Aren't you ready to go home? It's nearly nine o'clock."

"I thought I'd just get some things done before the men return."

"Don't you want to go home?"

"Why?"

"Don't you live there?"

Aislynn twisted her mouth, "Yes, but what are we going to do there?"

"What do you normally do?"

"They play chess, checkers, read. Tim is teaching No Nose to read."

"And you?"

"There's never a shortage of work for me at home."

Moran laughed, "When do you stop working?"

"I don't have the time."

Moran's face fell, and he asked her softly, "Don't you ever play?"

Aislynn thought his question indicated her lack of something. "Of course." Moran studied her. Aislynn felt defensive. She sighed, "I was the only girl; I still am."

He folded his paper and slapped it on the table. "Take the night off." He stood and said, "Lock up. Let's go."

In the cabin, he sat at the table and produced a deck of cards. "Know how to play poker?"

"Sort of." Aislynn eyed the cards with apprehension.

His brows rose with suspicion. "I think you know more than you let on. We won't be betting."

While they played, they discussed business. He asked her if she knew what stocks were. She shook her head. He settled into his seat and began a simple explanation. "Let's use Central Pacific stock as an example. The company, the CP, sells pieces of itself called shares. The people who buy the shares pay a price, like one dollar per share. Now, say the company is broken up into a thousand shares. The person who owes one share owns a one thousandth share of the company. When the company makes money, the owners make money equal to their percentage of shares. They receive dividends or part of the profits. Also, if the company makes money, the value of the company increases and the price of a share may rise, say from one dollar to two dollars. Now if that happens and you bought your shares at a dollar when you decided to sell your share how much profit would you make?"

Aislynn frowned at him. "Do you think I'm stupid?"

Moran stifled a laugh, "No, quite the contrary. Please forgive me. I lost my head. Now, with railroads, the government loans the companies money in the form of bonds to build the lines. In addition, the government allows us to sell bonds. You know what bonds are?"

Aislynn admitted ignorance again.

"Bonds are basically loans, like your mortgage. Eventually, they have to be paid back to the government or to those people who are doing the lending or as we say, to those buying the bonds. But, to help us pay off our loans or bonds, the government gives the company land, miles of it, along the finished line to sell so those debts can be

200

paid off."

"That's incredible. That's like the express office giving me money to pay them back for my mortgage. Why does the government give you so much?"

"They want the railroad, too. They learned a lesson in the War. This is a mighty big country. If we're going to hold together, we have to be able to travel from east to west, moving troops and stores. Railroads are the answer."

Aislynn was fascinated. He continued, "That's not all. For every mile of track completed, the government issues us more bonds. Plus we get paid for every mile of rail we lay and the payment per mile increases with the elevation."

"Meaning?"

"Well, we get $16,000 a mile for the flat lands. Between the eastern base of the Rockies and the western base of the Sierras, we get $48,000 a mile for building in the mountains and $32,000 for track between the ranges."

"That's so much money. How much does it cost to build?"

"Good question. The answer is it depends on where we're actually building. You know the rails are coming through the Sierra Nevadas. In the mountains, the grade can't be too steep, or the engines can't climb it, so at some points, we have to literally go straight through the rock. There, every inch has to be blasted. Some days the line only moves an eighth of an inch. And at the highest elevations, the snow makes laying the track even more difficult, and extremely expensive, hence the bigger payment." Moran sat back and scrutinized her for a moment. "Want to know a secret?"

Aislynn rested her elbows on the table and leaned her chin into her hands, nodding.

He moved toward her, "Let me ask you a question first. Do you think men can move mountains?"

"You're going to tell me they can."

Moran pulled back and frowned, "I'm either losing my poker face or you're beginning to know me too well."

Wide eyed, Aislynn bent closer and demanded, "Tell me."

"Well, how do we know where the mountains begin?"

"I guess where the land starts to rise."

"How much of a rise makes a mountain?"

"I don't know. However, I'm sure engineers and surveyors know."

"And what they say goes?"

"I suppose."

"Do you think a man could say the Sierra Nevadas extend, oh, maybe, twenty-four miles farther west than they actually do, so the track would be worth $48,000 a mile rather than $16,000?"

Shock escaped from her lips, "No! That's nearly three quarters of a million dollars."

Moran chuckled, "You're mighty fast with figures."

He scooped up the idle cards and started to deal.

"That's cheating." Aislynn moralized.

"That's business," Moran answered, laying down the cards.

"It's dishonest," she insisted.

"But profitable," he said as a matter of fact, studying his cards.

Aislynn sighed and picked up her hand. "Men can get away with cheating and lying. When you own everything, control everything, you don't have to be honest."

Moran looked up, his brows raised, "And women are honest?"

Aislynn looked at him from under her lashes. "More than men." She watched him make a sour face. Aislynn shook her head, "How do you trust anyone?"

A hard look flashed across his face. "I don't," he said, tapping his cards on the table.

Fighting her feelings of pity, Aislynn dismissed them

202

as superfluous. He was a man who had everything. They played a hand in considered silence.

Curiosity overcame her, "If you're so involved with the Central Pacific, why did you come here?"

"Ambition."

Leaning on the table, Aislynn studied him, waiting for his explanation.

"I want to go to Washington, not as a lobbyist for the Central Pacific or a messenger for Utah's governor, Mr. Durkee. I want to be a senator or congressman."

"The Mormons will never elect you."

"Now, Miss," he straightened the deck, "you have to learn to think ahead. First, there are a whole lot of Christians or Gentiles coming into the Territory. When the railroad is finished, and men hear about the silver, more will come. It's one of Brother Brigham's biggest fears." Moran put down his cards and continued. "Someday, the Territory will become a state and when it does, can a Mormon go to the Senate or the House and do any good in an arena where he would be reviled and despised?"

"No, I don't suppose so."

"Now, a man who is sympathetic to the Mormons..."

"How can you be sympathetic to them? You know how they treated me and Johnny."

"There are good and bad Mormons just like there are good and bad Christians. You have to remember Mormons came out here to avoid religious persecution. They walked themselves and their belonging nearly two thousand miles so they could be left alone to practice their faith. Along comes the "Gold Rush," and the very people the Mormons were trying to avoid come passing through their territory, some even wanting to stay and claiming land. They brought their objections to the Mormons and their practices with them. You traveled all this way to get what you want; how do you think you'd react to people who want to take all you've worked for?"

Aislynn nodded reluctantly, "I understand, but they

were so awful to us."

"They were just a few bad men. We Christians have them, too."

"I know. I suppose I could be more tolerant."

Moran leaned back and sent her a suggestive smile, "Yes, you could."

Aislynn felt the color rise in her face as she raised her eyes to the ceiling and shook her head. She turned the conversation back to his ambition, "How are you going to get them to nominate you?"

"By being a friend to Brother Brigham."

"My goodness," she marveled, "you want so much."

"Why not aim high?"

"Because if you don't get what you want, you'll be disappointed."

"It's a small price to pay. However, I believe I'll get my way. If I don't," he shrugged, "I've frequently found a journey can be more exciting than its destination."

Aislynn sighed and fell back against her chair, "You must take an awful lot of risks."

Moran aimed his flinty, unreadable stare and said, "I try to limit myself to safe bets." A smile crossed his lips, "Now, young lady, tell me what you've learned?"

"I need to make more money."

A whistle, blowing the signal to close the mine, pierced the morning air. It was an uncommon blast, only sounded in emergencies. Aislynn ignored the blast and continued to instruct Sung Lee, her new employee. Aislynn had developed a plan to increase her income. Although No Nose was her part-time helper, he refused to perform any tasks he categorized as women's work. With the help of this Chinese laborer, she could increase the number of tables and serve more people. She was explaining her routine when Murphy threw open the door, breathless, announcing, "Moran wants to see you! Better run!"

Murphy hung on the door for support, unable to say more. Aislynn grabbed her shawl. She feared some terrible tragedy had occurred. Puzzling over her purpose, she hurried up the street through the thin, sharp air. Then it hit her, "Tim!" She ran and burst through the office door.

Moran stood, solitary, his face dark and pinched in anger. The room felt small with him seething at its center. Weak morning light hazed around them, dusty and smoky from cigars and the burning stove. Her intuition sharpened; she recognized this had nothing to do with Tim. She was the object of his wrath. Aislynn waited, watching him ball his hands into fists.

Moran's harsh voice taunted, "You've never been down the mine. It's dark, wet and very dangerous. What with drilling and blasting, gas can explode, fires can start, timbers can cave."

Aislynn chewed her lip and nodded, her eyes riveted on his.

"I shut down the mine!" he shouted.

Aislynn nodded again, baffled by her role and his rage.

"I can't have men down there who can't communicate with each other." Moran took a step toward her. Her heart raced and she backed into the closed door. A blush burned her face, expressing her bewilderment. Moran dropped into a chair behind the nearest desk, leaned on his forearms and folded his hands.

His voice seethed. "You posted an advertisement up here, written in English."

"Yes," she whispered, not venturing closer.

"I have only three Chinamen who can speak and read English, one supervising the Coolies on each shift. One!" he pointed a finger. His volume increased with his command. "You tell Sung Lee to get his butt back up here and down that hole, pronto!"

She would not allow tears or even blinking; she wanted to see him clearly. Her hand felt behind her for the doorknob. Sidestepping, she flung the door open. She stumbled past Murphy standing on the stairs. Hurtful, angry tears came as she raced down the hill to deliver the message.

"I know you didn't mean any harm," Tim said when he found her curled on her cot in the dark cabin.

"No one has ever been so mean. I hate him. I will never speak to him again!" she cried.

Tim sat next to Aislynn and surrounded her with his arms. He rocked her and petted her hair. "He's a hard man sometimes."

"He has no feelings, so he doesn't have any idea what it's like to be hurt," she sniffed.

Tim waited for her tirade against Moran to extinguish. "He's insensitive, inconsiderate, just plain hateful. I can't imagine him being nice to anyone for more than a few minutes, unless he has something to gain from them." When her words were exhausted, he pulled away and looked for her eyes.

"The mine's open and running again." He paused and squeezed her. "I know he yelled at you, but I think he was more scared than anything else. I'm sure he was concerned that men could die, and the mine could close, and people would be out of work." Tim paused. "I think he's sorry."

Aislynn scoffed at Tim, disagreeing.

Tim tried again, "I do. Everything is fine, nobody was hurt, but I can see he's still troubled."

"Probably pining over losing a few dollars while the mine was closed."

"No, I think he's feeling very sorry."

"Good! I hope he's so miserable he leaves town."

Tim tilted his head and smiled at her, "Not likely; he does own the place." He rubbed her cheek with his knuckles. Aislynn grinned at his tenderness. Tim added, "Aislynn? You know we do all have to work together."

Aislynn's smile snapped into a frown. She straightened and faced him, "Don't you dare! I will not apologize! He was wrong!"

After considering Tim's opinion, Aislynn found herself dragging up the office stairs, repeating her mantra, "This is for Tim." Her strength was waning and she could hear her stomach churning as she rapped on the door. With Moran's, "Come in," Aislynn stepped gingerly through the door.

Evening had darkened the room, but she could see him sitting in a cloud of cigar smoke. She crossed her arms, shifted her weight and locked her eyes on his. Moran snuffed out the cigar. He walked to the front of the desk, leaned against it, his hands resting by his hips. Aislynn edged back toward the door. She saw his face fall. For the briefest moment, she was conflicted, she felt sorry, but she believed she was not at fault.

"I came..." she began, determined to have it over.

He held up his hand. "You should have waited; I would have come around ... eventually, and ... apologized."

Her sorrow was lost and her anger was found, although its direction was not clear. "That's what I told Tim," escaped from her lips.

His eyes flashed and his lips curled with suspicion. "What brought you here?"

She tried recover, "I came to apologize."

"Why?" His narrow eyes burned into her.

"I don't have to explain, I just have to apologize." She could feel her cheeks burning.

He reached behind him for a cigar and a light. "At least my attempt was sincere."

Aislynn remembered the morning's humiliation and stood indignant, "I said I was sorry."

"Wasn't it you who intimated men weren't honest?"

She spun and pulled the door open. Moran called to her, "By the way Rebecca, Ivanhoe ran home to Rowena

207

the first chance he got."

Aislynn slammed the door.

Chapter 19

For Christmas, Aislynn placed a tree in the restaurant and asked her customers to adorn it with any decorations they wanted to contribute. Rings, pocketknives, pieces of ribbon and all manner of effects the men held special hung on the little pine. Johnny wrought an iron star that presided over the room from the treetop.

Following their mid-day celebration, Aislynn, Tim, Johnny and No Nose were invited to attend a party at Moran's ranch with Murphy, the Spittlehouses and the Franks. Johnny had outfitted the wagon with runners, turning it into a sleigh. They herded into the bed, huddled on the low side benches, sang carols and pulled cider from a jug while No Nose steered them down the mountain to the ranch.

They could see the ranch from two miles down the canyon. The sky glowed golden from the light of lanterns lining the drive. The house was on fire with lamps perched on porch rails and candles in every window. When the group pulled up to the front door, everyone spilled out of the sleigh. Tim, Murphy and No Nose bounded up the steps. Tim held the door as Mr. and Mrs. Spittlehouse and Frank and his wife entered the lodge. Johnny guided Aislynn over the snowy walk. She stood in the doorway and took in the room.

It was a vast space with several, immense stripped tree trunks balanced on the floor, supporting the roof and the balcony skirting the second floor. A huge staircase twisted down from the story above and hugged the Christmas tree in its curve. The huge pine was trimmed with red ribbons and candles. Streamers of silver, red and green were swagged among the rafters. Fireplaces guarded each end wall. One side of the open room held two, long tables dressed in white linens, while the other had chairs and sofas arranged for conversation. Although the house was a spectacle, Aislynn's attention immediately fell on the women posed around the room. They wore satins, brocades and velvets fashioned into lovely gowns.

Aislynn heard Moran greeting her party at the door as she returned to the sleigh.

"Where's she goin'?"

Johnny replied, "It's her clothes." He motioned toward the sleigh. "She prefers this fine, frigid weather to your party."

"I'll get her," Tim sighed.

"No, it's my fault," Moran assured them, "I'll speak to her. You two get a drink and warm up."

Aislynn heard footsteps crunch across the snow and turned her back to the sound. Moran hoisted himself into the sleigh and took an opposite seat. She tried to avoid his scrutiny by pointing her nose in the air. He leaned forward about to speak when she snapped at him, "Why didn't you tell me this was a fancy dress party?"

"Would you have come?"

"No." Aislynn shook her head at him.

"That's why I didn't tell you."

"So you have us come to be humiliated like poor relations?"

"Is that what you think?"

Aislynn looked away from his eyes and focused on his hands, ungloved and gripping the bench. She twisted the ends of her scarf in her fingers. "No," she whispered contritely.

"I considered buying you a gown, but you couldn't accept it."

"Of course not. There are rules."

Moran laughed, "And Tim knows all of them."

Aislynn had to smile, "Yes, he does."

"I wanted you here to host one of my tables."

"What does that mean?"

"It means you make sure everyone has a full glass and food on their plates. You direct the conversation and bring everyone into it; particularly a discussion to get them interested in buying stock in Brother Brigham's railroad."

Aislynn gaped at his suggestion. "You want me to help Mormons, after they left Johnny and me to die?"

"Aislynn, I told you; you can't judge all people by the acts of a few. Besides, you're perfect for the job. After all, you know all about the Utah Central. And, you have such a smart mouth; I think it's time to put it to good use."

Aislynn's hands flew to her hips, "How very thoughtful of you." Aislynn jibed as she wagged her head, "But where's Miss Fairbanks?"

Moran frowned, "I didn't invite her."

"So you're offering me her job?"

Moran moved closer to her, "One aspect of it."

"You're crude."

"I am just offering you an opportunity to use your talents."

Skeptical, Aislynn asked, "What's it pay?"

"Would you accept the same remuneration I gave her?"

"I don't know what it was?"

Moran rested his hands on her bench, surrounding her. He brought his face close to hers. "Would you let me show you?"

As a flash of warmth spread through her, Aislynn pulled back, wrinkled her nose and shook her head. "Absolutely not."

"Good, it's too cold to get undressed out here."

Aislynn pushed him away. "You say the most improper things to me."

"If I stopped, you wouldn't have any reason to object to me."

"Ha, I'm sure I could find something."

"Come inside. We can debate my finer points where it's warm."

Aislynn was freezing, but she was still feeling drab.

"Please, Miss Denehy." He stood and pulled her to her feet. "It's very cold and if you catch a chill and die, I'll never have the opportunity to take advantage of you."

She followed him to the back of the wagon. "I don't have to die to make that an impossibility."

Moran jumped down and reached up for her. She placed her hands on his shoulders and he grabbed her waist. He lowered her slowly, holding her body against his. "I can hope," he laughed.

Aislynn squirmed out of his grip. "I hate it when you win," she grumbled.

"Well, that's encouraging, I thought you hated me."

Aislynn started to pick her way through the existing footprints in the snow. "I don't dislike you, I just don't trust you," she retorted.

"You are a very smart young lady."

She stopped and turned suddenly meeting his chest with her face. "Get out of the way," she fussed. "I forgot your present." She reached under the wagon seat and produced a bottle tied with a ribbon. She handed it to him, pride beaming from her cold, white face.

"What is it?" he asked.

"Huckleberry brandy."

"Where'd you get huckleberries?"

"They grow everywhere."

"In December?"

"You are so silly. I made it in September."

He looked at the bottle and his eyes returned to hers. "I ... I can't remember anyone ever making me a gift," he stammered. He looked down at her and softly said, "Thank you."

She thought it was the Christmas spirit taking hold of her heart, but she was willing to accept he might be capable of tender feelings. She took his arm and said, "Now we can go in."

He led her to a room off the huge hall. "I have something for you," he said handing her a small box. Aislynn opened immediately. It held two silver combs. "I can't accept these."

"Yes, you can. I'm giving one to each lady as a party favor. Not even Tim's sensibilities could be offended if it's a collective gesture."

"You're giving me two."

"You're earning it. Now, run upstairs. There's a bedroom to the left, at the end of the hall, with a full-length mirror. You can put in the combs."

Aislynn looked at the beautiful combs in her hand. She wavered. She wanted to wear them among these women who were so grandly decked, but she considered Tim's reaction.

Moran convinced her, "I'll explain it to Tim and Johnny." With his hands on her shoulders, he turned her about and pushed her to the door. "Now get going. I have guests to attend to and so do you." He held her for a second and whispered close to her ear, "By the way, there's a box on the bed. It's a jacket for my goddaughter. You might try it on. I'm sure she wouldn't mind you wearing it tonight."

Aislynn wheeled around and faced him. A sheepish smile spread across his mouth. Aislynn bit her lip and giggled. She became a willing conspirator. "Thank you."

The bedroom was twice the size of her cabin. In the center of the room, a huge oak bed stood flanked by nightstands and plush chairs. Against an interior wall, a gentleman's dresser with full mirror sat adjacent to a massive armoire competing with the bed for dominance of the space. A corner room, it had two exterior walls with large windows staring out into the night.

Standing before the mirror, Aislynn donned the jacket. It was bright green velvet with silver braiding running along its hems, collar and cuffs. Little silver stars, crescent moons and suns were randomly embroidered and shiny silver buttons held it closed. It covered her worn shirtwaist and the frayed waistband of her black skirt. She stuck the combs in her hair and twirled before the mirror, thinking of Cinderella. Laughing out loud, she imagined Moran's response to her fantasy of him as a fairy godmother.

Aislynn took her place opposite Moran, who sat at the head of a long table. Looking down at the array of silverware, a feeling of panic began to rise in her. She remembered her job-seeking experience in New York City and her inability to identify the purpose assigned to each piece. As the first course was being served, she searched for guidance. Moran held a small fork over his place as he waited for his meal. Aislynn found its match, waved it at him, smiling. She asked the guests around her to introduce themselves. With her questions about their origins and professions, the conversation flowed. Attempting to give the impression of wealth, she spoke about her business and her land.

She steered the discussion to the railroad spur Brigham Young wanted to build from Ogden to Salt Lake. Aislynn explained she and her people were fully invested in the territory and giving their complete support to the railroads.

After the meal, the women gathered by the couches for coffee and tea while the men remained at the tables with cigars and brandy. Aislynn attempted to keep everyone involved in the conversation by introducing women and talking about common bonds they might share. When she brought up the subject of children, she discovered some of Moran's female guests were not married to the men who escorted them. They had arrangements Aislynn could only speculate. She shifted the conversation to books and plays she had read, attempting to diffuse the awkwardness. She quickly had them all debating the greatest love story. Aislynn found she could extend this discussion by suggesting additional titles until the men arrived.

Music began to play and the chairs were pushed aside. Aislynn abandoned her job and sought out Tim and Johnny. She waltzed with Tim, reeled with No Nose and Johnny insisted she step dance with him. It was nearly 4:00 A.M. when Mrs. Frank pleaded for her bed.

As Moran bid her friends goodnight, Aislynn slipped up the stairs and returned the jacket to its cardboard home. She pulled her coat closed and stepped down the stairs, half expecting the see the sleigh transforming into a pumpkin. Tim and Johnny were waiting with Moran. He bowed. His voice was hushed, "You did a fine job. I believe we've sold a great deal of stock tonight."

Aislynn curtsied and said, "Happy Christmas."

While Tim took her hand, Moran swung his arm around Johnny. "She's quite a saleswoman. I'd like to borrow her again sometime."

Johnny grinned, "That's up to her; Aislynn makes her own choices."

"You two seem to get her to do what you want."

Johnny nodded and started down the stairs, "She loves us."

Chapter 20

Aislynn's eighteenth birthday celebration was small, with only her closest friends attending. It was an exciting occasion. Although it marked the end of Tim's guardianship, she liked the idea of being officially independent.

Her gifts were varied. Each one touched her with its special meaning. Tim gave her a brooch with a tiny, but genuine pearl. He said it reminded him of "their ocean." Johnny gave her gold earrings he had Moran purchase in San Francisco. With Johnny's assistance, No Nose had fashioned a silver cross for a necklace.

Moran's gift was an offer to take her, Johnny, and Tim to a concert at the Mormon Tabernacle. It had a choir in residence that Moran claimed was world-renowned. Aislynn had not seen Salt Lake City. When she considered the offer, she realized she had not ventured farther than Ogden in nearly a year. The affair was to be formal, and

Tim and Johnny balked at the expense of purchasing appropriate clothes. Murphy noticed Aislynn's disappointment and suggested she could attend with Moran and himself as chaperones.

Tim asked, "What will you wear?"

"I'm coming out of mourning, and I am having a fancy dress made for the Golden Spike Celebration. I could hurry along Madame Dijon, the dressmaker."

"We'll talk about it," Tim concluded, throwing his glance toward Johnny.

Aislynn surveyed the exchange of looks and asserted, "I can make my own decisions."

Johnny and Tim sent her twin blank stares. Aislynn did not know if they had discussed the transfer of power or if it were one more of those unspoken pacts men make between themselves that are not always shared with women. Nevertheless, the hand-over had been made, and it was clear she was expected to discuss her plans with Johnny. *Fine, it's easier to get my way with Johnny than with Tim.*

Salt Lake City sat like an oasis in the desert. Its wide streets were lined with the winter skeletons of full-grown trees. The white houses were clean and fenced. Brother Brigham's vision of a glorious city was being carved out of the Utah sand and stone.

The hotel stood five stories high. The lobby was a huge atrium rising to a colorful stained glass window in the roof. Brass railings trimmed the balconies that tiered down the four top floors. A massive, oak reception desk, an oak bar, an enormous, marble fireplace and the brass-railed staircase formed a circle around the lobby.

Moran sent Aislynn straight to her room with instructions to rest for an hour. "At four," he explained, "a maid will come with your bath and a light supper. Be down in this lobby by six."

She sprang up the stairs, excited by the splendor.

Her room did not disappoint her. It had large windows looking over the street, with plush velvet curtains the color of red wine. A thick carpet stretched across the entire floor. With brass twined into a shiny headboard, the bed rivaled the one standing in Moran's bedroom. A dresser and washstand completed the furnishings. Aislynn fell back on the bed and laughed out loud. The ceiling displayed a painting centered on two naked angels embracing passionately with small, winged cherubs flying happily around them. *Strange place for a painting, but there is just no accounting for taste.*

Aislynn awoke when the maid knocked on the door. Aislynn allowed the girl to lead her through her toilette, assuming she had assisted other ladies and knew how to proceed. The girl worked Aislynn's hair into a style Aislynn had seen in <u>Godey's Ladies Book</u>.

"What beautiful things. It seems almost a sin to cover them," the maid said, opening a box and displaying undergarments Aislynn had not ordered.

Aislynn wondered for a moment if she should just return them to the box, but the girl was pulling the scanty chemise over her head. Aislynn decided she would work something out with Madame Dijon when she returned. Corsetted, stockinged and shoed, Aislynn watched the girl open the largest box. Gently, the maid unfolded a bright green gown. She held it up for Aislynn to see. The dress was nearly the color of her eyes. The taffeta hung long and straight with a bit of gathering in the back. Two straps at the shoulders held up what little there was of the bodice.

Her mouth fell and her heart sank. Dijon had sent the wrong dress. Her mind scrambled for a moment. She had only her worn skirt and shirtwaist. Defeat was evident. "Go tell Mr. Moran I can't go."

"Why?"

"This is not my dress." She tried to contain her disappointed tears.

With two quick raps, Moran swung open the door.

Aislynn grasped at her dressing gown and said, "You can't come in here."

Moran shot her an angry scowl, and growled at her, "What is the trouble?"

His tone compelled her to explain.

Moran reached for the gown and held it up. "It's the gown I had made for you to wear tonight."

"Why?"

"I didn't want a repeat of our Christmas party problem."

"But it's so ..." Aislynn's hands stretched across her chest.

He looked down his nose at her. "I can assure you I know more about fashion than a girl who has spent the last year in a mining camp dressed in mourning."

She looked at the neckline and decided to stand her ground. She leaned toward him and cried, "I'll look like a whore."

His eyes narrowed into blackness. He raised his voice. "Do you think I'd dress you up like a whore and present you to my associates?"

She considered his perspective and shook her head.

He straightened and clenched his teeth as he stared at her for a second. Moran turned away from her and laid the dress on the bed. Calmer, he asked, "Why do you always think the worst of me?"

Chastised, she whispered, "Sorry."

With a frustrated breath, he grumbled, "You have five minutes to wiggle into that dress or I'll be back to stuff you into it myself."

Aislynn descended the stairs and found Murphy and Moran lounging at a table in the lobby having drinks. Murphy stood and exclaimed that Aislynn was the most beautiful girl west of the Mississippi.

"Are you saying there's a better looking girl in the east?" she demanded. With a sly smile, her eyes raked Murphy. "You are quite stunning yourself."

Moran stood and frowned, "You can fawn over each other in the carriage. I don't like to be late."

The Tabernacle glowed under huge chandeliers. Two wide aisles, radiating from the huge stage stretching across the front of the vast room, separated long rows of wooden pews. Murphy slid into a pew and Aislynn followed with Moran pushing in next to her. The Tabernacle was an enormous building with a white, barrel-vaulted ceiling, reminiscent the morning sky on the prairie. As God woke all the wondrous noises of nature, here, under this canopy, in this man-made shrine to sound, Aislynn listened to humans creating their own version of heavenly music. The mighty voices nearly pressed the air from the room. She could feel their strength penetrating her body, swelling her with emotion, and nearly bringing her to tears. She had never heard such sounds. They aroused feelings she thought might be indecent to experience in public. Between songs, Moran leaned close and whispered pieces of information to her, "It took railroad engineering to support the great ceiling." "The acoustics in this building are so perfect, you can whisper in the front and be heard in the back." "All the choir members are Mormons and they practice and perform voluntarily."

After the performance, they stood in the aisle while Moran presented her to a number of men. Murphy found an old friend and asked Aislynn if she would mind his absence at the dinner. Aislynn told him not to worry as she climbed into the carriage.

The leather seat felt stiff and cold through the thin fabric of her gown. The wrap Moran provided was velvet lined with taffeta, no barrier against the frigid March night air. She hugged herself and sank into the corner of the dimly lit coach. Moran sat opposite, studying her with a satisfied grin. His stare made her stomach flutter. Despite the chilly carriage, Aislynn began to feel uncomfortably warm. It annoyed her he could cause such discomposure with a look. She reminded herself to breathe naturally. Although she attempted to stare him down, she was sure she knew how a mouse felt being watched by a cat. Exasperated, she asked, "What is it?"

"What?"

"You seem awfully pleased with yourself."

"I am." He lounged against his seat, still smiling at her.

"Are you going to tell me why?"

"Men are very competitive about money, houses, women."

"Am I supposed to be flattered?"

"In this situation, your opinion is irrelevant."

"I don't believe they would be very impressed if they knew our situation," she teased.

He laughed, "Let's save that discussion for later. We're dining with Brigham Young and his favorite wife, Amelia."

"Talk about competition. How many wives does he have?"

"I believe number twenty-seven will be added next month."

Aislynn's mouth fell open.

"Close your mouth and remember, there are some things you don't question. I believe you are going to like Brother Brigham. I have a great deal of respect for him. He's an extraordinary leader, an accomplished administrator and one heck of a businessman. He raised this beautiful city out of the desert."

"Apparently, he's a very busy man," Aislynn giggled.

Young entertained at the Beehive House. It was a sturdy stone structure, solidly built, with a long hall for entertaining and a series of bedrooms for wives and their children tucked discretely behind closed doors.

Moran and Aislynn entered the dark-paneled foyer and were led up the spiraling stairs. She gave her wrap to a young girl sitting inside a window on the landing. Aislynn peered into the window and found several children strewn among the coats, rolling and laughing. "They call it the Fairy Castle Room," Moran explained, "They get to inspect their father's guests and poke fun at us."

Moran handed her up the stairs into a long room elaborately decorated with raspberry-red brocatelle drapes and velvet upholstery. A table for fourteen was set up on the far end, dripping with white linens and lace. At the entrance, a pretty, young woman floating in self-confidence stood next to an older robust man. Amelia looked past Aislynn and said, "Well, Mr. Moran we are so pleased to see you." Moran introduced Aislynn and the young woman surveyed Aislynn as she dipped into a curtsy.

"How nice to make your acquaintance," she said, again smiling past Aislynn, nodding approval to Moran.

Brother Brigham headed the table. Aislynn was seated opposite Moran between a Mormon church elder and a Christian banker. The table conversation centered on the Utah Central Railroad. Aislynn listened with polite detachment until she heard her name.

"Miss Denehy, I understand I should thank you for assisting with my venture."

Aislynn's eyes flew open, seeking an explanation from Moran.

Young continued, "It's not frequent that Gentiles help us and I do not want your kindness to go unrecognized."

Aislynn smiled and nodded, "You're welcome, sir."

"We don't have many friends among your people. Gentiles object to the way we live our lives." Aislynn could feel her stomach tighten anticipating a question she did not want to answer. "What do you think of our institution of multiple marriage?"

Silence fell over the table and her eyes met Moran's. She leaned into Young's view. "Well, sir, under the freedom of religion amendment, I think, as long as it's voluntary and no one gets hurt, you should be allowed to practice your religion as you see fit."

"But your government says it contradicts the laws of

the land," Young challenged her.

"If there is to be separation of church and state, I don't believe they should make rules regulating religions."

The men at the table grinned and nodded. Young pressed her, "Did Moran tell you to say that?"

Aislynn looked at Moran and giggled. "No sir, no one tells me what to say."

Young laughed, "I know a young woman like you." He smiled at Amelia, who sat adoringly at his side.

Amelia asked Aislynn if she were a suffragette.

"I do believe women should have the vote." Aislynn's eyes caught Moran's smirk.

"Oh, you're the young lady who asked for the vote in Moran's camp." Brigham remembered, "Well, I think we'll be extending the vote to women in our Territory."

Brother Roberts added, "Of course, we expect our women to vote as their menfolk direct them, in support of polygyny."

Emboldened, Aislynn asked, "What is the advantage of having the vote if you don't have the right to choose what you're voting for or against?"

"Young lady, women must follow the dictates of men." He paused and frowned at her, "Perhaps that's why you are not married."

"Or, perhaps, I'm looking for a man who is not a dictator," she scoffed.

Young's laugh rolled across the table. "Take heed, Moran. There's a warning there."

Aislynn could feel Moran's eyes but chose to move food around her plate rather than look at him.

The carriage was dark. Either the lamp had been dimmed or the oil consumed. She settled on the cold seat, shivering. Moran lowered himself next to her.

"Cold?" he asked softly. He brought his arm up and draped his cape around her shoulders, drawing her to him. She could feel his warmth through her gown and something close to panic surging through her body.

She strained to focus in the darkness. He found her gloved hand and began to slowly draw circles on her palm with his thumb. Her mouse-like fear had returned and she tried not to tremble. His free hand moved into her hair, and his mouth came down on hers. He felt like a humid day, hot and moist, and she levitated towards his heat. Moran reached under her thighs and lifted her into his lap. While he kissed her, he slowly pushed the broad strap off her shoulder and down her arm; detouring, his hand uncovered her breast. Her mind said, "Pull away," yet her back arched and his mouth followed his wayward hand.

Aislynn felt confused. Ideas and evidence collided in her mind. She stood on a ledge, dizzy with feelings of flying. Unbidden, she remembered Tim and took a step back from the precipice. Behind Tim, Johnny came tripping into her mind. She stiffened. His head rose and she murmured, "Liam, please."

His tongue dove into her open mouth. She could feel it probing in her most private parts. Resisting the temptation to melt into him, she found the hands she had lost in his hair. Pushing him away, she could see his pale eyes were soft. "Please, Liam. Stop."

"No." His moustache brushed her lips, "We're going to be so good together."

Aislynn was puzzled. She did not know what he was proposing. "Together?"

"I want you to be my companion, to live with me, travel with me." Moran was speaking into her neck.

Aislynn straightened, "Companion?" She reached for her strap and pushed it back. "Your whore?" Her words were angry. She tried to move off his lap but his hand held her hips.

"A whore is someone you spend a few hours with and throw a few dollars at. I'm offering you a home, an income.

"Your bed?" she spat back.

He smiled broadly and ran his hand up her side, "That's the best part."

"For you. What if I get pregnant?"

Startled, he joked, "How very direct. There are ways to avoid such an occurrence, but if it happens, we can work something out."

Aislynn was in a fury. She had heard about women who were forced to give up babies and those who lost their lives having abortions. She would have none of that and was rankled by his gall. "Let me go, you snake!" She slapped at him.

He grabbed her hands and she slid off his lap. "If you calm down and think about it, I'm offering you a good deal. You have no idea what you really want. You think you love Tim, and you're being backed into a marriage with Johnny. It's ridiculous. With me, there's no permanent commitment. You can leave whenever you like."

"So can you." She moved into the corner of the coach, crossed her arms over her wounded pride.

"It's better than being trapped in a marriage with no way out."

Aislynn fumed. "What I do is none of your business."

"You can't marry a man you don't love."

"I love Johnny; it's just ... different."

Moran studied her, "Let me ask you something very personal. Do you respond to Johnny that way?"

Aislynn's irritation grew. It rankled her that he would ask such a personal question, but it infuriated her to discover not only could she not trust Moran; she could not trust herself with Moran, and he knew it. Aislynn could feel the answer being revealed on her face.

"I didn't think so. He'll notice, Aislynn. It's a rather important issue for a man." She squirmed in her seat, wishing he would stop talking or disappear. "Even a boundless love like Johnny's can't survive in a frigid climate." There was softness in his voice, but she was not being fooled.

She bit her lip and wrapped her arms tighter around herself. "You're trying to scare me."

Moran shook his head. "No. I will admit I have, shall we say, a very personal interest in your not marrying him, but it's not a scare tactic; it's the truth. You don't want him, and believe me, Aislynn, when you're alone with him and naked, you're not going to be able to hide very much."

His frankness was astounding. A blush burned over her and she was grateful for the lack of light in the carriage. "You don't understand. I do care for him. Oh," she huffed, "it's what my father wanted; it's what Tim wants."

"Good God, are there no limits to what you'll do for Tim?"

Aislynn was furious. She would not make excuses for her devotion to Tim. She decided the interrogation was over. "It took two minutes to get here. Why is it taking so long to return to the hotel?"

"I told him to drive around."

"Oh, you are a skunk. Tell him I want to go back."

"You just have to knock on the front panel."

Aislynn leaned forward and pounded her anger into the carriage until it rocked. Moran took her hand and said calmly, "I believe he's gotten the message."

She fell back into the corner. She was defensive under his stare. "Johnny's a good man. He's kind and considerate and I can trust him."

"Mr. Maher is a wonderful fellow, but the point is you're not in love with him."

Aislynn looked down and replied, "But I can't hurt him."

"You only have one life, Aislynn; don't throw it away."

The coach shuddered to a stop. The light of the hotel spilled into the carriage. Aislynn reached up and repinned her hair. She was straightening her gown when he pushed a stray lock behind her ear. His long, warm fingers stroked her cheek and his eyes repeated his offer.

"Don't," she whispered, moving her head away from

his hand. "Don't ever touch me again."

She started for the door. His arm blocked her. "Let's try to remember our manners."

Aislynn sat back and waited for him to alight. He reached up and held her by the waist as he lowered her to the sidewalk. She bobbed a perfunctory curtsy and said, "Good night, Mr. Moran, and thank you."

"Should I see you in?"

"No, thank you. I can find my own way."

Aislynn gathered her skirt, tilted her head back and balanced her pride on her shoulders as she glided up the stairs.

She was greatly relieved when Moran appeared at breakfast to explain a business necessity would keep him from returning to camp with them. For most of the nine-hour carriage ride back, Aislynn feigned sleep, not in the mood for small talk with Murphy. Her mind jogged between shame and remorse. Although she was not ready for intimacy, she resolved to make more of an effort with Johnny. The carriage rolled up Main Street as the sun was setting and the lamps were being lit. When they reached the smithy, Aislynn peered out the window and screamed for the driver to stop. Her shrill cry woke Murphy who found her clutching the sill, her face white, with terror in her eyes.

Chapter 21

Johnny put his hand on her sagging shoulder, "I'm sorry, Angel. You probably weren't even out of town when No Nose saw the flames."

She studied the destruction of her restaurant with disbelief. It was gone. In its place, lay the pile of burnt timbers and a bitter, damp smell rising from the puddles of black water. "How?" she asked.

"Most likely the chimney. Seemed to spread right across the roof. We saved the cabin and the smithy."

"You think I could salvage my money jar."

"Not out of that mess. I'm sure it's broken and the paper's burned."

Aislynn nodded. She had two hundred dollars left on her loan and she was looking at her dashed opportunity to earn it. She dragged herself home.

"A hundred now and a hundred in April." She paced,

mumbling to the cabin. "I'll sell what stores I can. That will help. But I have to make that money."

Aislynn rose before dawn and began baking. Pasties would earn her the money to pay her debt. The miners liked to take these hardy turnovers down into the mine, and Aislynn believed she could pay off her mortgage with meat pies. She made eighteen and decided seventy-five cents each was a fair price.

Standing on the sidewalk, she hawked her pies. The men walking to the mine already carried their meals with them. A few loyal customers purchased her pies upon leaving the mine but most men passed her by. She met each shift change and at the end of twenty-four hours she had six dollars.

The following day, she lowered her price to fifty cents but business remained slow. She fed her men the leftovers. "For fifty cents, they want to eat in a restaurant. It's the Silver King's fault. They serve the same tired slice of steak and a pile of greasy potatoes at fifty cents and call it a meal," she complained.

"You get too many choices here 'bouts," No Nose explained.

Lying in bed, Aislynn decided that No Nose was right. She could not compete with the bakery, restaurants, saloons and boarding houses. In the darkness, she developed a new plan. With her remaining fresh meat and produce, she made three dozen large pasties. She packed one each for Johnny and Tim and sent them off to work. The remainders were stacked into baking pans.

"No Nose, hitch up the wagon," she ordered.

"What for?"

"We're going to sell our wares."

"Johnny's gonna wanna know where we'd be goin'."

"And what are you going to tell him?"

"I don't know."

"That's the right answer. Now go. Time's a'wasting."

North of camp, on the flat, sage-spotted plain, the

new city of Corrine sprouted to provide various forms of sustenance and entertainment for the Union Pacific railroad workers. The graders had had their stay and now the tracklayers were moving through. The new town was scattered with canvas and board shanties. With the exception of Sewell's two-story hotel, only low buildings grew, supporting large signs advertising their purposes.

Aislynn knew there were three hundred whiskey shops between Promontory Summit and Brigham City. Driving down Corrine's main thoroughfare, she wondered if most sat right here. As they rolled through, she also noticed that the "Silver King" problem persisted in this town. Signs announcing meals for fifty cents stood everywhere.

"Just drive on through," she commanded. "We won't get any takers here."

They rode for nearly an hour. Up in the folds of the frozen hills, "Hell on Wheels" had set up their tents and portable wooden shacks, unfurled their flags advertising every manner of sin for sale and waited for takers on a muddy semblance of a street. The people they encountered seemed dark and dirty. Aislynn could only guess at the nature of their occupations. It was said that these men and women would murder for five dollars and many had.

They rolled through the street under suspicious eyes and the persistent sounds of building. Toward the end of Main Street, they passed a shanty with a woman sitting in the window. She was clad only in a short chemise. As they rolled by, she called to No Nose, "Hey, ol' man, come in and warm up!"

No Nose's eyes bulged, "Did you see that gal? She ain't got clothes on."

"Don't even look at her." Aislynn turned away, but as the wagon veered and bounced over the ruts in the road, she suspected that No Nose was still peeking.

Aislynn knew the UP men were paid three dollars a day. She also knew they were fed plain beef and bread. Sure her pasties would appeal to their Irish stomachs, she pushed No Nose further down the rail to the attenuated work train.

The work train was a modern miracle. It was designed and built to assist in achieving one of the greatest feats of mankind, the Transcontinental Railroad. They passed supply cars, baking and cooking cars. Next came lounge cars where the men ate. Four "sow belly" sleeping cars followed, inside men bunked on three tiers of berths or to escape the stifling interior, they pitched tents on the roofs and slept in the frigid, fresh air. As they neared the head of the train, they came upon a car with a forge for blacksmithing, a flat car with tools and more boxcars bulging with supplies. The train moved forward on the new rail and sustained the thousands of tracklayers, graders, teamsters, timber cutters, bridge builders, carpenters, masons, and clerks. The activity and the hundreds of potential customers excited Aislynn.

As they approached the railhead, freight wagons were pulling alongside the boxcars and men were unloading heavy iron rails, boxes of spikes and bolts. Ahead, like ants on a hill, men swarmed. Aislynn and No Nose watched chaos become precision. A wagon, loaded with rails, pulled up to a group of men. The tracklayers began the process when two workers grabbed a rail and began to slide it off the wagon. Two more men stepped behind and joined the effort, until there was a line of ten, on both sides of the rail, rushing it to the end of the laid line. With a shout from the boss, they dropped the rail into place. The gaugers, spikers and bolters descended and the ring of iron hitting iron resounded through the steady roar of men in motion. They drove four rails a minute into a new era of transportation.

Aislynn and No Nose drove up to a group of men idling on a hill watching the activity. She smiled and offered her pasties. "They're made with fresh meat, carrots, turnips, onions and potatoes."

A man on horseback, charged at them, "What are you

doin'? Get outa the way."

"I'm not in the way."

"You gotta move off, 'fore Ol' Jack Casement sees you."

"I'm just selling some freshly made pasties; would you like to buy one?"

"No, ma'am. You better clear off UP land." The man was agitated and looking around nervously.

Aislynn put her hand on her hip and faced the man and spouted the knowledge she had learned from Moran. "It's not UP land until the tracks are approved and the grant is official."

"Don't give me no lawyerin' talk. You can't do no trading with the UP 'less you got a permit."

"Where do I get one?"

"UP office in Corrine."

"How much?"

"Fifty dollars."

Exasperated, Aislynn grumbled, "If I had that kind of money, I wouldn't be here."

"Well, no permit, no tradin'. 'Sides, can't trade at the work site."

Aislynn noticed a cloud of dust farther up the graded line. "Fine, we'll leave." She directed No Nose to drive west. They rattled away from the angry man. Aislynn waved when they met a group of wagons returning to the work train. "Can I interest you men in some fresh pasties?"

A small man with a full red beard rode ramrod straight astride his horse at the head of the wagons. General Jack Casement, the field boss driving the tracklayers, was dressed in a fur-trimmed coat and a Cossack cap; he aimed his bullwhip at her. He had thousands of men under his thumb and Aislynn in his way. "Young lady, I'm buildin' a railroad, not havin' a tea party. Get away from my men."

"I'm just trying,.."

Short on patience, Casement shouted, "Did you hear

233

me?"

Aislynn cowered, "Yes. Girl can't make a decent living," she mumbled to No Nose.

"You talkin' back?" he challenged.

"You can stop me from trading but you can't stop me from grousing about it. In fact, I'm going to write to the UP and complain."

"Fine. Address your letter to our boss, Dan Casement. He's my brother."

Hindered but not defeated, Aislynn changed direction. Moran had said that the Central Pacific had been grading parallel to the Union Pacific. Congress had failed to specify a meeting place for the two lines and had not set a limit on how far each could build, so both companies continued to press ahead. The UP pushed west and the CP snaked east until the graders were actually passing each other.

"Coolies don't eat pasties." No Nose declared.

"Not every worker on the CP is Chinese. Besides, we can say we know Moran. Bet we'll have no trouble with them."

They cut away from the UP road and rolled north over the hills, through the rocks and sagebrush, hoping to intersect the CP graders. From the top of a rise, they could see the CP, not five hundred yards ahead. As they wheeled toward the line, a blast sent sand, rocks and brush spewing into the clear, cold air. As debris fell, the mules panicked. They bolted across the hill. The tilted terrain and the obstructing rocks and sage caused the wagon to wobble on two wheels before No Nose pulled the frenzied mules to a stop. Their collective injuries included deep abrasions from the reins on No Nose's partial hands and splinters in Aislynn's palms from gripping the wagon seat. The pies were crushed or lost. Under the fading sun and No Nose's admonishments, Aislynn decided it was time to go home.

The lamps were glowing in the cabin when Aislynn

and No Nose pulled up. Tim was waiting with worry and an interrogation.

"Been to Hell," No Nose announced. "Nearly died to tell 'bout it."

Johnny and Tim were visibly shocked. "Where did you go?" Tim demanded.

"Hell on Wheels, just like I said." No Nose described their adventure.

"Good God, Aislynn," Tim's anger flared. "What are you thinking? Will you do anything for two hundred dollars? You could have been raped, killed!"

Aislynn withered under Tim's disapprobation, "I...I..."

Johnny tried to mediate, "She's doin' the best she can with what she has."

Tim continued, "What's next, Stella's?"

If he had slapped her, he could not have hurt her more. She wheeled around, slammed the door behind her and pressed down the sidewalk struggling against the current of Tim's disapproval. Aislynn realized that pleasing Tim had become too difficult, and perhaps, not what she wanted to do anymore.

Aislynn did not know where she was going. She had never wandered down Main Street alone after dark. It dawned on her that she was so tied to the restaurant and her cabin that she rarely went beyond the general store, and when she did, she was accompanied by one of her men. Brash light and vulgar sounds volleyed out of the dingy dens where men sought their pleasures. This was the world that moved outside her life, gritty, nervous and without restraint.

A hand came down on her shoulder. She stopped in terror. "Put this on." Tim shoved her coat at her. "Button it. It's cold." He took her hand and they picked their way through the groups of men and piles of dirty snow. Their walk ended at the bottom of Main Street where a pond had formed from mine water runoff.

Aislynn brushed wet snow off a log and sat down

while Tim threw stones at the skim ice. In the moonlight, Aislynn watched the stones hit the fragile surface and skid away while cracks snapped through the ice. Her father had been wrong, she thought; she had had her own dream. It was a fantastic idea of Tim, imagined by a young girl who wanted security, approval and love. When she was younger, in a different place, she fed her fancy without the interference of reality. It had become a habit. She had not noticed the transformation. Now, her dream drifted and diminished.

"What's happened to us?" she searched.

"You grew up." Tim stopped throwing stones and sat beside her.

"Sorry."

"No, I'm the one who's sorry. I'm still trying to make you into my idea of who you should be and I'm missing the woman you've become. I'm like the parent who wants his child to grow up and move out without leaving home."

Aislynn smiled, "What do we do?"

"Well, we don't get married," he joked. "You just stay the way you are. Johnny always says, 'Just give her time; she always does the right thing.' "

"I guess you can take credit for that."

Tim stood up and looked down at her. "I tried like hell."

"Tim!" Aislynn admonished his bad language.

He picked up a hand full of rocks and started throwing them again. "You know, one day, when you were about six or seven, we were out front and I hit you hard for doing something I thought was wrong. I sent you up to your room bawling. Mr. Rattawitz sat me down on the stoop and asked, 'You trying to hurt her or teach her?' Of course, I said 'Teach her.' But I understood his message. Then, he went on in his way; you remember how he talked." Tim attempted to imitate Rattawitz, " 'Who is the von person in the vorld who makes you angrier than any other?' Well, I knew that answer without thinking. I said,

'Aislynn.' So he asked, 'Do you know vhy?' I shook my head. He said, 'Because you care so very much about her.'" Tim paused for a minute, took his place next to her and swept his arm around her shoulders, "Frankly, I don't think anything is ever going to change that."

Aislynn lay in bed, her mind turning over the events of the day. She heard movement above her. Johnny's distinctive creaking came down the ladder. As the lamp flared up, he called her from her bed.

She rose and found him spreading some papers on the table. "What on earth are you doing?" she queried.

"I want to show you somethin'."

While Aislynn looked at the drawings, Johnny explained, "They're plans for a house."

Her interest piqued; she took the seat across from him and let him describe his vision. The plan showed a first floor with a kitchen, parlor, bedroom and a room for bathing. An incredible three bedrooms covered the second floor.

"We have to have a room for my mother and my sister. I'd like our girls to have a room separate from their brothers." He tapped the drawing of the first floor bedroom, "We should have some privacy."

Aislynn's stomach flipped and her face burned red. Her "Oh" was weak and wavering.

"I know you still have... reservations, but we could get a loan on the smithy and the cabin, and with the money I have saved, we could rebuild the restaurant and put up the house."

Aislynn could not look at him. Outside their pool of light, the cabin seemed to grow darker, the night's stillness louder. Speaking to the paper, she gently expressed her apprehension and hesitance, "Johnny, you know how very fond I am of you."

"Yes, I know." He replied flatly and began rolling up his plans. "Let's go to bed."

She could hear his dwindling patience and felt her own increasing anxiety. "Johnny?" she whined.

"Go to bed. I'll get the lamp."

Aislynn snuggled down into her feather mattress sorting through her confused feelings. She felt sorry for putting him off; however, she was relieved that he had allowed it. In the darkness, she heard him moving about. She pulled the quilt up, but, within seconds, Johnny pulled it down. He climbed onto the cot and stretched out next to her.

Chapter 22

Aislynn recoiled until the wall stopped her retreat. "What are you doing?"

"Goin' to bed."

"Not here," she asserted.

Johnny pulled her close and her hands flew between them, falling on his bare chest. Her entire body jerked away from his nakedness. He whispered, "Aislynn, I want you to put your arms around my neck and kiss me."

"I can't."

"Aislynn," he rested his forehead on hers. "Everyone is afraid of something."

"What could you be afraid of?"

"Wantin' you this much and never bein' able to have you."

She heard his ultimatum. With her "Yes" or "No," she knew their lives were going to change. A barrage of memories assaulted her. She could not sort them; however, they brought recollections of caring and consideration.

Under her hands, she felt the strength of his heart beating and remembered the last time she had touched his bare chest. His heartbeat had been nearly imperceptible. With intense trepidation, she slowly reached her arms around his neck and brushed her lips against his. She could feel the relief pass through him. He rested his head on her arm for a moment. She lay still, hoping he would drift off to sleep.

His hand came up and plucked at the ties of her nightdress. Her eyes strained in the darkness to watch his progress, an unnecessary effort since she knew the exact location of his hand. When his electric fingers slipped into her gown, she jolted from the shock.

"I'm sorry, Angel. My skin's rough." He turned his hand over and stroked her breast with the softer side. Johnny began kissing her and she discovered the desire to kiss him back. His mouth traveled down her neck and replaced his hand, while his hand wandered farther down her body. As he caressed the inside of her thighs, her hips found movement and pressed against him. Aislynn was embarrassed that she seemed to be burrowing under him but had no will to stop. Her world shrank to the size of her cot, a world like a warm river, flowing slowly. She realized Johnny could give her what she needed, and, suddenly, what she needed was what she wanted. Johnny covered her and she blossomed, welcoming him inside.

"Am I too heavy?" he asked.

"No." Aislynn was astonished by the truth.

Johnny started to move off her but she held him, "No."

"I'll hold you, Aislynn, but I don't want to hurt you." He pulled her onto his chest and surrounded her with his arms. Aislynn buried her face in his flesh and burst into tears. She cried for what she had gained and for what she had lost, for what she left behind and for what lay ahead.

She sat up and wiped her eyes with the back of her hand. "I do love you," she sniffed.

He chuckled, "I've always known that."

She pushed him, "How? I just realized it."

"Aislynn, you didn't say it, but you showed me."

Bewildered, she asked, "I did?"

He put an arm under his head and began, "Let's see, at dances, did you ever dance with anyone besides me or a Nolan?"

"No one else asked."

"That's because you said yes to me so quickly."

"Because you wouldn't allow it."

Ignoring her, he continued, "Did you write to any other non-Nolans during the war?"

"I had other things to do," she countered.

Johnny laughed, "And when you saw me on the street with my boys what would you always say?"

Aislynn was becoming annoyed with his conceit, "How should I remember?"

"You'd say, 'Johnny Maher, are you goin' to help me with these bundles?' and my boys would say, 'You're in, Johnny.' Sure enough, you'd ask me up to your flat so we could be alone."

"I never intended such a thing, I was being polite."

"And when we got here, you bought property for us. You don't get more tied to a man than that."

Aislynn threw her head back, "You are far too sure of yourself."

"You think so?" He pulled her down and leaned over her, "Well, tell me this, Aislynn Denehy, who are you lyin' with, makin' love to?"

"I, Aislynn Denehy, do solemnly swear," Ogden's short, balding justice of the peace, with stains on his shirt and beer on his breath, read the words for Aislynn to repeat. Aislynn smiled at Tim. It seemed right he should be giving her away. He had held her heart her whole life.

241

"...to love, honor and obey."

Aislynn stopped after honor. She exchanged glances with Johnny and Tim while No Nose laughed, "That won't happen."

Johnny asked the justice, "Does she have to say obey?"

"She's gonna be your wife ain't she?"

Johnny nodded.

"Then she oughta obey you."

"I'll be happy if she loves and honors me."

The justice insisted, "It's in the book."

"Well, if I don't mind, neither should you." Johnny closed the book and said, "I now pronounce us husband and wife." He pushed the Claddagh ring onto her finger with the heart pointing towards hers and kissed her hard and long.

Seated at the Western Union office, Aislynn struggled with the idea of taking another loan but she needed the restaurant and they needed a home. They mortgaged their collective property and Johnny assured her they would be debt-free in a year. It did not take long to find builders. Grading had slowed on the UP line and laid-off railroad workers were drifting into camp looking for labor. In ten days, they had the ruins of the old restaurant cleared away and new, mail ordered building slapped into place. Work on the house commenced as quickly.

With Tim and No Nose bunking in the loft of the blacksmith shop, Aislynn and Johnny passed their evenings alone in the cabin studying wishbooks. Johnny's only request was for a big bed. Aislynn selected their other necessities with frugality.

On April 10th, amid the smell of fresh paint and new upholstery, they moved into their new home. With the exception of Liam Moran, all their close friends helped them celebrate their housewarming. Moran was in Washington, DC where Congress came to a decision on the Transcontinental Railroad. It was resolved that the common terminus would be at Ogden, Utah and the rails would join at Promontory Point. Moran's wager was won.

In four short years, one of man's greatest engineering achievements, a solid testament to American ingenuity and imagination, had been completed. On May 10th, 1869, the entire nation held its breath waiting for the final hammer to push the "Golden Spike" through the last rail and strike the telegraph wire silently waiting deep in the last tie. Contact sent the message "Done" coast-to-coast triggering celebrations in San Francisco, New York, Washington and hundreds of towns in between. Ogden dressed for the occasion and joined the hurrah with band concerts, a fair and a dance.

With mourning behind her, Aislynn enjoyed the fair in a new yellow dress and a wide-brimmed, straw hat streaming yellow ribbons. Aislynn, Johnny, Tim, and No Nose wandered through the fair gawking at tall men, fat ladies, palm readers and snake charmers. They listened to hurdy-gurdy and hawkers, ate rock candy and popped corn. While the band concert commenced, they shared the dinner Aislynn had packed. When darkness beat down the sun, torches lining the dance floor were lit. Aislynn granted each of her escorts a dance.

No Nose and Aislynn waltzed back to Johnny and Tim just as Liam Moran approached. She felt her composure slip and her color rise. He greeted each man with a slight bow and extended his hand to Johnny, "Congratulations, I've been informed of your marriage. You must be very happy."

Johnny beamed at Aislynn, "Yes, sir."

As he turned and bowed to her, Aislynn's stomach churned. She had forgiven herself for her lapse of propriety in Salt Lake City, blaming his sophistication and treachery. Yet face-to-face with him, twinges of shame and guilt returned. "Mrs. Maher," he said, "my best wishes."

Aislynn mumbled a thank you.

He returned to Johnny, while the band struck up another waltz. "Perhaps, your bride would honor me with a dance?"

"That's up to her," Johnny shrugged. "She still tends to do what she wants."

Strengthened by Johnny's confidence, she consented. Moran offered his arm and led her into the middle of the crowd. They faced each other. He pulled her to him, staring down at her as the music moved their feet. Aislynn could feel his eyes and tried to push past her discomfort. Her marriage stood between them, protecting her from his indecent intentions. She knew she was a good wife and wanted him to know.

Aislynn offered conversation, "Your railroad is complete."

"Yes," he answered.

"You must be pleased."

"Yes."

Aislynn's anxiety rose. She could feel his condemnation filling the space between them. The crowded dance floor and the loud music made discussion difficult. He danced them to a dark, empty edge of the floor.

Aislynn nervousness became words, "How did you find Washington?"

"Trying, as always."

"Well, I guess we have to learn to take the good with the bad," she mused.

Bending close, the warmth of his breath on her ear raced through her. "You must be an expert on compromise by now, Aislynn, giving yourself to a man for a house and a restaurant."

Anger froze her feet. "That's not why I married him!"

"Do you expect me to believe that after all these years, you've suddenly realized you love him?"

She twisted out of his arm and seethed, "I don't have to explain myself." Wrenching her hand from his, she snarled, "I only have to answer to one man, and that man isn't you!"

Stomping away she heard him shout, "He isn't Tim Nolan, either."

Chapter 23

After Aislynn's breakfast customers had left the restaurant, she headed out the back door. The Golden Spike celebration left her tired and her legs aching. As she passed the woodpile, she heard mewling, "Missus Maher? Missus?"

Startled, Aislynn searched behind the logs and found a young girl. As quickly as the girl's dark skin and coarse hair registered her as a Negro, her dress told Aislynn she was a whore. The girl crawled into the light. Aislynn's eyes were drawn to a fresh gash across the whore's neck, still moist and red although the stream of blood on her dress was dry and brown.

"Good Lord!" Aislynn clapped her hands over her breasts. She struggled for an appropriate response. Her sensibilities were shaken, but her sympathy was stirred. "Come in the house; we'll clean your wound."

Aislynn sat the girl on a kitchen chair and started to heat water. The whimpering girl introduced herself as Carrie. She spun out her seventeen-year-old life. She had been a plantation slave until a man purchased her and put her to work on the road. She turned tricks under his command from Georgia to Denver. When her pimp was shot dead, she ran. Stella gave her work but Carrie sniffled, "Miners be a rough lot. Last night, one cut me bad. I had to get."

The ruffled neckline of Carrie's dress interfered with Aislynn's attempt to clean the wound. Carrie pulled down her dress, exposing herself, and causing Aislynn to gasp. Raised scars burned round by cigars marred the girl's black skin. She had purple remnants of human bites and dark souvenirs of slashes on her breasts, shoulders and back. Aislynn filled the bath. Carrie soaked herself clean and washed away her former profession.

Aislynn was ready to close up when Moran, Jeb and Buck blew into the restaurant, covered in trail dust and worry. They took seats with her fellows and she brought them the remnants of the night's offerings. Jeb, silent as always, dove right into his meal, but Moran and Buck explained their frustration.

"She be gone or dead. Can't find her nor any trace of her nowheres," Buck offered.

"I'm going to have a real problem if another woman is dead." Moran added.

Aislynn's curiosity was piqued, "Who's dead?"

"Carrie, one of Stella's whores." Johnny explained.

"She's not dead; she's asleep," Aislynn stated.

The men were astonished. Even Jeb emitted words of surprise.

Tim spoke up, "Aislynn, Mr. Moran has been looking for that girl all day."

"Well, no one asked me about her."

"You don't even look at the whores." Tim explained.

Aislynn shrugged, "She's not a whore any more. She's my... assistant." She nodded at No Nose, "You can help in the smithy, Carrie's going to replace you here." Starting for the door, she called, "You can lock up. I'm tired and I'm going home." She looked over her shoulder at Johnny. Wide-eyed and expectant, she invited him to bed asking, "Are you coming with me?"

Moran heard her proposition and chagrin raced across his face. As he spoke up, Aislynn could hear his disbelief. "Johnny, would you mind if I walked your wife home? I'd like to have a word."

Aislynn could hear Johnny's irritation. "It's up to her. After all, it seems she's making all the decisions now."

With a few long strides, Moran reached her. The pout she sent to Johnny fell into a frown for Moran. He opened the door and she passed before him. Outside, he said, "You're full of surprises, aren't you?" His eyes raked her. "I should have known you'd ... adjust to certain aspects of marriage."

"What do you want?" Aislynn burned. She had expected this reprisal and chose not to dignify it.

Following her across the yard, he started in his superior tone, "She's going back to Stella's."

"Why, so next time they can kill her?" she challenged.

"Don't be so dramatic. It's her job."

"It's not." She halted abruptly. "I...I know what she's suppose to be doing," she looked down at the ground and twisted the toe of her shoe in the dirt. "She said she can bear the, you know, but they torture her."

Moran huffed, "Some men are pigs."

"It's not right. There should be rules, some kind of protection."

Moran chuckled, "There are rules; the first one is- when a man's paying, he does what he wants."

Aislynn was determined to make her point. "I don't pretend to know a great deal about this, but it seems there should be limits."

Frustrated, Moran explained, "These men don't want limits. That's why many of them came west in the first place."

"Mr. Moran, I have rules and the men follow them just fine."

"Aislynn, Stella's is not a restaurant." She could hear the condescension in his voice and it angered her.

She looked up at him and declared, "Liam, she's a human being. She has a right not to be burned or bitten or sliced or scarred." She could hear herself becoming shrill, "You go tell Stella that Carrie is not coming back." She marched up the front steps and put the key in the door.

She heard him kick the dirt and stomp up behind her.

As Aislynn stepped inside, he called, "Don't shut me out!"

She slammed the door behind her. It flew open and crashed against the wall. She backed into the hall and inhaled, "I didn't ask you in."

An over-wound spring, he seemed ready to snap. "Too late," his breath came short and hard. Aislynn stood her ground. He hovered over her, and she could feel his heat as he hissed, "I want that girl."

For an instant, she thought she saw into him, into a place where he kept his secrets, his pain. He caught her looking, and anger flared in his eyes. She lifted her face up to his and shook her head. She whispered. "You can't have her."

"Aislynn," he shouted in a voice that pushed her back two steps, "she owes money and she's going back."

"So, it's money you want, Mr. Moran." Aislynn wheeled around, opened the closet door and stooped. Out of the dark, quiet space, she produced a glass jar full of coins and a few greenbacks. She held the jar out at arm's length, "Here, Liam, the most important thing in the world."

Her eyes never left his as he raised his hand and swept it before her. The jar shattered against the wall. Coins flew, clattering to the floor, rolling, and entwining them in invisible circles until they lay exhausted.

Chapter 24

Aislynn stood at the front door of the restaurant watching the rain fall in long, shiny strings against the window. People on the sidewalk passed like soggy specters. Carrie was helping Mrs. Spittlehouse care for three chicken-poxed children. With No Nose helping Johnny, Aislynn found herself alone and lonely. Anxiety had risen with her that morning, and the longer she idled, the stronger it grew.

She pulled her thin scarf over her head and ran across the yard to the smithy. Aislynn rarely visited the blacksmith shop. It was a place for dirt, animals and sweaty men. She stood inside the open, barn doors and watched Johnny. He was standing before the fire pounding a piece of glowing iron. His broad back faced her. Through his shirt, she could see the waves of his muscles roll as he raised his mallet and brought it ringing down on the metal. The concussion made his arm tremble and sent drops of sweat showering off the strands of his hair. Aislynn's eyes traveled down to his thick legs. She felt herself blush as she recalled those legs pressing on hers.

Johnny must have felt her eyes. He turned and sent her a quick grin. The beauty of his eyes and the sweetness in his smile struck her heart. His gaze did not bring her the flash of heat Moran's could, but Aislynn now knew the value of a slow steady flame.

Johnny laid down his work and walked toward her. "What brings you here?" he asked, wiping his hands on his pants. Shyness grabbed her. Now that she was with him; she was not sure what she was going to do. She bit her lip and stared down at the dirt.

Johnny cocked his head, trying to catch her gaze. He held her hips and pulled her close for a kiss. She reached for his mouth with hers and ran her tongue over his lips. Johnny's head jerked back and he gave her a startled look. She spread her hands over his chest and pressed her pelvis forward. A soft moan rose from his throat. He turned to No Nose and announced he would be back in awhile.

They rushed into the kitchen. Johnny stopped at the sink and pumped some water over his face and his hands while Aislynn pulled his shirt out of his pants, and over his head. She led him into their room and told him to sit on the edge of the bed. She knelt down and pulled off his boots. When she stood up, he started to urge her down. Aislynn pushed his hands away and said, "You just watch."

A smile burst across his face, "I can do that."

Standing between his legs, Aislynn slowly undressed, letting each layer of clothing fall to the floor. She reached up, pulled the combs from her hair and shook it loose. Johnny leaned toward her, but she pushed him down on the bed. "You have to wait," she said kneeling next to him.

Johnny had always taken the lead. "For what?"

"Just wait."

Aislynn started to kiss his mouth and worked her way down his chest and over his belly. Her hair swept him as she moved. When she came to his pants, she hesitated. She unbuttoned the fly and pushed his pants open, however, she discovered a dilemma. She had rarely looked at him and had never actually touched him. Rocking back on her heels, she faced him. "I don't know what I'm supposed to do now."

Johnny laughed and pulled her down on the bed, "I do."

While Aislynn studied her ledger and calendar, Johnny started to clear off the table occupied by Murphy and No Nose.

"Johnny Maher, you doin' women's work?" No Nose chided.

"I'd eat your socks if it would get me home in bed with my wife sooner," he answered.

Aislynn's eyes flew open. "Johnny!"

He approached her and she whispered, "Must you let them know."

"Aislynn, they know. It wouldn't be natural if we weren't."

"But... it's private."

"I'm sorry, Angel. But I do want to get home. It's our last night alone."

Tim had gone to Ogden to meet the morning train bringing the Mahers and Emma to Utah. The house stood empty and quiet as Aislynn and Johnny bustled into the kitchen. He started to pull off her apron as soon as the door clicked shut. They left a trail of clothes as they kissed and groped their way through the hall, the parlor and into the bedroom.

Lying in the afterglow, Aislynn mused that at times, it was hard for her to know where he ended and she began. She had always thought there would be parts of herself she would to keep for herself, but now, it seemed Johnny asked for so little, she wanted to give him everything.

Resting on Johnny's chest, she propped her chin on her hands. "I have something to tell you."

"I know," he smiled.

"How is it you know everything?"

"Well, first off, you haven't bled since March and second, I can feel your body changin'. Lastly, I don't believe we could have worked harder at it unless we gave up our jobs," he laughed.

"Well, I knew you'd be happy."

Johnny's tone turned somber. He petted her hair, "Aren't you?"

"Yes, I'm just a little scared."

"We'll be fine, Angel. It's the greatest thing that can happen. Babies bind us eternally. They make our love last forever."

She bent forward and kissed his chest. "I do love you."

"I know that, too."

While Johnny slept, Aislynn thought about their baby. *It is a wonder how our lives have been tied together. There are forces in the universe, strong forces that can align the planets. They direct our destiny, and all we can do is follow.*

Sleep settled briefly on Aislynn, when the fire alarm startled them awake. With fires a frequent occurrence in the camp, Johnny jumped into what had become a routine. As he pulled on his pants, Aislynn dragged herself out of bed.

"If you're comin', you have to hurry," he announced.

She pushed her feet into her shoes and searched for her work dress. It had been lost in the kitchen, so it was there she pulled it on.

It was easy to spot the fire, a great glow at the bottom of Main Street. This time it was the boot shop, a wooden building situated hard up against the newspaper office, not fifty feet from Stella's big, new pleasure house. Flames were eating their way through the walls and ceiling, as men doused the adjacent buildings with buckets of water.

The pumper clanged down Main Street from the mine. Hoses were stretched and filled. The shouting of the men competed with the crashing and crackling of the fire. The air filled with smoke and the smell of burning leather.

The fingers of flames stretching out the windows transfixed Aislynn. Johnny was instantly engaged with his brigade, strategizing the best approach. The fire swallowed the roof. As it collapsed, it gushed a great gust of heat. Aislynn screamed.

Johnny's arms rushed around her. In her ear, he suggested she go back to the restaurant and brew some strong coffee. "These men are half asleep or full drunk. It would be a big help."

"Alone?"

"You have your gun?"

Aislynn nodded, the tiny pistol lived in her dress pocket. "But the marauders?" The entire town had heard the tales of havoc laid-off rail workers were causing in Utah. When the Transcontinental Railroad was completed, some ten thousand men were left unemployed in the remote territory. Most had recklessly squandered their pay at "Hell on Wheels." The honest men accepted their circumstances and quietly wandered away. The miscreants were scouring Utah: stealing, raping and murdering.

"They aren't in our area," Johnny said.

"I want to stay with you."

"I have a fire to fight. Now show these men what a good, lovin' wife you are." He lifted her chin and kissed her mouth. Patting her behind, Johnny turned her up the street.

Aislynn's anxiety flared. She tore up the boardwalk. Her eyes strafed the street and alleys, while her ears strained for unfamiliar sounds. Her pace increased as she passed through the dark spaces between the lighted buildings. When she reached the restaurant, she unlocked the door. Peering into the dimness, she squinted to see if anyone was inside. She reached for a lowered lamp and turned it up. The restaurant appeared empty and safe. Aislynn returned to the door and locked it behind her.

While the stove grew hot and she waited for the coffee to brew, her curiosity brought her to the door. She stepped out on the boardwalk. Above her, the sky was black, but at the end of the street, the orange glow reached into heaven. Flames were shooting up, releasing tiny stars rising gently above the chaos. They floated into the darkness until they extinguished themselves. Like the shooting stars she and Johnny had seen over the Trail, Aislynn wished on these as they had wished on them.

As she watched, one huge ball of light flared up over the camp, sending thousands of big, brilliant cinders skyward. The embers, caught on the waves of heat, danced into the darkness and waltzed toward eternity. She heard a crash, a whoosh and a roar from the crowd. Hypnotized by the fireworks, Aislynn forgot her pots until one sizzled and sputtered, boiling over on the stove.

Aislynn ran to move the pot off the flame. She began collecting her metal mugs and attempted to devise a means to transport everything down the hill. While searching for a large basket, the door creaked open behind her. Instantly, she remembered; she had forgotten to lock it. Her hand dove into her pocket and found the pistol. She cocked the hammer and wrapped her finger around the trigger.

Chapter 25

Aislynn spun around and discovered Moran standing in the doorway. His hair and his beard were singed white and the ruffles running up the front of his shirt were charred black. A sorrowful expression hung on his face.

"Get out!" she yelled across the restaurant.

He reached his arms out to her. His hands were wrapped in bloody handkerchiefs. "Aislynn, I'm so sorry," he uttered with gravity, swallowing hard.

Aislynn screamed, "Get out. You've got nothing to say to me!" Her hands clapped her ears.

He started across the floor, shaking his head. "Aislynn, please."

"No!" Her fear and its attendant shriek came from a dark place she had never touched before. They were not directed at Moran. It was what he had brought in with him. There is a phantom that flies with the banshees. It strangles the throat, pierces the heart and consumes the body with pain that only time and tears can expel. It turned her bones to fluid and she flowed to the floor.

Moran crouched next to her. "I'm sorry," his voice was thick with tears. "There was nothing…" The tragedy lodged in his throat. Each time he reached for her, she cringed and cried out. Rising, he doused the fire with the coffee and returned to Aislynn. She had curled into a small heap; her hands clutched her hair and soft whimpers escaped from her trembling body.

Moran placed a hand on her back, "I'll take you home."

"I have to get him … I have to help him."

"No one can help him. We tried. He rushed in to rescue Bowman, and the roof collapsed."

"You don't know for sure."

"Aislynn," his voice was cracking, "no one could survive that kind of heat and fire. Believe me, we tried."

Aislynn took a long, silent look at his red, raw face. Moran calmed under her scrutiny and continued, "Murphy and No Nose are there. When the fire is out, they'll take care of Johnny; I promise." He pulled her to her feet. "Let me take you home."

Moran took her arm and she blindly followed him home. He turned up a lamp and they stepped over the clothes scattered on the floor as he led her into the parlor. Aislynn took a seat while Moran disappeared into the kitchen. She heard him searching for something but made no attempt to help. When he returned, he handed her a drink. "Take this," he ordered. Without thinking, she swallowed the potion; its bitterness stirred her into reality. There had to be an explanation; she had to find it. "Didn't anyone see the danger?" she demanded. "Why didn't anyone stop him? Who was with him?"

She grilled him until the drug numbed her mind and her body, then she sank into the chair. All the tension holding her body taut and upright snapped, and she collapsed like a marionette.

The first thing Aislynn noticed when she opened her eyes was her throbbing head. She pulled herself up on one elbow and looked out the window. The sun on the window was hard and bright. Through the accumulated dirt and dust, everything she saw was reduced to dark shapes and light spaces. She fell back and turned to Johnny's side. As soon as she realized he was absent, panic hit her heart, but, at the same moment, she heard pots clanging. Hope bolted her into the kitchen. Liam Moran was standing in front of the stove. The shock took her breath.

"I made you some coffee," he offered.

Aislynn stood with her mouth moving and no words escaping. She felt herself swaying.

"Maybe you should sit down," Moran suggested.

Her hand rushed to her mouth, "I think I'm going to be sick." She brushed past him and ran out the back door. Leaning over the porch railing, she vomited. Moran followed her with a damp cloth and a helpful hand.

When she was wiped clean, they entered the parlor to find No Nose and Murphy. After they extended their condolences, Murphy proudly explained the arrangements. "We want him to have a hero's send off. He deserves all the honors, Aislynn; he died in the line of duty. We'll wake him at the Claimjumper tomorrow, and the day after, we'll have a grand funeral."

Aislynn nodded. She listened to the words, but they made little sense. All she could hear was a soft buzzing, like seashells were being held to her ears. She sat in a chair at the front window and watched the street. As she waited, the buzzing grew louder.

When the wagon pulled up, Aislynn rose and stood solid as stone on the front porch. She greeted Mrs. Maher and Kathleen with silent kisses. Murphy and Moran quickly guided them into the house, entreating them to sit so they could better bear the awful news. Trembling, she labored down the steps to Tim. He was unloading the wagon. Without turning around, he grumbled, "Emma couldn't come. She's too frail."

Aislynn stared at his back and made no comment. He turned and faced her, placing a valise on the ground. His eyes scanned hers and terror jumped across the two feet of Utah sunshine separating them. In a voice full of fear, he asked, "What happened?"

Most things in Aislynn's life became truly real when she shared them with Tim. As the buzzing in her ears burst into a roar, she collapsed against his chest and sobbed, "He's dead."

Moran's carriage carried Aislynn, Mrs. Maher, Kathleen, Carrie and a priest, who seemed to materialize from nowhere. He spoke words of comfort that Aislynn did not hear. They followed the fire wagon bearing Johnny's body, strewn with red, white and blue bunting. Standing next to the grave, between No Nose and Tim, Aislynn could hear the distant thumping of the stamp mill out on the flat. It beat steadily, the heart of the camp. It reminded her that her heart, fragile and near collapse, was still beating.

The thudding of shovelfuls of dirt hitting the wooden casket brought her out of herself. She watched the mourners passing by, each taking a turn with the shovel, depositing their own form of condolences before her. Their numbers seemed endless. She could see by the movement of her dim shadow, ticking off the minutes that a great deal of time had passed. *Time is just the space between then and now.* With each second, she knew she moved further away from Johnny, a journey she did not want to make.

The crowd diminished. Most had gone to the Claimjumper to drink Johnny's spirit into the next world. Only Aislynn, Tim, and No Nose remained at the grave. No Nose proudly pushed the iron cross he had wrought into the ground. She gave them a sad smile and sank to her knees. Aislynn rested her cheek on the mound of loose earth and pressed an ear against the silence. In the warmth of the freshly turned soil, she imagined she could feel him. She could hear him in the wind and smell him in the wood smoke drifting down from the camp but all she could see was the dark, damp dirt. Her tears slid off her face, onto the grave and were absorbed quickly. Aislynn hoped they would touch Johnny.

"It's time to go," Tim announced. The Mahers were waiting in the carriage with the priest.

Aislynn looked up at the dark clouds bunching around the summit. "He's going to get wet," she whispered and spread her hands over the soil, making no attempt to rise.

No Nose shrugged as he and Tim exchanged looks. Tim crouched next to her and tried to catch her eyes. "Aislynn?"

She stretched her arms over the grave, her eyes pleading for help.

"We have to go," Tim stated, but she did not budge. He scanned the cemetery and released a heavy sigh. Shaking his head, he unbuttoned his jacket. After he smoothed it over the raised earth, he placed his arm around her shoulders and whispered, "He'll be protected now."

Aislynn nodded. Tim rose and pulled her to her feet. "Take my hand, Aislynn. We're going home."

Aislynn drew the drapes and climbed into her cold bed. Searching for Johnny's scent, she hugged his pillow. She felt like a dark star, with grief pulling her in so tightly, it squeezed everything out of her. For two nights and two days, she lay in the dark. Her mind struggled to find a reason for her loss, but no explanation was apparent, so she waited in the darkness for a sign.

On the third evening of her isolation, Mother Maher broke through. "You've got to eat somethin'."

Aislynn sat up in bed and nibbled on jam and bread. She sipped tea while Mrs. Maher opened the drapes and cracked the window. Aislynn could hear the world beyond her room. She wondered how other lives could go on while hers had stopped.

"The world hasn't ended. It just feels that way to you," Mother Maher said, "Life's still gotta be lived."

Aislynn thought on this for a few minutes. "You're right," she murmured, realizing there was something important she had to do. She rehearsed her words while she dressed. She reached the cabin and knocked softly. Tim called for her to come in. He was lying on the bed, reading a letter. He sat up and said, "It's good to see you."

Aislynn took a deep breath, "You can go home, Tim. You don't have to stay here on my account. I'm going to be fine."

"Aislynn..."

She held up her hand. She was tearblind and choking, but she wanted to deliver her speech. "I want you to live your own life. You should be with Emma." She bit her lip trying to hold in her sobs.

"No, I can't leave you."

"You have to. She can't come here, so you have to go there. Please, Tim. I'm not alone. I have Mother Maher, Kathleen, No Nose and everyone else.

"No."

Aislynn placed her index finger across his lips. "You have been telling me what to do my whole life; now, I'm telling you. Go, Tim. Go now before it's too late." Aislynn choked on her tears, "Love each other while you can, or you'll miss your chance."

Tim wiped his tears. "I do want to go, Aislynn. I'd feel so guilty."

Aislynn took a breath. "Tim, I have enough to feel bad about; don't add to my sorrow by making me feel responsible for keeping you two apart."

Tim held out his hands and pulled her next to him on

the bed. He wrapped his arms around her and she buried her face in his shoulder. With a sigh, he whispered, "I'll go as soon as I can afford the ticket."

Chapter 26

It did not take long for the practical aspects of widowhood to make themselves known. The mortgage payment on the smithy and the cabin, so easily met by Johnny's labors, was difficult to scrape together for June. As July spiraled to an end, Aislynn knew they were in trouble. She had four people depending on her for food, shelter and employment, and she feared losing the very things providing these essentials.

She called them all together to explain the problem. If she were to meet the mortgage, no wages could be paid, and she would understand if anyone wanted to find work elsewhere. Loyalty brought suggestions to increase their collective incomes. No Nose would try to collect the old debts Johnny did not have the heart to press on customers. Mother Maher would attempt to take in washing and ironing, but the influx of Chinese men, laid off by the railroad, drove the prices of these services so low, it was barely worth her effort. Kathleen and Carrie thought they could serve two more tables if they could be added to the restaurant. Aislynn dragged in two old tables knowing the ones they had were not always full.

Tim cornered Aislynn and offered to contribute what she lacked of the July payment. Aislynn had long fed and housed him accepting minimal monthly payments. She knew he sent stipends home to his father and Emma while he tried to save for a ticket home and college. Aislynn had never wanted to hinder his effort. "No, we'll pay it."

"It's just not right. It's time you accepted my fair share." He threatened, "I'll move in with Murphy if you don't."

Aislynn told herself she wanted him to leave, but it broke her heart when she thought he might actually go. He held out his arms and called her into his hug. She rested her head on the shoulder that was always there for her. His strength and constancy held her together; he kept her from falling to pieces in her grief. She thought his presence sheltered her from the interested and curious miners starved for female company. "We'll work this out," he said. "Everything will come in its own time."

"Fine," she acquiesced, "but it's a loan."

Worry, sorrow and fatigue were wearing on Aislynn. Every morning she donned a white, starched smock over her ever-tightening mourning dress and arrived at the restaurant with a forced smile. Days were spent in suspended reality. When grief washed over her, she pretended Johnny was at the smithy, working as always. Failing that, she would go to a place in the deep creases of her mind that was shared with no one. Here, she held the suspicion his death had been a terrible mistake. She spun fantasies she wanted to believe were plausible explanations for his disappearance and would justify his amazing reappearance.

At night, the fingers of darkness crept over the window ledge and strangled her with sadness. For protection, she would wrap herself in one of Johnny's shirts, but the pain clawed at her heart. She would lie in bed, cry herself awake and wonder why she was being punished. Aislynn questioned why so many crude, useless people lived, and Johnny had to die. Sometimes, she would lie very still, waiting for a sign. She reasoned a love as strong as Johnny's could transcend the barrier between life and death. Yet, as she moved further into a life without him, she received no message.

Sorrow subdued Aislynn. She let Carrie and Kathleen serve the customers, while she soldiered at the stoves and the sink. Carrie had caught Buck's attention and Kathleen, a girl who could not hear, attracted the interest of Jeb, a man who did not like to talk. Each night Moran and his men left the girls large gratuities, sometimes worth more than the meal. Aislynn saw it as charity. Although she found it excessive, it was the girls' earnings and she was in no position to condemn acceptance.

When Aislynn couldn't make the August payment, the girls produced nearly one hundred dollars between them. Aislynn accepted the money with gratitude and embarrassment.

"You're spoiling those girls," she reprimanded Moran. She was sitting at a corner table studying her ledgers as he approached.

Moran sat across from her, leaned back in his chair and leveled his eyes at her. "I hear they're not earning anything else."

Distress swam through her, "Are people talking about me?"

"I believe people always talk; it's human nature."

"They shouldn't speak about me or my money."

"It's the lack of it causing discussion."

Her sensibilities offended, Aislynn snapped, "Money should not be discussed."

"You've… spoken to me about money," he smirked.

The memory made Aislynn's eyes widen, "A minor indiscretion."

"Let me help you," he offered.

"How could you suggest such a thing? I do not need anyone's charity." She slammed the book closed.

"It's not charity."

"I have no more collateral."

He bent over the table and whispered, "I'm not asking for anything in return." There was a kindness surfacing in his voice that turned her red. His pity humiliated her.

Aislynn drummed up her dignity. "Thank you," she replied stiffly. "I only have a few more payments, then things will be just fine."

Moran fell back in his chair, "Well, at least take some meat from me. I've got a man coming in from Kentucky. He's a veterinarian who's thinking about raising horses and cattle. I'm having a steer slaughtered; you can have what's left."

"Why aren't you using it?"

"I'll use some, but the steer is big and I can't just kill the part we want to eat."

"I'll pay you for it."

Moran rolled his eyes. "Just take it off my hands. Serve it to your customers and save me the trouble of doing something with it."

Aislynn demurred, "Well, if it will help."

The September sun was still bright, although its strength was diminishing. Aislynn pulled on her Golden Spike bonnet as she settled in the wagon seat next to No Nose. The mules were happy to be out on a jaunt. They seemed proud trotting down Main Street toward Moran's ranch.

No Nose was singing some silly song, glad to have Aislynn alone and trying to bring back her smile. At the mouth of the canyon, the sides of the road were rocky and the understory dense, but from here, the way lay flatter and wider, making the trip easier. Aislynn was just about to join No Nose in a chorus, when two men sprang from the brush into the middle of the narrow lane. The mules balked and came to a stop. The intruders held the harnesses as they crept up to the wagon. The man on No Nose's side gripped a gun while the man facing Aislynn held a hunting knife, its wide blade flashing in the sun. Aislynn and No Nose stiffened, straight and silent in the seat.

"Well, what have we here, Beauty and the Beast?" the gunman asked stepping up on a spoke of the wagon wheel.

The knife wielder looked up at Aislynn. Grabbing the side of the wagon, he hoisted himself up to her level, saying, "Ain't you sweet?"

Aislynn's drew her hand out of her pocket. The first bullet exploded into the gunman's chest. Blood spurted out of his shirt, as he flew backwards. Before her heart took another beat, she turned and shot the knife-holder in the forehead. He gave her a look of surprise before he fell forward. As he slipped down the side of the wagon, his knife sliced Aislynn's left arm and came to rest deep in her thigh.

The mules jolted at the sound of the shots. They tore down the road. No Nose held the reins and struggled for control. Aislynn felt the warm stream of blood running down her arm before the pain seized her. She grabbed No Nose's arm with her right hand and attempted to stay upright. She looked down and noticed her blood billowing into a dark red cloud on her white smock. As she slumped against No Nose, he slashed at the mules with the reins, speeding them toward the ranch. Aislynn's head slipped into his lap. She saw the arch standing in Moran's drive pass over her. In the distance, she could see Moran leaning against the corral fence with two other men. They seemed blurred in the dust. No Nose held her with one hand and called for help as the wagon bounded forward. The dust grew thicker and a cloud hid the sun. Darkness descended while Moran called out her name.

Chapter 27

Aislynn's ears woke first. She listened as the unfamiliar sounds spoke to her. The walls creaked, paper rustled, a lamp hissed and thunder roared. When she opened her eyes, the room was dark, but for a small pool of orange light radiating from behind a large chair. Her vision fell on a solid figure occupying the chair. "Da?" she breathed. "No," she recalled. "Da's gone, Johnny, too." She bolstered her voice, "Tim?" Lightning flashed and engulfed the room in an eerie, white light. The figure moved. Aislynn felt a searing pain in her arm and leg; she moaned.

"Aislynn, are you awake?" it asked.

"Are we in hell?" she ventured.

"No, Utah," it softly chuckled

Aislynn recognized Moran's voice. "Why am I burning?"

"You were wounded very badly." He sat on the bed,

reached an arm around her head and held a cup to her lips. "Try to drink some of this."

The warm drink smelled bitter, but she felt parched. She swallowed a few sips and pulled her head away. Moran lowered her on the pillows while she tried to piece together her whereabouts and the circumstances that brought her here. Thoughts flew at her like snowflakes in a blizzard. She remembered the men, the shots and hoped, if she had murdered, No Nose had returned and hidden the bodies. Panic and nausea rose up through her body. "Oh God," she grabbed Moran's arm, "I need to see Tim."

"What is it?"

"It's something terrible. I have to speak to him."

"About the men?"

She gasped her shock. "You know?"

"Of course. No Nose told us."

"Are … they dead?" She needed to ask but feared the answer.

"Yes," he said flatly.

Aislynn started to cry, "I'll hang."

"Aislynn! Don't give it one moment of thought. You don't hang for a clear case of self-defense. I won't even permit an inquest. It's over." His voice was adamant.

Relief rushed through her. She lay with her thoughts for a moment. Realizing she was not in the clear, she started in a small voice, not wanting those who sit in judgment to hear. "It's a mortal sin to kill. I suppose I'll go to hell now and never see Johnny again." Tears were streaming down her cheeks, and she covered her eyes.

Moran laid his hand on her hair. "Let's believe God isn't as harsh as all that."

He leaned toward her as he slipped his arm behind her again. "Try to drink this. It's a Chinese remedy to fight pain and infection. You were cut up pretty bad. The vet stitched you, but you lost a lot of blood."

Aislynn drank the bitter brew. She quieted for a moment, but her mind still raced. "Do you believe in ghosts?"

He shook his head and scoffed, "No."

"But they might haunt me; I did kill them."

"I've never been haunted."

"Have you ever killed anyone?"

"On occasion," Moran admitted.

"How many occasions?"

"Enough to know there are no such things as ghosts."

Aislynn contemplated his wisdom. "Well, when you go, I think I'd feel better if you left the light burning."

Moran laughed softly and patted her hand, "How about I just sit here while you get some sleep. If any haunts come, I'll chase them away."

The sky was white and the color returning to life when Tim arrived. Her pale face and red-rimmed eyes smiled at the sight of him. He sat on the edge of the bed, holding her hand and murmuring words of comfort.

Shadows outside the wide windows shortened as Tim coaxed her into conversations. He stood at the broad windows looking over the wide valley into yellow hills. Tim was speculating on the size of the Great Salt Lake when a cramp seized Aislynn. She doubled over, squeaking in pain. Within seconds she could feel fluid flowing between her legs. Fear and disbelief strangled her words, "It's the baby."

Tim rushed for help and returned with Moran's housekeeper, Pee Yeh. She clamored into the room laden with towels, string and a knife. A boy carrying two pots of boiling water followed her.

Tim's eyes darted between Aislynn and Pee Yeh, "Should I go?"

Aislynn reached for his hand. He resumed his seat on the edge of the bed. Pee Yeh shooed the boy from the room and pulled the sheets down. Aislynn curled toward her and grabbed her arm, "Please, save my baby," she pleaded.

Silently, Pee Yeh stared at Aislynn and then, at Tim. She looked down at the soaked sheet and quietly went to work. Aislynn gripped Tim's arm until his fingers turned from red to white. With his free hand, he stroked her face with a cool, wet rag. "Everything is going to be fine," he declared. Aislynn gasped, grunted and growled. Tim whispered, "Don't worry, Katherine, it will be fine." A few loud screams, and Aislynn felt the baby pass. Pee Yeh tied the cord and cut it. She grabbed the tiny infant and swaddled it in a clean towel.

Wide-eyed and breathless, Aislynn asked, "Boy or girl?"

"A very tiny boy," Tim's voice brimmed with concern.

Aislynn held her breath and listened to the stillness. She pulled herself up on Tim's arm and begged, "Please, Pee Yeh, don't let him die."

Tears were rising in Pee Yeh's eyes; she shook her head. "Please," Aislynn wailed.

Pee Yeh spun and swept Moran's silver brushes off the dresser with her arm. She gently laid the baby down and bent over him. Aislynn could hear her sucking and spitting, breathing and blowing.

Tim fell to his knees and held Aislynn's hand while he frantically prayed. Aislynn's mind split. She prayed, saying the words, but she watched and listened, willing the baby to live. After a few hour-long minutes, Pee Yeh stood and began wrapping the baby in the towel. Aislynn cried, "No!"

Tim's head snapped up. He jumped to his feet and rushed to Pee Yeh. Grabbing the baby, he dipped his hand in the steaming water and sprinkled it on the baby's head. "I baptize thee in the name of the Father, the Son and the Holy Ghost."

Aislynn tried to crawl to the end of the bed, but her useless arm and leg denied her. "Give him to me."

Tim stiffened and held his terrified breath. He shook

his head.

Aislynn entreated, "Jesus Christ, Tim, please."

Tears streamed down his face. He whispered, afraid to tell her the truth. "He's dead."

Aislynn nodded slowly, "I know."

She took the bundle onto her lap and unwrapped it. She slowly stroked the tiny purple body. "Oh, how I wanted you."

Cramps grabbed Aislynn, and she felt like her body was going to turn inside out again. She handed the baby to Tim, and he started to the door. Pee Yeh rushed to help Aislynn finish the delivery. Aislynn tried to tell Tim she wanted the baby back, but a spasm took her voice, and he disappeared with her son.

The fruitless pain had been endured simply for its cessation. After six months of pregnancy, she had nothing. With the delivery over, she closed her eyes and straightened her legs on the wet bed. She lay bloody, empty and exhausted.

She watched Pee Yeh scramble around her, pulling the sheets and replacing them with clean linens. Pee Yeh washed Aislynn, rebandaged her bleeding wounds and dressed her in one of Moran's clean nightshirts. She left Aislynn staring at the desert, dry and dusty with silvery waves of heat rolling toward the hills. Her eyes lost their focus and the landscaped shifted into a blur.

Tim returned with tea Aislynn now knew was laced with laudanum. He sat on the bed, but she did not stir, her eyes were glued to the window. "I was just remembering the day you took me to the ocean," she murmured, "how it shone in the sun, so brightly I could barely look at its waves." Aislynn inhaled deeply, "You said, 'It's as bright as our futures.' But, it was so overwhelming; I was afraid. When I asked you if there were dragons in it, you said, 'No.'"

Tim took a thick breath, "I'm wrong about a lot of things."

Aislynn did not have a remark. She lay silently as Tim stroked her hair, "Aislynn, someday we'll go see the ocean again, and I bet it looks a whole lot smaller and less scary."

She stared out the window for a moment and with great effort turned her face toward his, "There's not much left that can scare me, Tim."

Chapter 28

When Aislynn opened her eyes the room was dark, and the chair stood empty. Crammed with confusing thoughts and the weight of the laudanum, her head hung heavy. *Everything is gone, nothing's left.* She felt torn in so many places; she decided to bleed to death. Her strong hand picked at the bandage on her arm, but she could not loosen it. With feeble assistance from her injured arm, she tried to untie the wrapping around her leg. *If I could just pull out my stitches.* She struggled, cursing Pee Yeh for her effectiveness.

Her mind whirled. *There has to be something in this room for me to use... Moran's murdered. He must have a gun... I'm sure he does.* She scanned the armoire and the dresser. Her brain blurred. *A knife would do; worked for Romeo, no, Juliet, worked for someone; worked for someone.* She dropped her legs over the side of the bed and tried to rise, but she felt dizzy; her head would not stay erect. She fell back on the bed and slid to the floor. Dragging her limp leg, pulling herself along on her healthy arm, Aislynn attempted to crawl toward the dresser. However, once there, she forgot why she had wanted to reach it. Thoughts seemed to be flying toward her, but they landed briefly and disappeared. She rested her head on the hard floor. While she studied the grains of dirt ground between the floorboards, sleep consumed her.

It was early light when Pee Yeh pushed a tub into the bedroom. "Company come."

Aislynn had been crying for two nights. Other than sharing a few words with Pee Yeh and taking care of bodily necessities, she lay listless and undirected. She had fallen into a dark place where her family of friends had little meaning. She yearned for Johnny and her baby. Yet, with Pee Yeh's words, she remembered those closest to her.

Pee Yeh helped her bathe and shampoo her hair. When Aislynn was dressed in one of Moran's ruffled shirts and back under the covers, Pee Yeh pushed the tub out of the room, leaving the door ajar. Aislynn sat struggling with the matted hair hanging in her face. Armed with one of Moran's hairbrushes, she tried to unsnarl the thick mess with her one usable hand.

"Can I help?" she heard Moran ask from the hall.

Aislynn peered through the dark curtain, "Are you a tonsorial artist?"

"I don't think we need to go to such extremes," he quipped. "Let me try. I don't want your friends to think we aren't taking care of you." He held out his hand for the brush and sat behind her on the bed.

Tear sprang to her eyes, "You've been very kind." She wiped her cheeks, "You have to excuse me, I've been crying a lot."

"You've got plenty to cry about."

"I just don't seem to be able to stop. Pee Yeh says my body is out of balance." Aislynn's wounds throbbed, her breasts swelled on the verge of bursting and her spirit sagged. "I feel like I was at the bottom of the mine without a candle, and just when I thought I was moving toward the light, I fell back into the pit."

Moran tugged at her hair, "I've been thinking for days about something to say, something to make you feel better."

Aislynn sniffed in her tears, "I appreciate that, but there aren't any words. I learned that when Johnny died."

Moran pulled her hair to the back of her head with broad strokes of the brush that stopped abruptly each time it snagged on the tangles. "I've been feeling rather useless."

"Useless? You saved my life, gave me your bed and... I know," she pushed the words out, "you buried the baby. You brought the priest back, too. I thank you for that. I couldn't speak to him last night. I know he wanted to see me, but... I'm afraid I'm questioning my faith."

"That's understandable." Moran gently pulled the brush through her hair and stroked his hand behind it. The rhythm felt soothing and Aislynn's tears stopped flowing. Silence spread between them until Aislynn sighed and her head fell back.

Aislynn felt Moran's breath on her hair. He whispered, "Pee Yeh gave you my soap; you smell like me."

"You don't smell like sandalwood," she declared.

"Should I ask what I smell like?"

"You smell like brandy, cigars and horses."

"Is that good or bad?" he ventured.

Aislynn shrugged, "It's just you."

No Nose, Carrie, the Mahers and Tim crowded into the room. Tentative, at first, they stood stiffly and carefully chose their words. Her feelings for her friends were resurrected at the touch of Tim's hand. As she relaxed back into them, they became boisterous and blatantly attempted to rouse her into good humor. Moran and Pee Yeh pushed a table into the room and spread supper for them. Aislynn sank into her pillows and when she woke, the room was dim and the visit a memory.

Pee Yeh restricted her to bed, insisting Aislynn could not walk until all her wounds stopped bleeding. Three days passed while she and Moran read aloud, played checkers and card games. This was a kind Moran, respectful of her grief, patient with her weeping and considerate of her silent brooding. She appreciated his effort. On the morning Pee Yeh checked her bandages and found them clean, Aislynn begged Moran for a change of scenery.

Moran tenderly carried her to a porch chair and propped her legs on a hassock. Tucking a quilt around her, he ordered, "Stay put. If you need to get up, call me; I'll be in my office." He started toward the door, "If you want anything, call." On his way through the door, he turned and began again, "Aislynn, if you get cold…"

"I know," she set her jaw, "call."

Aislynn was swaddled so tightly she could barely move. As she wiggled her healthy arm free, two wranglers rode up.

"Mornin', Miz Maher. Nice to see you lookin' so well," Dollar Bill announced tipping his hat.

"You're lookin' fine, ma'am." Sam, a young cowboy, was a recent addition to the ranch, and Aislynn had met him briefly at the restaurant. He sent her a perfect smile. As he removed his hat, his long, blond hair fell into his bright blue eyes. He jumped down from his horse and tore a dusty yarrow from beside the porch and brought it to her. Aislynn thanked him and gazed at the flower, with several broken buds hanging limply from its stem. Sam dropped a nod and raced back to his horse. Bill told her to stay put, and they rode on.

The flower's strong smell spoke of its determination. Prolific, yarrows grew in the dry hard soil, pushing up every spring after tons of snow and frigid weather beat them down each autumn. Aislynn inhaled the scent, and the lid that had slammed down on the box of her life cracked open.

In a few moments, the men returned with a fine, muscular horse prancing behind them. " 'Member him?" Dollar Bill asked.

Aislynn studied the proud animal and with doubt guessed, "Cuchulainn?"

"Thas right. Your horse."

"Oh," Aislynn gasped, "he's hardly my horse."

"Well, that's what Mr. Moran said to the Kentucky gent. He said he couldn't sell 'im, cuz he'd promised a special, young lady she could ride 'im."

The disclosure flustered her, and she could feel her cheeks redden. Dollar Bill's eyes darted toward the porch door, and Aislynn could hear Moran's tread come up behind her. "Ain't that right, Mr. Moran?"

Aislynn could feel Moran lean on the back of her chair. "Yes, Bill, that's exactly what I said." Moran turned his attention to Aislynn, "He's turning into a fine horse. I believe we're going to be very pleased with him."

Aislynn could feel the wranglers assessing them. Her stomach fluttered nervously. "I suppose you'll just have to wait and see," she said attempting to sound detached from his "we."

Moran nodded to the cowboys, "Maybe we'll take him to Saratoga next summer."

"To New York?" Sam's eyes grew wide.

"Fine racing there." Moran smiled at the men and explained, "Mrs. Maher's father raced in Saratoga. He was a jockey."

Aislynn wondered how he knew this bit of intimate intelligence and instantly credited it to Tim. Her cheeks burned, guessing the men must think she and Moran talked about traveling to Saratoga together. She noticed the wranglers shifting in their saddles as they exchanged glances.

"We'd best be getting back to work," Sam said with relief. "It was nice to see you, ma'am." They tipped their hats and rode away pulling the thoroughbred behind them.

Moran moved his hand under her chin and lifted her face to his, "If you're tired, I can tell the men not to bother you."

Aislynn bit her lip, wondering if he already had. "No, actually they're a diversion."

Moran shook his head. "You need to rest." He left her on the porch alone.

In the pink evening light, the ranch quieted. Aislynn closed her eyes and listened. From the kitchen, she could hear Pee Yeh preparing dinner. The horses in the corral gave occasional whinnies, and she heard their hooves tamping the sandy soil. At the end of September, Utah could not decide if it was cold or hot. The sun could burn, but the wind could be frigid. This time of day, with the sun yielding, and the breeze beginning to swirl, it was pleasantly cool. The scents of brandy and cigar smoke reached her, and she knew Moran was near. She feigned sleep, listening while his wooden heels softly hit the planked porch. She heard him settle on the rail.

Peeking under her lashes, she found him leaning against a porch post, one leg raised and his foot resting on the railing. He wore a relaxed, contemplative expression, not his usual sharp, searching visage; there was nothing threatening or dangerous about him. Moran was quick to feel her eyes.

"Are you awake?" he asked.

"Yes."

"Why didn't you say something?"

"I was just enjoying the quiet."

"And watching me?"

"You're blocking the view."

Moran pushed a chair against hers and stretched

out, resting his boots on her hassock. "It is a nice view," he agreed.

"You sound surprised."

"I've never sat here before."

Amazed, Aislynn asked, "Isn't this your home?"

"No," he replied, "it's where I stay when I'm in the area, but I built it for business."

Aislynn was shocked with the information. "Where is your home?'

"I guess I don't have one."

Aislynn could not accept the concept, "You must have a home somewhere. Where are your parents?"

"Don't have any."

Aislynn thought he was teasing. "Well, you had to have had them at one time, somewhere."

"No," his tone was hard and serious. He took a long drag on his cigar and looked at her bewildered face. "I never had parents. I was raised by nuns in a foundling home, in Chicago."

Sympathetic, she turned to look in his eyes, "What happened to them?"

"My mother was a whore. She probably didn't know who my father was. She just dropped me there when I was born." Anger rang through his voice.

Aislynn felt pity for him and his mother. She contemplated the situation for a moment and offered, "Maybe she didn't have a choice."

"No choice? Let me ask you Aislynn; what would you have done to keep your child?"

She fell back against her chair as a few tears escaped.

"Sorry, Aislynn. That was very cruel." Turning away, he glanced at the sunset and sipped his brandy. "I'm sorry."

Aislynn had many thoughts but settled on one, "It's not a fair question."

"I know; you weren't given any choices."

"No, you've been poor and alone, Liam, but you've never been poor, alone and a woman. It's different; we don't have the same options."

He turned to her and sighed, "It doesn't matter."

"Maybe you could find her."

He shot her a look of disbelief, "I don't need a mother." There was finality in his voice.

Aislynn frowned at him. She had always wanted her mother, and although she could not believe he was not curious about his own, she left the subject. "When did you leave Chicago?"

Moran gave her a critical half smile. "If you must know..." Aislynn nodded and he continued, "When I was twelve, I was sent to live with a couple in the country. They needed help on their farm. The woman, I grew fond of her, but her husband was violent. He'd beat me regularly. She always promised to make him stop." He shook his head. She watched the muscles in his face grow taut, as his eyes squinted bringing the past into view. "She didn't. I guess if he weren't beating me, he'd have been beating her. In any case, I realized I couldn't trust her either, so I skedaddled. Eventually, I got to the gold fields and I believe my dear friend Mr. Murphy has told everyone the rest."

Aislynn fidgeted for a moment, trying to pry without sounding too bold. "And you never married."

Moran leaned toward her and smiled slyly, "No."

Aislynn raised her chin in the air and looked away from him, "Do you have any children?"

"Mrs. Maher, you are nosey."

Frustrated, she stormed, "Liam, you know everything about me and I know so little about you. It's only fair."

Moran laughed. "Have I ever given you the impression I'm fair?"

Aislynn tried to cajole him. "Yes, well," she reconsidered. "Maybe not, but answer my question anyway."

"Not that I know of." She gave him a confused look.

"Aislynn, I'm a wealthy man. If any woman thought I was the father of her child, she'd be after me for money. To date, no one has approached me for a penny, so I assume the precautions I have taken worked." She bit her lip, dying to know the precautions people could take to avoid pregnancy, but far too inhibited to ask. Moran noticed the question in her eyes and said, "The interview is over."

They sat quietly until Aislynn said, "I'll be well enough to go home soon."

"Aren't you enjoying my company?"

"Yes, I'm surprised to say I am." She raised her brows and added, "But I have to get back to work."

"Can I give you some suggestions on how to ease your financial burdens?"

Aislynn looked into her lap as the color rose to her face.

"Listen, sell the smithy to No Nose. He'll be paying you and you won't have to worry about paying him. Then sell the cabin. Tim can live in the house with you and the other women. God knows no one could find anything immoral about that arrangement. Mother Maher is there to chaperone. Carrie will be marrying Buck soon. I wouldn't be at all surprised if Kathleen and Jeb aren't married before long, either. If Emma does come, you can accommodate them both."

"What could I get for such a tiny cabin?"

"Who knows? Maybe four hundred dollars. Jeb might buy it just to be next door."

Aislynn's mind ran from appreciation that he had given her situation so much consideration, to amazement over his seemingly workable solutions, to frustration that she had not thought of the options herself. "Those are wonderful ideas."

"I have one more. Keep the restaurant open for the midnight shift. Those men want to eat before they go to work, and the men coming off their shift are hungry, too."

"I'd be working until 2:00 AM."

"Yes, but Mrs. Maher could work the morning shift, Kathleen and Carrie could do the evening, and you could cover the late night round."

The sun dipped beneath the hills and the wind churned. Aislynn was considering his proposals when Moran reached for her hand and asked, "Are you cold?"

Aislynn was about to deny the fact, but he growled, "Your hand is freezing; I'm going to take you in."

"Please, Liam, not just yet. Do you realize how long I've been cooped up?" She turned her sad eyes on him.

Moran settled back in his chair, rubbing her hand between his. "Just don't think I'm always going to give in."

He placed her hand on his thigh and covered it, his long fingers reaching over the tips of hers. Aislynn studied his hand for a moment. Hard physical work showed in the lined skin baked brown by the sun, but his nails were clipped and buffed, reflecting the privileged side of his life. It was a confident, forceful hand and it completely engulfed hers. Aislynn thought this contact far too intimate and considered removing her hand when a group of riders cantered up to the porch. Before the four horses came to a halt, Lank was tipping his hat at her, asking how she was feeling.

Aislynn saw his eyes fall like a weight on her concealed hand. She tried to pull it away, while she casually responded, "Thank you for asking. I'm much improved." Moran's grip tightened. Redness rushed to her cheeks, and she attempted to wiggle her fingers and dislodge her hand without causing further embarrassment.

"We jes heard you was up, and we thought we'd pay are respects. Sorry 'bout your troubles, Ma'am."

Aislynn's dilemma was interrupted. His comment reminded her of her loss. Sorrow and vulnerability surfaced. She bit her lip and fought the urge to weep. She nodded at the men, and with a small voice said, "Thank you."

"We'd best be gettin' on. Ga' night, Ma'am." Lank tipped his hat at her and Moran. "Night, sir."

Aislynn trembled, and Moran squeezed her hand. His strength penetrated her weakness, and Aislynn yielded.

Chapter 29

Tim had just stepped out the back door when Aislynn heard a knock at the front. She rushed to answer it and found Moran looking down at her, dripping rain. He stepped over the threshold and hung his hat and coat on the rack.

"I can't socialize; I'm canning," she announced as she limped toward the kitchen.

Moran followed her. "Should you be hobbling on that leg?"

"It's the only way I can get around right now."

"Maybe you shouldn't be standing and canning?" he accused.

"Liam, I run a restaurant; food is essential," she snapped. "Instead of criticizing, you should help me."

"I don't know how."

"A monkey could learn to do this."

Moran's mouth twisted, "A male monkey?"

Scowling, Aislynn pointed a ladle at him. "Just fill the jars with the jam. I'll follow you and seal them with the paraffin."

Moran held his hands up, "Do I get a reward?"

"You are such a child," Aislynn declared. He gave her a questioning look. "Fine." She consented, as she pushed the ladle at him.

"Do I get to choose my reward?"

Aislynn slammed her hands on her hips, "No. Get to work before the jam burns."

The task completed, Aislynn instructed him to sit at the kitchen table. She cut a piece of cake, piled it high with huckleberries and poured thick cream over the top. Patting his head, she said, "You did a good job." She placed the plate before him and took a seat.

Moran studied the cake. He raised his eyes to her. "Cream," he stated as though it were important to him.

"I thought you liked cream?" she wondered.

"I love it." He stared at her for a silent moment.

Aislynn endured his scrutiny without comprehending it. "Eat," she ordered with impatience. "I'll get you some coffee. Are you still wet?"

With her comment, Moran seemed to recollect his purpose. "Slightly. I came here with news. Your cabin has been sold."

"So soon?"

"I told you Jeb would buy it."

"He's going to propose to Kathleen, isn't he?" Aislynn tried to contain her excitement. "She'll say yes. Of course, she has to wait until her mourning is over before they marry."

"Aislynn, no one out here expects women to stay in mourning for a year. Why, widows remarry in a matter of days."

"Well," she conceded, "I suppose it's her choice." Aislynn stiffened, rigid with rules.

"Don't you want to know what you sold it for?" he

teased.

"Oh, yes." She leaned toward him anticipating.

"Four hundred dollars, just like I said."

Aislynn reddened, "That seems like a lot."

"It's fair compared to other properties." Moran pulled the bills from his coat pocket and laid them on the table. "I'm giving him a mortgage, so you can have your full amount right now."

Aislynn leaned away from the cash, wondering if the money changed anything between them.

"It's yours," he assured her. "You can do anything you want with it, even give it away." He threw his hands in the air.

Aislynn was absorbing the significance of four hundred dollars. "There's so much I could do. I could pay off the mortgage. Gosh, in New York, families live for a full year on four hundred dollars. Why it could pay for..." Aislynn's words stopped short. She held her thought to herself. Moran raised his brows and searched her eyes. She continued, "Lots of things."

Rain blurred against the window. Aislynn looked toward the cabin, thinking how clarity is relative. She pulled her shawl against the wet wind and crossed the yard. Her heart beat as loud as her knocking on the door. When Tim appeared, she brushed past him. She threw the money on the table, as if it would hold her down if she did not let it go.

"Where'd that come from?"

"I sold the cabin. You have to leave."

Tim was visibly searching for words.

"It's yours," she declared. "I want you to go home. Use it to get married and pay for college."

"Aislynn! I could never..."

"It's a gift; you have to take it."

"No, never..." he stuttered.

"You have to stop waiting or it will never happen," she

293

insisted.

She watched him shaking his head. "You have debts that come first," he reminded her.

A deep breath moved her forward. "Money doesn't do me any good, it can't stop my pain. Please, Tim, at least one of us can be happy."

His faced flushed red and he shook his head. "I can't leave you alone."

"Tim, please." Tears were spilling over her eyes. "We'll never really be separated, remember? We're a part of each other." She paused, trying to keep her voice from cracking. "Besides, we'll only be time and space apart." She turned toward the door and pretended to be sure. "Go; I want you out of here by tomorrow."

Aislynn stepped out into the night and looked up to the dark, weeping sky. Raindrops hit her face, slid down her neck and into her dress. She stood wondering where to go. The lights in the restaurant burned and the hum of her patrons reached her. The mine engines whirred and music rose from down the street, while No Nose clanged in the smithy. She started toward the warm glow of her house, but she had sunk into the mud. Mired, her movement sent her off balance. Stumbling backwards, she strained her wounded leg. Pain shot through her and stole her breath. Aislynn waited, sure the burning would pass, believing she could get herself home.

Chapter 30

Aislynn decided if she were too busy to think, she would be too busy to hurt. She worked until 2:00 AM and returned to the restaurant to serve customers coming off the 8:00 AM shift. Cooking, cleaning, washing, drying, setting, clearing. Days and nights full of movement that brought her back to where she began.

With Tim gone, she had no hand to hold. She was emotionally drained and detached. It seemed everyone in her circle was drifting away, getting deeper into their own lives. Aislynn stood outside, only entering when necessary.

Letters came with news of Tim's marriage and acceptance to college. Aislynn was pleased and proud, grateful his life was moving forward.

As the undecided autumn gave way to the determined winter, Aislynn was drawn into the preparations for Kathleen's wedding. Trying to embrace the excitement, Aislynn organized the December wedding celebration. She offered her home, cooked and baked. But, when the party began, she hung back, skulking like a kitchen maid, serving food, wiping spills, and clearing plates. Her hands were in a sink full of dishes when she heard a familiar tread behind her.

Moran leaned against the table and crossed his arms. She could feel his disapproval. "I think you enjoy being in mourning," he began.

Aislynn's first reaction was anger, "What do you know?"

"I know you wear it like a sign saying 'stay away.' It keeps you apart from everyone else."

"I do hold it dear; I hold them dear." Her voiced wavered.

"Mrs. Maher holds them dear, but she's not burying herself."

"You don't understand; it's too soon."

"It doesn't matter how long you wait." He bent his head toward hers and added softly, "they cannot come back."

Aislynn pulled her hands out of the sink and watched the water drain through her fingers, "I lose everyone."

Moran touched her arm and nodded toward the parlor, "No, not everyone."

The Christmas spirit settled on the camp, and its energy caught Aislynn. Her finances were growing more secure, and she was appreciating what remained in her life. On her daily walks to the cemetery, she was met with respectful nods and light, formal conversation from the men and the camp's few women. She found herself looking forward to the possibilities of the new year.

Aislynn's family of friends assembled for Christmas dinner. The group expanded to include Murphy, Moran and Kathleen's and Carrie's new husbands. Aislynn prepared an elaborate meal of rib roast, potatoes, pies, cakes and candies. She attempted to keep the tone respectful of their mourning with few decorations and a small, unlit tree. Spirits were consumed, small tokens were exchanged, and the excitement rose. Murphy and No Nose raised their glasses and their voices with competing ditties, causing a great deal of laughter around the crowded table strewn with discarded wrapping paper and the remnants of the meal.

Aislynn suggested the group move into the parlor chairs for coffee and brandy. Once everyone was seated, Buck stood and pulled Carrie to his side. "I got en announcement to make." The room quieted. Everyone listened. Aislynn knew what he was going to say. Her nerves stood at attention.

"Carrie and me be havin' a baby."

The words fell like boulders into Aislynn's empty womb. With a great gasp, her hand flew over her heart. She shocked her guests into stunned silence. Moran jumped out of his seat and held out his hand to Buck, "Congratulations." He turned to Aislynn, "That's fine news, isn't it?"

Moran's narrowed eyes reprimanded her. She found the air to fill her lungs and crossed the room to Carrie. "I'm so happy for you."

"Are you? I don't wanna do nothin' to hurt you."

"Don't be silly. Of course I'm thrilled. It's just what we need around here, a new life."

Carrie hugged Aislynn and softly said, "I'd have nothin' if it weren't for you."

Before turning in, Aislynn stuck her head in the closet and sniffed at Johnny's shirts. They had all taken on the scent of the raw wood. She climbed into the big, cold bed and curled around Johnny's pillow. There was an aching in her belly. *My baby should have been born this month. Now there's no one to center my life around.* She squeezed her eyes against her tears, rested her chin on the pillow, and stroked it for a moment. With a sigh, she placed it on the other side of the bed and rolled away.

On New Year's Eve, Aislynn sent Mrs. Maher and No Nose to Moran's party at the Claimjumper. She closed the restaurant to retire early. Aislynn and 1869 were running down like unwound clocks. She had no strength to stay awake and bid the disappointing year good bye.

In her dark room, she lay reviewing the year in her mind. Despite the tragedies, she tried to recall happy moments. "Remember the smiles," she told herself, but changed her phrasing to, "Try to smile." That was her resolution. She wished she had a photograph of Johnny's smile. Aislynn closed her eyes and tried to see his round face, his grey eyes, and his broken tooth.

Loud rapping on the front door jolted Aislynn from bed. She pushed her feet into slippers and struggled into the sleeves of her robe, rushing in the darkness to answer the call. Throwing the door open, she found Moran, smiling.

"What's wrong?" she implored.

"Nothing." He walked into the parlor and lit a lamp.

Aislynn's anxiety was in full bloom; she insisted, "Is it No Nose?"

"No." He rubbed his hands over the stove. "It's cold in here."

"The fire's been out."

Moran opened the stove door and filled the box with wood. He stuck a friction match and started the kindling burning. He turned to Aislynn and asked, "Get me a brandy, please."

Aislynn studied him for a moment in confusion. She decided it was easier to comply than argue. When she returned, he had removed his coat and was warming himself before the stove. She stood at arm's length and handed him the drink, "Why aren't you at your party?"

"I was bored," he responded.

Disbelief dripped from her words, "So you came

here?"

He nodded, his eyes holding hers as he sipped his brandy.

Apprehension spread across Aislynn. "You can't stay."

"Why not?"

"It's 11:45."

Moran chuckled, "Are you the town-crier?"

"I'm alone; you have to leave."

"I don't want to."

"You've had too much to drink."

"Is that possible?"

"I believe your evidence," she retorted.

Moran stated, "I'm as sober as a judge." He reached for her hand and suggested, "Let's sit down."

Aislynn pulled away. She could feel something between them, something big, important and terrifying. It was growing like a physical being and was blocking her escape. "Liam Moran, all the other men respect my mourning."

His eyes flew open in disbelief. He was incredulous, shaking his head, "No, they don't."

His tone told her she was wrong. The truth hit her. In a world were no single woman was single for long, not one man had approached her since Johnny's death. She suddenly realized women were like land, claimed and owned. *All this time, they've been acknowledging his right not my widowhood.*

He pulled her to him and surrounded her, kissing her hard. Aislynn's body remembered intimacy. She was not sure if it wanted Johnny or Moran, but it wanted to be held. The smell and the taste of him, reminded Aislynn of Salt Lake City. She shoved him, "I won't whore for you."

His grip tightened. Looking down at her, he smiled. "Fine, wife for me."

The first thing Aislynn felt was fear. She wondered if she could survive his intensity. But fear melted into doubt; she did not think she could resist him. He kissed her again. *He's like mountain fever.* At an altitude of 8,000 feet, Aislynn remembered her heart racing, her vision blurring, and her breath shortening. Mountain fever made her dizzy, warm and very weak. She kissed him, realizing he was as inevitable as the sunrise.

Moran's hands moved over her. Aislynn squirmed away, "Liam, wait. I have to think. I'm still in mourning."

He looked to the ceiling and moaned, "Aislynn, no one expects you to mourn for a year."

"It's important to me."

"But it's five more months," he protested. "I feel like I've already waited a lifetime."

"Then five months should be easy." She took his hand and pulled him toward the sofa.

He sat and grabbed her hips, steering her into his lap, "We'll see. In the meantime, I can spark you."

Aislynn sat upright. "Only respectable sparking."

"We'll see about that, too." He wrapped his arms around her. "Let me tell you what I have planned."

Aislynn leaned into his chest and listened. "I'm going to take you to Sacramento, San Francisco, Chicago and Washington."

"And New York?" she interrupted.

"No, you've been there."

"But we could go back and see Tim," she added.

Moran stiffened slightly, "There are too many places we haven't been, like London, Paris, Rome. Why, I thought you might like to see the Pope."

Aislynn was awed as she listened to him describe his many ideas. "Liam," she sat up and put her arms around his neck. "Could we just stay here?"

"Aislynn, you can't expect me to live with Mrs. Maher."

"No, but we could live at the ranch. We could make it into a home."

He pulled his head away and searched her eyes, "You

mean a nest."

Aislynn felt her face redden. He continued, "You want a baby?" He kissed the tip of her nose and spread his hands across her back. "We can make a baby anywhere."

The topic made her entire body blush and her cheeks burn. Aislynn did not want to discuss what needed to be done in order to get what she wanted. The idea of making love with him for the rest of her life was exciting but extremely intimidating. Aislynn looked away from his hungry eyes. "I just thought we would be more comfortable."

"When we know you're pregnant, I'll bring you home. But when you're close to confinement, I'm taking you to San Francisco, to a hospital with good doctors."

For Aislynn, having babies was a private affair and should be done at home, but she understood his concern. Aislynn feared losing another baby more than maintaining her privacy. She nodded and kissed him for his thoughtfulness, "Whatever you want."

Chapter 31

Although they had agreed to keep their intentions secret, Moran made no effort to hide his affection. He appeared nightly when the midnight crowd thinned and greeted her with a touch on her arm, a hand on her shoulder or a pat on her head accompanied by an endearing salutation. As blatant as his overt gestures were, they paled when compared to the excitement in his eyes. At first, his attention embarrassed Aislynn, but he was a potent, insistent force. She was carried along like a leaf in a river current.

Residents of the camp had long speculated Liam Moran was in love with Aislynn and intended to marry her. By Aislynn's birthday, it was common knowledge, information traded in the street. Moran had insisted Aislynn celebrate her birthday with a party at the Claimjumper, where everything would be done for her. With clandestine assistance from Stella, he planned an elaborate affair. Expensive food was prepared, ice was sculpted, champagne was poured, and music played. At the end of the grand evening, Aislynn blew out nineteen candles. Moran raised his glass and wished, "Happy birthday to my darling Aislynn." The guests cheered and sipped their wine as Moran slipped a square-cut, emerald ring on her finger, covering her tiny Claddagh.

Moran commanded Aislynn's total attention. She rarely had a free moment he did not fill. He no longer traveled, not even returning to the ranch at night. He conducted all his business from the mine office and slept at the hotel. Overwhelmed by the intensity of his esteem, she was learning what pleased him and trying to conform. In deference to his sensitivity toward her former intimacies, she began to refrain from references to Johnny and Tim. Her walks to the cemetery were curtailed, only taken when she knew Moran was otherwise engaged. She stopped mentioning the arrival of letters from Tim and did not share the news they contained.

The restaurant was quiet when the boy from the express office trotted in with the telegram. Afraid the missive held bad news, Aislynn braced herself as she read the brief message from Papa Nolan. Her heart filled with grief for Tim when she read Emma had died, but her thoughts turned to Liam. She was afraid to tell him, afraid of his response. Reconsidering, she realized her concern should rest with Tim. She fell into a chair and remembered the shock, the void, the recognition, and the hard-biting pain that could still stop her heart. Aislynn knew the desperation Tim was feeling without Emma.

Aislynn announced to her few patrons she was closing. She put up a sign and went home. She was sorry Mother Maher was asleep; she wanted a companion. She made a cup of tea, crawled into bed and wept for Emma, for Tim, for Johnny, her baby and herself.

With the banging on the door, she remembered

Moran. She could see the concern in his eyes. "Oh, Liam," she sniffed into her handkerchief, "something awful has happened. It's Emma; she passed away."

He gave her a tender hug. "But you can't get yourself so upset about something you can't do anything about. Tim has his family and her family. He's not facing this alone." Aislynn nodded behind her hankie. Liam tried to peek behind her cover, "At least they had five months together."

Liam pulled her close again, but this embrace felt different; it had direction. He asked, "Makes you think about wasting time, doesn't it? Why do we wait for things we want when they're within reach?"

Aislynn struggled with her thoughts while the air seemed to drain from the room. Her breathing became labored, and her heart raced. She wondered if she had to protect herself or please him. She realized that once she gave in, she could not get out. However, if she loved him, should she be asking or acting? Hesitant, she tipped her head back and her lips sought his.

He led her to the bedroom. In seconds, his practiced hands had her robe and her nightgown untied, unbuttoned and in a heap on the floor. Liam lowered her on the bed and began to explore her body. His movements were slow, lingering each time he heard or felt a reaction. It was the most pleasurable agony. He found a place where he could break through her reserve, reveal her rawest emotions and drain her will. She thought she was dissolving into him, yet she opened herself wider. He was searching for a specific signal. When her body shuddered, and she gasped and moaned and called out his name, he answered her.

He slipped off and leaned over her, running his fingers over her lips. In the explosion, Aislynn had scattered. Her breath returned as she was trying to pull herself back into who she was. As ecstasy waned, guilt rose up to replace it. "Liam, we shouldn't have..."

"Regrets, so soon?"

"We aren't married and I wanted to wait."

He said, "Mourning is over," in a manner that told her not to pursue the topic again. "And for all intents and purposes, we are married. Except for a few legal ends to tie up, our relationship is clear and consummated."

Aislynn chewed at her lip as an unsettled feeling stretched over her. She reached up and held his face in her hands, wanting to absorb his certainty. "Aislynn," he whispered, "the payroll is due on Friday. Saturday morning, I'm going to take you to Sacramento and have Father Kelly marry us."

He had meant to reassure her, but the idea of marrying in a church raised a new concern. If she married him in a church, would God make her spend eternity with him instead of Johnny? Aislynn's loyalties were conflicted. With a shiver, she passed from confusion into apprehension.

"My poor darling, are you cold?" Before she could respond, he said, "I'll just have to warm you up again."

His hand brushed her breast and she tried to assess him. "Liam, I am beginning to think you only want me for my body."

He was kissing her neck, his beard scratching her shoulder. "No," his voice was thick and hot, "I want your mind and your heart and your soul and your spirit."

Aislynn wanted to ask, "What does that leave for me?" but he was stealing her breath, taking away her words.

Chapter 32

Aislynn woke when Mother Maher closed the front door. The first thing she felt was Liam's arms holding her and the weight of his leg on hers. She realized his hat and coat were hanging in the front hall, and Mother Maher must have seen them. Her shame escaped in a sigh.

Moran stretched as he lay blinking in the sunlight. He brought his arms back around her, and she could feel his intentions. He made hot, fast love to her. When he rolled off, he took the covers with him. Aislynn yelped, "Liam!'

A soft laugh came from deep in his throat. "I can touch you and kiss you, but I can't look at you?"

Aislynn tried to grab for the blankets, but he held them fast. He bent over her and kissed her belly, "You know Aislynn, we might have that baby sooner than we thought."

She rubbed her hands in his hair and said, "I hope so."

He rose and began dressing. "I want you to go to Ogden today. See Madame Dijon and get yourself some dresses."

Pulling a blanket around her, she replied, "I don't have money for clothes."

"I know, but I do." He started to list the clothes she needed. "Tell her if she can just get you the basics by Saturday morning, I'll pay her double."

Once Aislynn arrived at work, she realized how much needed to be done before she left. She began ordering food, reviewing bills, and teaching the women bookkeeping. She had no time to take the eight-hour round trip ride to Ogden. She knew Liam would be disappointed. As soon as he appeared in the restaurant, she promised she would go the next day. He gave her a disapproving look, but she gave him a public peck and his feathers seemed to unruffle.

Moran assumed Aislynn's nights belonged to him. He walked her home, and he led her straight to the bedroom. Aislynn was a bit hesitant. However, she was easily persuaded and slipped into bed with him.

"When you go to Ogden, I want you to see Jim Flanagan. He's an attorney."

Aislynn, squinting in the morning light, gave him a bewildered look, and he continued, "I think you should turn the restaurant and the house over to Mrs. Maher."

Aislynn's mouth fell open. "Why? They're all I have."

"Aislynn, I'm surprised at you; you're usually so generous."

"Liam, you're asking me to give away everything I've worked for, everything I own."

Moran buttoned his pants and sat next to her on the

bed. He scooped her into his arms, resting her on his knees. "You have no idea how much we have."

"You have…"

"We have; you're part of me, now." He placed a kiss on her cheek. "Darling, you don't realize how much responsibility you have being my wife. You have a ranch to run, a business to learn. You are going to have to know all about my holdings and how to manage them. If anything happens to me, you can't trust other people to protect your interests. You have to do that for yourself and our children. You are not going to have time to come into camp every day."

"You do."

He frowned at her, "Aislynn, you know marriage changes a woman's life far more than a man's. Your time and your attention belong to me, to our marriage and eventually to our family."

Aislynn understood her role and his expectations. "But why do I have to give everything I've worked for to Mother Maher?"

"Because she has nothing."

Selfishness shamed her, but Aislynn wanted to keep her property. She put her arms around his neck and purred, "Liam, can't I just let her run the restaurant?"

He frowned and said, "No. I'll send the mine wagon down for you in an hour." He tipped her off his lap and deposited her playfully on the bed. He rose to leave. "And don't forget to see Madame Dijon."

Aislynn pouted, annoyed by his "No." In the back of her mind, she remembered something, something she had nearly forgotten, something she knew she should not be remembering.

In Ogden, Aislynn met with Jim Flanagan. When she explained what Liam wanted her to do, he asked what Aislynn wanted to do. She searched herself, but she could not answer him.

Madame Dijon was thrilled to see Aislynn. She slipped clothes over Aislynn, pinning and chatting ceaselessly. She had heard of Aislynn's engagement. "Je sais, I knew." Madame said in her affected accent. "I could see eet en hees eyes, I could hear eet en hees voice. When he came last year, for zee green dress, he deed not say zee name, he describe hees girl and I knew. Eet was love. He was hopeful but not sure. I could not eemagine, tres beau, tres reech. Then, vous picked zee boy." She shook her head. "Well, maintenant, vous mend hees heart."

Aislynn was shocked to hear this information. Memories of Salt Lake City assaulted her. Her heart sank as she recalled the past two years. She had met his advances with callousness and cruelty. *Love? I didn't even credit him with feelings.* The conversation made her regretful and ashamed.

Aislynn left the dressmaker's and returned to Mr. Flanagan's. She fell into his empty office chair and dragged the words out, "Draw up the papers to transfer ownership of my property into the name of Mary Maher; I'll be back on Saturday to sign them."

When Aislynn returned to camp, she rode the wagon straight up to the mine office and surprised Liam, who was still working at his desk behind a cloud of smoke. She strode across the floor, threw her arms around his neck and announced, "I did everything you wanted today."

He gave her a broad smile and a quick kiss. "That's my good girl." His expression changed. His eyes grew soft and narrow as his hand moved down her leg, "Now, are you going to do everything I ask tonight?"

"Liam Moran," she put her hands on her hips and shook her head, "are you never satisfied?"

Aislynn had only been in the restaurant for a few moments when the door flew open and the express boy jogged in. Carrie and Kathleen had gone home, and

Aislynn was alone, preparing for her last midnight shift.

"You're popular." He held his hand out for a tip. Aislynn handed him two pennies, but when he offered her the telegram, she hesitated. She could feel the threat. It was there, being shoved at her. Her heart was pounding so hard her hand was shaking. The boy's eyes were wide. "You gotta take it."

Trembling, she lifted her hand. He slapped the paper on her palm, raced out the door, throwing it closed. The bang made her jump. Biting her lip, she opened the telegram. She breathed a sigh of relief as she read it, "Tim in despair. Come home."

Five words for a dollar. A sob broke in her throat. *At least, he's alive.* She folded the paper into a small square and slipped it into her waistband.

Aislynn considered Papa Nolan's request as her customers came and went. Moran breezed in as the restaurant cleared. She was washing the last dishes when the final miner strolled out the door. Liam came up behind her and cupped her breasts. She bolted upright and spun. "Liam! Not in public."

"Let's go someplace private." He handed her a towel.

As they reached the parlor, his arms went around her and the paper at her waist made its presence heard. "What's that?" His eyes were bright, "A surprise?" He was reaching into her waistband.

Aislynn grabbed his hands, "No, Liam, stop." He pulled out the telegram with a flourish and shook it open. "Please. I was going to show it to you."

He stared at the message. He set his jaw, the muscles in his face grew taut. He crushed the paper in his hand and tossed it into the stove. He turned his hard expression on her, "I believe we were on our way to bed." His voice was cold and his eyes were sharp, poised for her response.

"Why did you burn it?"

"You can't go."

"Oh, Liam," she rested her hands on his shoulders, "can't we get married in Ogden and..."

"No, I've made plans for Sacramento. People have been notified, guests. No, we can't."

Aislynn surrounded his face with her hands. "Would it be so difficult? New York would make a wonderful wedding trip."

Liam pulled away from her, "With Tim in mourning?"

"But," she stammered. "Papa Nolan says he needs me."

"He has his family."Aislynn heard his increasing irritation.

"Yes, but I know them. They're out of their realm; they can't help him. How can I turn them down?"

"They turned you out." His voice was a low growl.

"Not Tim, never Tim. You know that. He's always been there for me. He stayed, Liam; he stayed when he wanted to leave, had good reason to leave. I simply can't say no."

"Yes, you can."

Fretting, Aislynn tried again, "You've never had a relationship like ours."

He crossed his arms over his chest. "What exactly is your relationship?"

A hand went to her hip. Her anxiety was drifting into anger. "You know very well. He's my friend, my family. Oh," she huffed, "can't you see?"

"I see you're running to him as soon as that impediment Emma is out of the way."

Aislynn was shocked, "It's not like that!"

"Then explain it to me, Aislynn." His words were cold and critical. He was building a wall. She sensed he had already decided there was no explanation.

"He held my hand." She was grasping to find the words to describe what she meant. "He reached down, gave me his hand and pulled me up. Tim's always held my hand. It's what I have to do for him." Aislynn met his unreadable stare. "It's what we do for each other." She sighed, "I know them. He needs compassion. The Nolans can't give it to him."

Aislynn bit her lip and waited for his response.

"It sounds as though you've made your decision." His words frosted the room.

"Liam, maybe you've never loved anyone like..." She was trying to reassure him.

"Like you love Johnny and Tim."

Something terrible was stalking them. She could feel it ominous, expanding and ready to spring. She had not invited it, but she realized she had known it was coming. She bolstered herself with a breath and handed him what he would not accept. "Loving them does not mean I don't love you."

He was hardening himself against her. "Is this how you show it?"

"I have to go; I won't be staying there; I'll be back in a few weeks."

"You made me a promise, Aislynn. In fact, there isn't a man in this Territory who wouldn't agree you're already my wife."

Recognizing the truth, and the consequences of what she had done, for what she was doing, she said, "I know. I intend to keep my promise." She felt contrite.

"Fine, then you'll obey me."

The word bit into her. Aislynn stepped back. Her memory was vivid, "Aren't loving and honoring enough?"

"No." He threw the word at her. "Tell me, my darling, are there limits to your love for me?"

Trying to reach what she feared might no longer be reachable, she pleaded with him, "I have tried to show you; I've done everything you've asked."

"But there are limits." He sounded as though he were at the end of a tunnel, his words echoed in her ears.

Her hands crossed over her heart. "You can't tell me how to feel, what to think and do. Being your wife doesn't mean I stop being me, the woman I've always been, the woman you love." Her statement was a question. Holding her breath, she waited for his answer.

"But you'll put him above me," he sneered. "He's first, Aislynn, always first." She felt Liam's love draining away like the color in his face.

Her hands gripped her head. Everything was changing. The earth shifted, and she was being thrown off balance. The room blurred as her eyes filled. "Please Liam, don't." Aislynn tried again, "Can't you just trust my love?"

"You're choosing him!" He seemed to be growing larger, more threatening.

Understanding settled its weight on her; she was not going to New York for Tim. "Liam, I have to live with myself, with my choices."

"And you don't have to live with me."

There was nothing left. Her strength and her feelings were exhausted. She fell into a chair and shook her head slowly, "You want too much."

His body was ready to pounce. His hands were rolled into fists. His face was distorted with rage. "Go to New York, Aislynn," her name slid out like a curse. "Go to hell! But I won't come after you, and I won't be waiting here for you to come back!"

The door slammed, its wood split, and she wondered why she wasn't crying.

Aislynn bought her ticket at the Ogden depot and struggled out to the platform with her luggage. Her carpetbag slipped from her hand, hit the ground and her delicates tumbled out, scattering in front of her feet. A gentleman started toward her, "Can I be of assistance?" he asked.

"No, thank you. I'm fine by myself," she answered.

Aislynn gathered her clothes, laid them in the bag and snapped it shut. Up the line, the roaring locomotive

314

rolled. Its whistle screeched and the earth shook. Belching steam, spewing cinders, the engine ground to a stop. Aislynn picked up her bags and boarded the train.

ACKOWLEDGEMENTS

I want to acknowledge and thank everyone who gave me their support and encouragement:

TD and Timmy for accepting my dream and being a continual part of it. I love you both.

Sheila Garry Avery for reading every word and every revision. You are truly a "woman of strength."

Amy Goodman, who has the tremendous responsibility of bringing truth and reason to a crazy world, yet found the time to read and critique my manuscript.

Curt Nowell for generously turning my manuscript into a book.

Kristoffer Pearson for his patience and persistence while creating the cover.

To everyone else who read the book, shared their reactions and encouraged me to publish it: Derbigny, Meg, Annie, Midge, Mary, Kim, Betty, Dina, Denise, Candace, Heide, Lisa, Linda, David, Vanessa, and the wonderful book clubs, I am forever grateful.

CPSIA information can be obtained at www.ICGtesting.com
Printed in the USA
242286LV00001B/119/P